A PACT WITH THE DEVIL

LIFE ON MARS MEETS THE DIRTY DOZEN

TOM FINN

CONTENTS

PROLOGUE

Isaac Okoro lies dying on the pavement of a South London street with blood oozing through his school jacket. He has stab wounds to his stomach, back and chest, together with slash marks down his arms where he tried in vain to protect himself from the attack. His schoolbag, containing his homework, gripped firmly in his other hand, while the puddle of blood spreads by the second.

Three youths, none of them older than fifteen, dance around the prostrate boy, the adrenaline of the hunt and the kill still in their veins, pointing their knives and machete at the unresponsive body, daring it to retaliate.

Isaac drifts in and out of consciousness as the ritual continues. He wishes he could have run faster; he wishes he hadn't cut through the estate, and he wishes his mum was here with him to make the pain go away. As consciousness slips away, he remembers everything his mum told him--too late now. He hears the sirens; however, he can't be sure if it's the police or ambulance. He doesn't care. Anyone to help him and make the pain go away.

The dancing youths also hear the sirens and, as an ultimate act of defiance, one of them kicks their victim in the back and they run back onto their estate.

Before the sirens can get any closer, the pain for Issac Okoro goes away, permanently

CHAPTER ONE

Terry Reid was on his fifth coffee and sixth cigarette by nine a.m. on a sunny spring Monday morning in April. His routine–up at six a.m., walking his dog by half-past, and grabbing a paper from the newsagents - had remained the same for the last fifteen months. Originally, it had been his crossbreed rescue dog that had guilt-tripped him into the walks. However, now it was Terry who felt the need for structure in his day. As he took a sip from the mug Denise had bought him for his sixty-fifth birthday with 'Old Git' emblazoned on it, he allowed himself a small smile. He hadn't smiled much in the last two years, not since the news of Denise's cancer and her painful death six months later.

Now, looking over the slightly neglected garden of his detached four-bedroom house in Chigwell, Essex, he thought, 'Not bad for an East End boy. Nobody would have guessed the snotty-nosed kid at St Edmunds Secondary Modern School in Bethnal Green would have ended up a high-flyer in the police.' When he'd received the telephone call asking him to take the role of Detective Inspector of the Flying Squad, he'd thought it was a wind-up. It was Denise, sitting in this very kitchen, who persuaded him he was good enough.

Seven years later, when they offered him a promotion to Detective Chief Inspector, he and Denise had once again hunkered down at this table and discussed his options. Although it meant leaving the Flying Squad with only five years to retirement, they both agreed the increased pension would come in handy. She was right-she, she always was.

He'd missed the action of the Flying Squad - being in the middle of it all - and those last five years of his service as Detective Chief Inspector were miserable; he had felt more like an administrator than a police officer.

Terry's mobile phone rang, and he scrabbled in his pocket to answer. The screen revealed it was Bob Simpson, a former Detective Chief Superintendent who now ran the Ex- Detectives Association. This threatened Terry's morning peace, but the rest of the day yawned with nothing other than reading the paper at his side and pottering, so he picked up. "Hi, Bob."

"Morning Terry, how are you keeping?"

"I'm good, mate. Any news in the world of ex-tecs? Don't tell me someone else has died. All your emails are obituaries these days."

Bob snorted, "Oh, Terry, it's only us old guys left. Not many of those detectives they employ these days think to join us once they retire."

What did they do, Terry thought, all those others who retire? Golf? Grandkids? He wasn't interested in the first; as for the second, he and Denise had been enough for each other and never wanted kids. Terry said, "It's great to talk to you, Bob, although I'm sure you didn't ring just for a chat. What's happening?"

Bob cleared his throat–a phlegmy gurgle. "Do you know Detective Chief Superintendent Alan Jones?"

"Never heard of him. Should I?'

"Not really. He was probably joining the police as we were retiring. He rang me yesterday, wanting your phone number."

"Me? What for? I don't know him."

"Told him I wouldn't just hand out a member's details. He pulled the old 'Do you know who I am?' routine on me."

"I'm sure that impressed you,"

"He got real shirty," said Bob. "Gave me his number for you to ring him and said it was a matter of high importance."

Terry felt a nudge of excitement, then reminded himself that it was probably about a form he'd forgotten to fill in before he left the Police. "Not much of a copper, is he?" said Terry. "Any decent detective could find my number."

"Not sure about that nowadays," said Bob.

They were silent for a moment–a reckoning of the good days.

"Jones is up his own arse," said Bob. "Privately educated and all that. Never been on the streets getting his hands dirty. Pretends to be big on police corruption–likes to rake over old stuff, and prosecute the old guys. Would be happy to close down the CID given half a chance."

Corruption? Thought Terry. Well, sure, he'd crossed the line a few times, hadn't they all? But nothing to warrant him getting into trouble now.

"Don't worry," said Bob, as though he could read Terry's mind, "I got the impression he wants to work with you, not bang you up."

Work with me? Thought Terry.

"But don't ask me anymore," said Bob. "I've no more details."

Terry stared at the wedding photo on the mantelpiece when he rang off. "What do you think, Denise?" he said to the empty kitchen. "Shall I call this Jones bloke?"

Ring him; she would've said, what have you got to lose?

Peace and quiet, he thought, then again he'd never been much of a fan of that either.

At eleven-thirty, Terry made the call. After two rings, he heard. "Detective Chief Superintendent Jones, Commissioner's Staff Officer."

That's a mouthful, thought Terry. Especially with all those plums inside his gob. "Good morning, Alan," he said, grinning as he used Jones' first name. "Terry Reid here. I understand you want to speak to me."

There was a moment when it sounded as though Terry was being taken off speaker phone. "Yes," Jones said in a low voice. "I was rather hoping you could come to the Yard today for a meeting."

Terry raised his eyebrows at Denise's picture. "A meeting?"

"Correct."

"About…?"

Terry could hear footsteps and the sound of a door being closed. When Jones next spoke, it was almost a whisper. Good job Terry didn't need hearing aids yet. "We have a problem with an Albanian drug dealer," Jones said. "Who, unfortunately, because of circumstances outside of our control, is how shall we say it?"

Get on with it, Terry thought.

"... well, he's been pretty tricky to catch. His drugs are supplying the estates and are escalating the knife crime and murders."

Terry glanced over at his newspaper - CRYSTAL PALACE RISING STAR MURDERED.

"I'm not saying it's out of control," said Jones. "Obviously, we have systems in place of the highest calibre-"

Oh, for God's sake, thought Terry. "So, you want to take back control," he said, looking at the picture of the smiling young boy in his football kit.

Jones cleared his throat. "The, er, new Commissioner and new Home Secretary thought that maybe..."

Jones seemed incapable of finishing the sentence. Terry supplied him. "They want me involved?" What as? What could I do?

"If... well, yes, perhaps... we were thinking of a team of men, maybe. Go into the estates as-"

Oh, that's it, Terry thought and interrupted, "Community liaison officers. No, thank- "

'Not quite. Bear with me."

Terry switched the phone to his left ear and leaned his elbows on the table. Denise was smiling at him: eternally twenty-four in her wedding dress.

Jones hesitated. "The Commissioner thinks you may have certain skills unavailable to officers today."

Ha! Thought Terry. So they want a bit of old fashion policing. So much for prosecuting corruption. Bet this sticks in his craw.

Jones sounded defeated when he said, "There are matters I don't want to discuss on the telephone. However, we believe one person involved with our suspect is a man called Kenny Pierce. Someone from your era,"

Kenny Pierce thought Terry, now there's a blast from the past.

"Tell you what," Terry said, sending a wink to Denise, "I'll meet you at eleven-thirty tomorrow morning in The Peacock Pub in Stepney."

"The Peacock- listen - I'm not sure about meeting you in a public house. I have no idea where that is. What's wrong with you coming here?"

"I'm sure your driver will find it," said Terry and hung up.

~❖~

Jones slammed the phone down. He was already having a bad few days, what with the news that his younger brother and his glamorous wife had just moved to a six-bedroom house in Surrey. That was bad enough. Now his wife, having got wind, had been making digs. Shouldn't he have become a barrister like his brother and eventually a judge like his father? At least then, he'd work reasonable hours and wouldn't always be so goddamned tired. She meant grumpy. Still, he'd show her and his parents when he was Commissioner.

When he *was* Commissioner, he wouldn't be making stupid plans like this one. The idea of recruiting dubious ex-detectives to resolve a current problem in London was ridiculous and, at worst, dangerous. It could easily bring down the careers of both the Commissioner and the Home Secretary. Which wasn't so bad, he thought: Leave room at the top.

Aware of where blame might fall in the future, he had already taken the precaution of warning both bigwigs of the potential dangers whilst supporting the idea in principle. Perhaps this might work out. He scribbled a note to himself, *Press coverage?* And sat back in his chair.

Now all he had to do was find out where the hell The Peacock was.

CHAPTER TWO

Terry Reid strode up to the bar at The Peacock, his feet registering the stripped wooden floorboards where once had been sticky floral carpet. The wallpaper had gone, and they had removed the plaster from one wall, exposing the brickwork, whilst they had painted every other wall with a rich magnolia. Terry assumed the refurbishment was a standard package used by the brewery. He was sure he had been to dozens of pubs that looked identical.

The server, a young man with a nose ring like a bull and a name tag baring the name 'Jake', nodded to him. 'What can I get you?'

Terry read a sign on the wall: *We sell coffee now! Ask our barista for a cup of our finest roasted Arabica.* 'There used to be lots of barristers here,' he said to Justin.

'Sorry? What?'

"The old Thames Magistrates' Courts used to be over the way, next to the old Arbour Square Police Station."

The server stared at him blankly.

'Never mind.' He pointed to a fancy machine on the counter. 'I suppose that makes coffee?'

'Cappuccino? Latte?'

'Black.'

The cup was the size of a soup bowl, and Terry took it to a table opposite the door. The only other customer was sitting behind him, an elderly man studying the racing pages of the Sun with a half-drunk pint of lager in front of him.

At eleven-thirty, Alan Jones, wearing a dark grey pin-striped suit with a mop of public school hair and an angry face, strode into the public house carrying a briefcase. Terry stood and offered his hand, which was gripped firmly. The man introduced himself. "Detective Chief Superintendent Jones."

"Good morning, Alan," Terry said.

Jones scowled.

"Would you like a drink?"

"No, thank you. We should get on." Jones sat down, removed a newspaper from his briefcase, and placed it on the table. It was the same paper Terry had bought the day before. "I expect you've seen this," said Jones. "Damned nuisance, it is. He was in the wrong place at the wrong time. No sign he was ever involved in drugs."

"Only thirteen," said Terry, "and already the hot ticket for Crystal Palace."

Jones sighed, "And he did charity work. Thing is…" he looked around him and shifted his seat closer, "we were under tremendous pressure anyway - now we have the press and public on our back."

So that's what you care about, thought Terry. "And you think it's drugs-related?" he said.

"The estates are lawle-" He caught himself. "What I mean to say is that, yes, it's definitely drug-related and there has been a certain amount of, how shall I put it, collateral damage. Believe me, we have been working night and day and have discovered the supply. It's an Albanian who is-"

Terry interrupted. "Would that be Arian Mehmed?"

Jones' mouth hung open. "How do you know that?"

Terry smiled.

"Never mind," said Jones. "The point is, despite our strong, may I say, determined efforts, we can't get him. Two years of a thorough process-led investigation and, unfortunately, we are no closer. Mehmed doesn't appear to have a fixed address, doesn't own a car or even drive one, and he seems to have a different driver daily. Every day he changes his mobile phone. We have the highest calibre surveillance and technology, believe me, and yet…" He looked wistfully at the brick wall.

"What about informants?" said Terry.

Jones folded the newspaper so that Isaac Okoro's face was no longer looking up at them. "Mehmed only employs Albanians, and they are all petrified of him. Not without reason."

"Yes, I've heard he likes a bit of torture - either before or after he murders their family." Before being asked, he added, "I may not have a computer, but I still keep my ear to the ground."

Jones sniffed. "Well, I can confirm that our informant supports your claim."

"So, why do you need me?" asked Terry. "Has your grass got cold feet?"

Jones lowered his voice. "Look, this is very sensitive. Our informant was very low level in the organisation, although we were hoping, given time, he would make his way up the gang."

So they still play the long game, thought Terry.

"However," said Jones, "he has disappeared and we fear the worst."

Jake, the barista, came to the table and said to Jones, "Can I get you anything?"

"I would have indicated if I wanted something," said Jones.

Terry gave him a hard stare and then looked back at Jake. "Pint of lager, thank you."

Jones looked at the still-full coffee cup. "I don't want-"

"Who said it's for you?" He smiled. "So, tell me about Kenny Pierce. How's he involved in this?"

Jones' eyes were on the coffee cup as though it could give him answers.

"Kenny Pierce?"

"Oh, yes, right… The surveillance team followed Mehmed to a firm of solicitors, Baker, Radcliffe, and Wright in Mayfair."

"Harry Baker's office."

Jones gave his impression of a goldfish. He didn't ask Terry how he knew. "Our highly trained team set up a permanent observation on the solicitor's office," he said. "Over the two years, Mehmed visited the solicitors a further twelve times, and on each of those occasions, Pierce was there as well."

"Huh," said Terry, accepting the pint of lager he really didn't want from Jordan.

"It may just be a coincidence," said Jones, "as intelligence suggests Pierce may well have retired. He is seventy-five years old."

"Is he?" Although, Terry thought retirement was highly unlikely. Men like Kenny Pierce never retire. "What about Mehmed's finances?"

"Extensive enquiries found nothing, and the Foreign Office warned us not to make enquiries in Albania. They told us a man of his wealth and connections would have corrupt officials over there, and therefore he would realise our interest in him."

"Interesting," said Terry. And it was. It'd been a long time since he'd been privy to anything more than overhearing snippets snatched in the streets and second-hand news passed on by the old boys:

Folding his arms, Terry asked. "Why am I here?"

"Look, it's not been easy." Jones stabbed the folded newspaper with his finger. "If we can't get to Mehmed and stop his drugs, we can't control the estates. The papers have been ringing me non-stop and-" He looked behind him to the door as though he wanted to be through it and back to his paperwork. He took a deep breath. "Thing is, we have a new Commissioner and Home Secretary who are both, I would say, more robust than their predecessors. Having spent around two million pounds so far, they are open to exploring… alternative methods to solve this problem."

"Alternative?" Terry wasn't making it easy for Jones.

Jones shifted in his seat. "Shall we say that officers of your era-"

"I'm not dead yet,"

"If you'd let me finish. We believed that in your time, you and your colleagues could solve problems using… shall we say… unorthodox methods."

Hold on a second," said Terry, lifting his hands. "Do you think we were all corrupt, fitting people up and probably stealing their money? Unlike today, we didn't have the luxury of mobile phone tracking, CCTV cameras on every corner, or even DNA. We worked on instinct, gut feeling, and informants. Yet the crime rate was half of today and the conviction rate was double. Sometimes you have to rule by fear and not by the book."

Jones inspected his fingernails. "We don't get the allegations of wrongful convictions now, unlike before."

"That's because the only people convicted now are those that plead guilty! In the old days, villains feared us while the public respected us. You aren't anywhere close to claiming that." Jones flushed a little, and Terry softened. "I'm sure you are doing the best you can under the circumstances." Thinking of Isaac Okoro, he tried a smile. "Listen, we are on the same side. Something has to be done."

"I agree. The Commissioner and Home Secretary have come to a decision and…" He breathed in through his nose. "They are hoping you would consider forming a squad of 'like-minded' ex-police officers to take on Mehmed and, if possible, rid some estates of the gangs. We are confident we can take back control once their influence is no longer there. "

A squad? They both sat in silence while Terry thought of who he could ask: he would need some muscle and some resources the police wouldn't be able to supply. It wasn't until moments later; he came to his senses. Why should he work for Jones?

"So, explain to me how this would work?"

Jones sat back in his chair as though he was more comfortable now. He was onto brass tacks. "Well, we currently employ some ex-police officers to investigate historical murders, and the plan is to give you and your team two unsolved drug murders, one in North London and one in South London. That will provide you with cover and an excuse to investigate drug crimes. We have an office set aside for you at Scotland Yard and will provide you with computers and anything else you need, including an officer to liaise with you, on a strictly non-operational basis. This will allow us to pay you."

With a paltry wage, no back-up, no security; old men running after drug lords who murdered and tortured, Terry could see no reason he or any of his friends should be involved. Yet he felt more energised than he had done for a very long time. He took a sip of lager, almost content.

Jones then looked Terry straight in the eye. "Should things go wrong, we will say you were a rogue outfit. The sort of things you did back then, you can't do now. The world has changed."

Terry banged his fist hard on the table, causing Jones to flinch. "For fuck's sake, maybe if people like you hadn't forced change, you wouldn't be in the position you find yourself in now. Who knows? And yet I'm here, and remember, you called me. Explain that?"

Jones' shoulders fell. "Maybe I've imparted my views more than I should have."

"This is just a publicity stunt for you, isn't it?"

Jones gave a tight smile. "There is a certain amount of that involved. However, if this works, it could be a formula for all the estates in London. Think of that."

Terry glanced at the folded newspaper and remembered the boy's bright smile inside. He stood and held out his hand. Warily, Jones shook it. "You have a deal," Terry said. He withdrew his hands. "There are conditions: you meet me here on Thursday at the same time; you give my men a minimum six-month contract and you will pay us all at the Detective Inspector rate."

"But…" Jones shook his head. "Don't you see that…? Fine."

"On Thursday, I need you to bring along someone from the Home Office who deals with prisoners' parole and someone from the Director of Public Prosecutions who deals with extradition; they both need to be at a level where they can make high-level decisions."

Jones looked uncomfortable. "I'm not sure why you can't tell me what you require, and I'll contact the relevant authorities with your queries and get back to you."

There was a temptation for Terry to tell Jones why he didn't trust him to pass on his request; instead, he said, "What I need from both of them is complex, and they may need clarification. I don't think it's right or fair to use you as a messenger between us."

"Well, I suppose that makes sense, although I'm not sure I can get them to meet you here."

"If, as you say, the Home Secretary is on board with this, I'm sure she will get her staff to slum it for one day. If not, the deal is off. Oh, and by the way," said Terry, smiling, "are you aware that Commander Power, who runs the Anti-Terrorism Squad at Scotland Yard attended the same school as your new Commissioner? They are still close friends and play golf together most weekends."

Jones looked puzzled.

"Well, I'm godfather to his son and I'll be sharing our conversation and asking him to ensure you briefed his good friend, the Commissioner, accurately."

Jones snatched the newspaper off the table, put it back in his briefcase, and left. As soon as the door swung shut, the old guy on the table behind came and joined Terry and sat in Jones's chair. "Did you hear all that?" asked Terry.

"Most of it," said ex-Detective Sergeant Nicky Whybrow. "He's not very discrete, is he?"

"No. And as for charisma, he thinks that's the 25th of December."

"Are you going to contact Paddy Power?"

"Course not, but he doesn't know that."

Nicky grinned: a flash of bright white dentures. "Is that drink going spare?"

Terry pushed the pint of lager towards him and Nicky took it with hands gnarled by arthritis. The backs of his hands were a deep brown from gardening and golf. He took a sip. "Bet you're glad you asked me here now."

Terry sat back. "Definitely," he spread his hands. "What do you think? Do you want in?"

"I'm game," said Nicky.

"Could be dangerous. Won't you miss your allotment?"

Nicky laughed, which turned into a hacking cough from decades of fags. "One last adventure won't harm me," he said when he recovered.

"And what about the others?"

'Who are you thinking of?'

"We're going to need informants to get us on the estates - so probably John Olde and Jimmy Smith?"

"They'll be handy if things get lively."

"True," said Terry. "I don't want to keep going back to Jones for resources, so how about Peter Rhodes?"

"That's a good shout. You'll need to speak to him, though. I'm not sure if he would want to be involved."

"Can you arrange a meeting for me with Peter, and will you visit Jimmy and John?"

Nicky sighed contentedly and said, as though he was a character in a children's book: "The old team back together again."

Terry laughed. "What could possibly go wrong?"

Nicky asked, "What about those other two phone calls? Shall we make them now or wait till after Thursday?"

"No, let's make those calls first. When you make yours, arrange a meeting for Friday morning. I'll arrange my meeting for Friday evening."

After Terry finished his call, he felt happy with the way it had gone. When Nicky Whybrow hung up from his call and relayed the conversation to Terry, he didn't seem as convinced of the outcome.

Terry was staring at the bar, unsure whether to order another coffee or a pint of lager. He was deep in thought: Today was what he needed; he had enjoyed messing with Jones's head. But what if he couldn't put a team together? What would he say to Jones and the two civil servants on Thursday? The next forty-eight hours were crucial.

CHAPTER THREE

As Terry stared up at the high glass building which housed Peter Rhodes' security business, he felt a little defeated. Why on earth would Peter want to join the team when he was so well set up?

He pressed the button on the intercom system and was buzzed through. As he made his way to the shining teak reception desk, his footsteps sounded on marble. A young woman with hair scraped into a bun and flawless makeup flashed him an expensive smile. "Mr Reid, for Mr Rhodes, I presume? Please, follow me."

Her heels struck the marble with confidence as she led him through a maze of open offices filled with brash young men in blue suits, talking animatedly through microphones attached to headphones. "Stairs, okay?" the woman asked him over her shoulder as she started to ascend.

I'm not that old, thought Terry, as he climbed after her.

At the top of the stairs stood Peter. He wore a pair of chinos and a blue pencil-striped shirt unbuttoned at the collar. His thinning hair beautifully groomed. "Great to see you, Terry," he said, holding out his hand. "It's been a long time. You're looking good."

Peter's grip was firm. "I'm not sure about that," said Terry. "You look as though you've lost some weight."

"Personal trainer," he said. "I don't get to run around as much as I used to - I'm mainly sitting at my desk." He put a hand on Terry's shoulder and ushered him into a large office with windows overlooking the River Thames.

The high-rise offices of Canary Wharf opposite reflected on the glittering grey water. Inside, there was a large mahogany desk and a separate seating area. The shelves were neatly curated with pictures of Peter's family and of him with politicians and other celebrities.

"So sorry to hear about Denise," said Peter. "It was five years ago last week when I lost my Barbara. I know how tough it is."

"She was a good woman. They both were."

There was a knock at the door and a young man brought in a pot of coffee. As he left, Peter said, "Black with no sugar, right?"

"Bloody hell, you've got an excellent memory," said Terry.

Instead of sitting behind his large oak desk, Peter moved a chair to sit next to Terry and said, "Nicky's call was very mysterious. Is there a problem?"

"No, nothing like that."

Terry told him about Jones and his plan to rid drugs from the estates. "I'm looking to put a team together." He looked him in the eye. "People I can trust. Who will do the job the way it used to be done."

Peter leaned back. "Me, you mean?" He spread out his hands, indicating his office, all he'd worked hard for since leaving the police. "What makes you think I'd do a thing like that?"

Terry looked him straight in the eye. "You were a bloody good detective. They should never have forced you to resign. This would be your second chance."

Peter turned his head, looked out of the window, and was silent. "Maybe they did me a favour," he said.

"You think?"

"I mean, yes, I can't say I wasn't… bothered. Or haven't missed things… But I picked myself up: I've got a huge team now. Most of them ex-coppers who are good at security."

"The type of men who could run your business for a bit?"

Peter gave a wry smile.

Terry stood and wandered over to the pictures on the shelf. "This one, your grandson?"

"Jamie, yes. He's Sarah's boy. He was thirteen last week."

"Same age as Isaac Okoro."

"The young footballer who they stabbed?"

Terry turned back to him. "If you don't want to join me for yourself, join me because I know we can make a difference." He waved his hand across to the Canary Wharf. "That place is full of drugs, and guess who supplies them? Young kids on the estates who then turn to violence and kill innocents like Isaac. We can hold back the tide. I'm sure we can."

Peter thought for a moment. "There's no way they should have made me retire. So what if I sold tracking devices and electronic bugs in my spare time? I'd been the one to show the drug squad how effective they were in the first place. The rule about second businesses in the police doesn't even exist now. It lost them a good man."

"Does that mean you're in?"

Peter stood and shook Terry's hand. "I'm in."

~❖~

Nicky stood outside Jimmy Smith's semi-detached house in Ilford. He rang the doorbell, which sounded the theme tune from the Rocky film. They must have got a new one because, as far as he remembered, the bell used to have a plain old ring from all the times he'd visited with his wife. Nicky was still grinning as Debbie, Jimmy's wife, answered the door. "Hello, Nicky. You alright?"

"I'm great, Debbie. I've been trying to telephone Jimmy. Is he about?"

"The silly sod dropped his phone. He's waiting for a replacement. I thought you were the courier." She took her coat from a peg in the hall. "I'm just going shopping. He's in the garage – round the back." She slipped past him and said over her shoulder, "Tell him to listen out for the delivery driver."

"I will," replied Nicky.

He walked through the kitchen and out the back door, around the side of the house to the door of the garage. He could hear the banging coming from within and as he opened the door, he saw Jimmy hitting a huge punch bag hanging from the rafters of the garage. The bag appeared heavy, though it was swinging from the force of the relentless punches. Tamala Motown music was blaring from a CD player on a small table and Jimmy, wearing a T-shirt that was soaked in sweat and clinging to his body, didn't notice Nicky's entrance.

Not wanting to stop Jimmy's fun just yet, Nicky perched on an old metal chest and took in the garage. On the wall to his right was a large framed photograph of Jimmy posing in boxing gloves, wearing a Repton Boxing Club vest. Copies of posters of the great heavyweight fights of years gone by surrounding it. Nicky estimated the photograph showed Jimmy as either a light-heavyweight or cruiserweight, although he was certainly a super-heavyweight now, with little or no fat on his body. With his closely cropped hair, he looked an intimidating figure. Maybe I should have looked after myself a bit better, thought Nicky, smoothing his shirt over his paunch.

Jimmy gripped the bag to stop the movement, took off his bag gloves and turned off the CD player. It was only then that he saw Nicky; nonetheless, he betrayed no surprise.

"Cup of tea?"

They walked back into the house and Jimmy switched the kettle on and excused himself to have a quick shower. As he waited for the kettle to boil, Nicky wondered if Jimmy ever regretted giving up the opportunity to be a professional boxer to pursue a career in the police.

When Jimmy returned to the kitchen and, over a cup of tea, Nicky explained the reason for his visit. "So we're looking to put together a team."

Jimmy sniffed loudly through a nose broken many times. "No police back up?"

"No, though they'll put a young officer with us."

"And Terry's definitely got a plan?"

Nicky laughed. "You know what he's like. Runs rings around the rest of us."

Jimmy took a slurp of his tea. "Debbie would kill me,"

Nicky grimaced. He cradled the tea in his hands, warming the ache of his arthritis. "Didn't you say the private investigation work was drying up? Just a few insurance jobs." He looked at the chipped Welsh dresser and the ancient oven. "When we were here last, Debbie said she'd love a new kitchen."

Jimmy sniffed.

"Or a holiday in Greece."

Jimmy laughed. "Alright, Nicky, mate, you don't have to pull a Terry on me. If you want me there, I'll be there."

"Oh, that's great news. What about John Olde? I've been trying to ring him. Has he changed his number?" asked Nicky.

Jimmy stood and fetched a cake tin. Inside were five perfect scones. "Butter?"

Nicky looked down at his paunch. Sod it. "Go on then, and a bit of jam if you have any."

Jimmy ducked into the fridge and placed everything on the table.

"So - John," said Nicky, smearing butter on his scone.

"He's been involved in personnel protection," said Jimmy with his mouth full.

"Yeah, bodyguard to lots of big names. The last time I spoke to him, he was best mates with Scarlett Johansson." He laughed. "Surprised he didn't ask her to be wife number four."

"Well," said Jimmy, "Thing is, the studios started asking for risk assessments and health and safety reports. All that razzamatazz. Well, with John..."

"Paperwork was never his strong point," said Nicky, running his finger along the plate to pick up crumbs.

"That's right. It all got on top of him and he bailed out."

"Poor bloke. I should've been in contact earlier. Called round of something,"

"He's not in that flat in Pimlico anymore. Too expensive. He's living off his state pension and whatever pennies the police pension gives us. He moved back to Peckham to live in a bedsit."

"What the hell did he move back there for?" said Nicky, eyeing up the remaining scones. "He only joined the police to get out of that hellhole."

Jimmy put the lid firmly back on the cake tin. "Not only that. The chances are his phone's cut off."

Nicky threw his hands in the air. "No wonder he didn't answer. How are we going to get in touch?"

Jimmy tapped his broken nose. "I know where he works."

"So he has got a job?"

"Only part-time and all cash in hand. He works as a minder in this illegal drinker just off Peckham High Street. He's there when there's a footie match on the telly, and… Guess what?"

Nicky smiled. "Crystal Palace are playing tonight!"

Jimmy sniffed. "Listen, I'll take you there, although we shouldn't get our hopes up. I don't think he'll want to join. It's not as though being part of the police did him any favours.

I only had one broken marriage because of it; he had three go down the swanny. No one ever thanked him or appreciated his hard work on the Flying Squad and Regional Crime Squad. At one time, his informants were providing work for two teams full-time. He knows being forced to leave was his fault. However, he got little or no support once he was out and he resents that."

"He did put his girlfriend's husband into hospital," Nicky said. "He could easily have found himself nicked for attempted murder. It may seem harsh, but he was lucky to get out of the police without being charged. If that was today, he'd be doing a ten stretch." He shrugged. "We can only try. It's not the police he'll be working with; he'll be working with us. That's got to count for something."

~❖~

As they descended the stone stairs to the basement drinking club in an alley off Peckham High Street, Nicky realised he would never have found the place without Jimmy. The paint of the narrow door was blistered and scratched. After knocking three times, the door opened and John Olde filled the frame. Nicky had forgotten just how big he was.

"Nicky, my old mate. Jimmy!" John had an enormous smile on his face. Dispensing with handshakes, he hugged them both tightly. Nicky felt like a small child.

"Let me get you a drink," John said.

They pushed their way through a crowd of about fifty or sixty young men. They were all staring at a fifty-inch television showing Manchester United v Crystal Palace. With only twenty minutes gone, the score was already 2-0 to Manchester United and the mood was sombre: not yet turning to violence.

John ordered three pints of lager and they traced their steps back towards the door, away from the television. There was a small, ripped leatherette banquette and the three of them squashed together. Nicky felt like a child between two uncles. Good-looking ones at that - John looked fit and strong and still had a full head of black hair; Jimmy had his muscles and a rakish charm despite his twisted nose and thinning hair. Maybe I should go to the gym instead of the golf course, thought Nicky, and then what's the point? I'll never catch up.

On-screen, a Crystal Palace player gave up an easy ball, and the room filled with curses. Nicky turned to John. "I don't understand why you are doing this. If it kicks off here, what can you do on your own?"

John chuckled. "You've got to realise Nicky; it's all bravado with these kids nowadays. In reality, if you slap one, the rest of them cry. None of them wants to take the risk of getting a good hiding from a sixty-five-year-old bloke. Remember, it's not the dog in the fight that matters, but the fight in the dog." He took a sip of his beer. "Anyway, tell me, what do I owe this pleasure for?"

Nicky explained the reason for their visit, giving an outline of the task in front of them. "We're going to make sure that boys like Isaac Okoro are free to walk the streets."

John drained the last dregs of his pint. "Sure," he said.

Nicky had been expecting some resistance or at least some questions. "You mean you want to join us?"

"Yeah, why not? Fancy another pint?"

"Well-"

"Not here." He stood, walked over to the bar, and reached over it to retrieve his leather jacket. "Come on," he said. "I know a nice little boozer."

"Don't you have to finish your shift?" said Jimmy.

"I'm a Hammers supporter. This lot can kill each other, as far as I'm concerned. We are what's important now."

CHAPTER FOUR

On Thursday morning at eleven, Terry sat in the empty bar of The Peacock with a large black coffee, putting the finishing touches to his notes. Finished, he threw down his biro and stood to adjust his suit. He remembered buying it at Marks and Spencer in a New Year's sale over twenty years ago. The suit trousers were digging into him, despite the elasticated waist, and he could only secure the jacket button if he held his breath.

Just as Terry finished re-buttoning his jacket, Alan Jones strode in. In his hand was the same briefcase as before. However, Jones was wearing the distinctive blue and burgundy Brigade of Guards regimental tie this time. You old fraud thought Terry. He'd done his background on Jones and knew he had never been in the armed forces or had any military background. "Nice tie," Terry said with a grin.

Before Jones could reply, two more men entered the pub, and Terry got his answer why Jones had chosen this attire. One of them was wearing a Coldstream Guards tie and the other a Parachute Regiment tie tucked into their immaculate Saville Row suits.

"Gerald McLean," said the one with the parachute colours, holding out his hand. "Home Office."

"Michael Freeman," said the other. "Director of Public Prosecutions office."

"Just as you asked," said Jones

"Got it, thanks," said Terry. "Please, take a seat. Coffee? Tea?"

Freeman opened his mouth to reply. Jones said, "Let's just get on, shall we?"

"Fair enough," said Terry, sliding over a piece of paper to McClean. "Here are the names of two brothers in prison for importing drugs, Ozzie and Omer Hassan. They are five years into a fifteen-year prison sentence," he said. "I may want them to be paroled early. By which I mean, within a couple of months."

McClean raised his eyebrows.

Terry smiled. "Prisons are terribly overcrowded, I hear."

McClean glanced at Jones, who gave a slow nod.

"I suppose it could be possible. Have they been model prisoners, for example?"

Terry interrupted, "One of them is in HMP Frankland in Durham, and the other is in HMP Wakefield. Before we decide on paroling them, I'd like them transferred to Belmarsh prison in South London on Monday morning. They are both from London and it would make it easier for their families to visit them."

McClean looked over at the bar as though it was not coffee he wanted and would prefer a strong brandy. He turned back to the table and twitched the paper under his neatly manicured fingertips. "If that's what our superiors deem necessary, Mr Reid, of course, our office will oblige."

"Terry, please," said Terry. "We're all friends here. And, don't worry, if my idea doesn't go to plan, then the pair of them can rot in jail for all I care. Now! Onwards!" He grinned at McClean, who shuffled in his seat. Pushing over another piece of paper towards Freeman, he said, "Here are the details of the Pierce brothers, who are in Kenitra Prison in Morocco, awaiting extradition for their involvement in importing drugs. If necessary, would the Director of Public Prosecution office send a 'defective' application that would fail to get them extradited?"

Freeman's eyes widened. "Are you asking me to pervert the course of justice, Mr Reid?"

"Terry, Terry, and absolutely not." He laid his hand on his chest. "I'm thinking of justice: of the long term." He took a sip of coffee and looked over the cup at Freeman. "At present, it's almost impossible to extradite someone from Morocco. Am I right?"

Freeman gave a reluctant nod.

"These two kids have no previous convictions and were chancing their arms, trying to shift ten kilos of cocaine. I'm not saying that's alright, except when you look at the bigger picture, they are small fry compared to our goal."

"How do you suggest we go about this, Mr Reid?"

"Well, then. What I say is that sometimes… just sometimes, paperwork isn't up to speed. When the Pierce brothers are released from Kenitra Prison, they will not want to stay in Morocco and they are unlikely to come home, are they? They'll choose another country and bingo, you arrest them there, where your chances of extradition are greater."

Freeman sighed. "This is all very irregular."

Terry patted his arm. "My friend," he said, "I am not exactly happy either. We're on the same side, believe me." He sat back in his chair. "I keep thinking of that Isaac kid, on the ground, bleeding."

The three men nodded solemnly.

Terry gestured to Jones. "The police force is working flat out. Our man here is trying his damn best - the best we can do is give him our support."

Jones opened his mouth and closed it again, as though not knowing whether to acknowledge the compliment or disclaim Terry's entire plan.

"Well," said Freeman. "You can count on our support."

"Great. So, one more thing - you are dealing with the Pierce brothers' solicitor, I assume? Serving them all documents relating to their case?"

"That would be the normal procedure," said Freeman, adjusting his tie.

"Please contact them on Monday and inform them there will be a delay of three months before you serve documents on them."

"But… why?"

Jones put his hands on the table. "I'm sure Mr Reid knows what he is doing."

"Terry," said Terry.

"Very well," said Freeman. He stood, and Terry submitted to two firm handshakes before the men left.

As the door shut behind them, Jones shook his head. "Are you mad? What I have just been a spectator to, is insanity. Are you trying to get us all put into prison?"

"I thought-"

"I just needed it to end," said Jones

Terry laughed. "Alan, it's fine. Honestly."

"My biggest problem is that you don't even seem to realise there is a problem."

"Look, Alan. I'll deny you were ever here if it comes down to it. And, let's face it, the Home Secretary would get the rap, not you."

Detective Chief Superintendent Jones sat in silence, like a sulking child.

Terry broke the silence. "Here is the list of the ex-officers with their bank details for payments to be made." He handed over a sheet of paper. "You'll find the serving officer's name I want to be attached to us; he is a Detective Sergeant on Operation Trident."

"I will arrange for him to be seconded to you," said Jones flatly.

"That's fine. We've already reached out to him, and I'm meeting him in the next couple of days."

"Of course you have," said Jones.

Terry ignored him. "All contact will now be through him."

"Some good news at last."

"I'll get him to provide you with a new telephone number, which you can contact me on in case of an emergency."

"Goody."

His poor wife thought Terry; he certainly knows how to stretch out a sulk. "When can we start?" said Terry.

Jones furrowed his brow. "Haven't you already-"

"I mean, if we are about to close the drug supply on an estate, how much notice do you and the Home Office need to start the clean-up of the estates once the gangs are out?"

Jones replied, "At least a week."

"Not happening."

Jones' chin snapped up.

"Of course, we'll try to give you some notice of what council it is and one day for an approximate location."

"It's not enough."

"We need shock and awe. Look, Alan, this is important…" Terry spread out his hands, "we can't afford a leak."

Jones' jaw tightened. "My men-"

"You can't tell the press until after we are done. Do you hear me? If there is any leak of information, it will only have come from your end, and the deal is off and we are out of it."

"Now, listen to me-"

Terry put his hand on Jones's arm. "I need to say something that has been on my mind since we met on Tuesday. I'm not telling you how to do your job. Honestly, I'm not. If we put Mehmed out of the drug business, there will be only a brief window of opportunity for the police to regain control of London."

Jones withdrew his arm, although it appeared he was listening.

"It will be very costly and manpower intensive," Terry said. "You'll need help from the National Crime Squad. Even, initially, the armed services. The sort of operation that helps a man make a name for himself."

At that, Jones leaned forward.

"The first thing to happen will be the price of cocaine will go through the roof in London, which will encourage gangs in the rest of the UK to fill the void. This may lead to out-and-out warfare; you need to be prepared."

Jones nodded and gave a tight smile. "I note your concern."

"Good, glad we've got that cleared up." Terry looked towards the bar. "Did you want a drink?"

Jones dusted the arms of his suit. "No, I really must-"

"Oh, and, yes, I need five thousand pounds in cash for incidental expenses,"

"Incidental expenses? What are incidental expenses?"

"We need information fast; we haven't got time to cultivate informants, so we may need to spend money to buy that information. You won't be getting any receipts."

"Terry Reid, you really are…" He looked around the room as though he could find a good enough insult hiding in one corner.

"I know, I know. Don't worry; you'll get results." He grinned. "You'll even get credit for them."

Jones stood up so quickly the chair squealed on the wooden floor. "Good day, Mr Reid," he said.

Terry wanted to call. "It's Terry", after him, but decided he'd put the bloke through too much for one day as it was. You'll thank me, though, he thought, tracking Jones' outline through the pub window. You'll thank me one day.

CHAPTER FIVE

Just after Jones had left, Terry checked his watch. There were still a couple of hours before Nicky, Jimmy, John, and Peter would arrive. Plus, the new police officer which he had requested. Terry ambled over to the bar. Jake, the server with a ring through his nose, was there. 'I don't suppose there is still a function room upstairs, is there?'

"Well…" he started.

"Is that a familiar voice I hear?" came a voice from the back. The owner of the voice appeared. The landlady was a short woman made even shorter by osteoporosis, giving her a slight hunch. She had carefully made up her wrinkled face and her hair was the same as it had been since the eighties.

Terry had thought she must be dead. "Diane!"

"Hello, Terry! Long-time no see. How are you, my dear?" Her cheek was soft and fuzzy as she kissed him. "What on earth are you doing in this neck of the woods? I imagined you and your dear wife in Marbella sipping cocktails."

He didn't want to say Denise was dead, nor that his retirement comprised of walking the dog, mowing the lawn and lonely cups of coffee in his kitchen - until now, of course. He laughed, "No such luck. Actually, I've got a bit of work coming in from the police - nothing major - just wondered if you still had the function room?"

"Well…" she said, with a well-executed pause. "The brewery didn't want to spend any money upstairs, so… it's a bit of a state."

"Could I see?"

She raised a painted eyebrow.

"Please?"

"For you, my dear, anything."

As they slowly made their way up the stairs, Diane clutching the bannister tightly, they chatted about all the people Terry had come drinking with in her pub. They ticked off the dead, and he told her Nicky, Jimmy, John and Peter were coming.

"Oh, they're lovely fellas. John found wife number three yet?"

"He's been through number three. Looking for number four."

"You men," she said as she creaked open the door.

The place was stuck in a time warp. On the floor was an Axminster carpet which once would have sung with red and green, although it was now the colour of sludge. The oak-panelled walls could have been beautiful; unfortunately, someone in the mid-eighties had thought to paint the panelling over in grey and pink stripes. There was a roundel of brown oak left on the wall closest to Terry with little pinpoints of damage around it - obviously where a dartboard had once been. Hanging, with a smattering of mildew, was a pair of floral curtains that neither matched the carpet nor the walls. On a sturdy table with six chairs sat a glass Rothman's cigarette ashtray, complete with cigarette butts. Diane swiped it away. "As I say, we don't use it much."

"It's perfect," said Terry.

"Then it's yours," she said, "For as long as you need it on this not very important police business." She winked. "Coffee, dear, while you wait for your team?"

Terry gave her a peck on the cheek. "Yes, please."

"Charmer," she said as she left.

Terry sat, making notes in the room, sipping his coffee and waiting for the men. The meeting with the Home Office and Director of Public Prosecution had gone as well as could be expected, and he knew Jones would come round once he saw results. That was going to be up to him and his men. Could they pull it off? None of them was getting any younger. Still, Dave Driscoll, the police officer who he'd requested to join them, was young and full of vim. His father had been a good man - one of Terry's mates in the Flying Squad. Poor Paul, thought Terry, keeling over from a heart attack at sixty-five. And poor Monica too. Working her way up the force–struggling - as the only black woman detective for years and years. To do all that and then - bang! - Just as you are about to enjoy retirement, your husband dies.

The door flew open. "Blimey," said Nicky. "I've not been up here for years. Do you remember dangling that newbie out that window one night? From his ankles - squealed like a pig."

Terry blinked. "Not me."

"Someone then."

Nicky sat down and the chair creaked. His suit was as ill-fitting as Terry's and the seams looked as though they might burst as he crossed his arms. He was about to speak when Jimmy, John, and Peter arrived. They too exclaimed about the room. Terry noticed they were all wearing the famous Flying Squad tie with the swooping eagle motif. There had been no mention of a dress code. They all instinctively knew this was the correct attire for their first meeting. For the first time, he felt confident they could pull this off.

The door opened again and Dave Driscoll walked in. Terry got up to shake his hand. Dave had a firm grip. At thirty-five, and blessed with handsome - some might say, beautiful - good looks. The good genes of a Welsh father and Kenyan mother. He too was wearing a suit; however, this one fitted perfectly. He had unbuttoned his shirt at the neck and on his feet were a pair of what Terry might describe as leather trainers.

"Come in, come in," said Terry. "Take a seat."

As Terry sat, the buzz in the room subsided. "First, welcome, and thank you for agreeing to participate in this adventure. Nicky has spoken to each of you, nonetheless, I'm not going to apologise for repeating what he's told you. We are going to get little or no protection from the police; if things go wrong, we will be on our own. However, I can't think of a nicer group of people with whom I'd want to get into the shit."

The men laughed, although Terry knew they were aware the warning was real. "You old buggers know each other. Some of you won't have met Dave Driscoll."

Sitting next to Dave, Peter shook his hand and Nicky, Jimmy, and John waved. They looked toward the younger man at the end of the table.

"Dave is a serving Detective Sergeant on Operation Trident. They deal with black-on-black murders and his knowledge of all things gang related will be very welcome. His father was our old flying squad friend, Paul Driscoll."

"Oh, Paul!" said Peter, grinning, "How is-"

Nicky leaned past Peter and said, "I'm sorry for your loss."

"He was a good man," said Jimmy.

Dave gave a slow smile. "Yes, he was."

"Are you a West Ham supporter, like your old man?" Asked John.

"Yea, I'm a season ticket holder. Do you go to the games?"

"You're joking," interrupted Jimmy. "He gets married most Saturdays."

"Charming," said John, punching Jimmy on the arm.

"At a later stage," said Terry, "I'm going to ask Dave to explain to us the structure of these drug gangs." He then introduced Peter Rhodes - "a technical genius" - Nicky Wybrow - "knows a key informant." Terry then struggled to describe John Olde and Jimmy Smith's roles. Heavies? Bruisers? "Good solid men," he said.

After they had said their 'Hello's," Terry said, "Other than Dave, none of us are police now and there are no ranks. I know I don't need to say this, anything that is said within these four walls or," he gestured to the door, "whatever happens out there goes no further, ever."

They all nodded. "Course, Boss," said John.

"So," said Terry, "Let's go over what they have asked us to do. Its two jobs really, both involve Arian Mehmed. The first thing they want us to do is clear two estates of drugs." He held up his hand. "Like you, at first I thought - it's just a glorified PR stunt and the drugs will come flowing back in after a couple of days. However, the more I've thought about it, the more I like the idea." He leaned back and folded his arms. "These bastards make residents' lives a misery. Without the drugs on the estates, it should cut down on the stabbings and shootings, especially if the police get back on them in numbers and I'm assured they will. Also, it will hurt Mehmed, not so much financially. His authority will take a knock. Cocaine may be his business, but I guarantee power is his drug."

"Sounds good," said Nicky. "What do you want us to do? Start searching for old informants?"

"That's the ticket," said Terry.

"Reckon mine will all be dead," said John gloomily.

"Not all, John," said Terry. "Not all."

"We're still here," said Nicky.

Jimmy laughed. "Just about."

"Okay," said Terry, "Let's try. I reckon some of the old guys would be happy enough to finger some of these new bucks. I'm going to have a few quid in the kitty, although I'm rather hoping we can get some help for old times' sake."

He turned to Peter. "Do you reckon you can do the social media and computer searches to help find informants we have lost touch with?"

"Sure. I'll pull one of my guys from his usual stuff and get him doing just that."

Terry said, "With any luck, you might get them on their old home numbers." He turned to Dave. "We are relying on you to do all the police and housing authority checks."

Dave smiled as though pleased to be included at last. "No problem."

Peter said, "Logistically, for police manpower, it might be better to target one estate south of the Thames and the other north of the Thames. This should help confuse Mehmed, who wouldn't have a clue what was happening next."

"Good idea," said Terry.

John folded his arms. "So, if we identify targets who are moving drugs, what then? Even if we disrupt the supply, if they get out on bail, they'll be back up and running in no time."

Terry grinned. "I thought we would go 'old school' and 'Tilbury' them."

Peter, John, Nicky and Jimmy gasped and then started laughing.

Tentatively, Dave raised his hand to his shoulder. "I'm sorry. What does 'Tilbury them' mean?"

"Nicky, perhaps you would explain," Terry said.

Nicky flicked his eyes to the door and then back to Terry.

"Listen," said Terry, "whatever we say in this room stays in this room." He smiled at Dave. "We trust you not to say a word to Jones or anyone else."

Dave swallowed, then nodded.

"Back in the eighties," Nicky began, "we caught a young lad driving a getaway car for a team of armed jewellery shop robbers. They were hitting all the big jewellers in the West End. He was only a kid, and they'd bullied him into stealing a car and driving them. Of course, he didn't have a clue how to steal a car and ended up using his dad's. When we arrested him, the petrified boy informed on the rest of the gang. We convicted them for fifteen armed robberies. The biggest clean-up record in years. We told the judge about the lad's help, and he got let off with a suspended sentence." Nicky leaned back in his seat. "His family was very grateful, and it turned out his old man was the Harbourmaster at Tilbury Docks. Now he would do anything for the Flying Squad."

Dave blinked as though wondering where this story was going.

"So," said Nicky, "If we wanted to get somebody out of the way for a while, we would take them down to Tilbury Docks blindfolded and the harbour master would give us the keys to one of the damaged containers, kept at an isolated part of the wharf. We would then bang them up for a few weeks."

Dave's mouth opened, "Isn't that-"

"Highly illegal? Yes. False imprisonment? Yes."

"Worked a treat," said John.

"Squealing like stuck pigs after a couple of days," said Jimmy.

"We never used it lightly," said Terry. "Desperate measures and all that."

"Wasn't the first time we did it during that gang warfare in Walworth?" Asked Nicky.

"That's right," said John. "Both gangs had guns, and it was looking to be a bloodbath–they had already shot and killed some poor bloke caught in the crossfire in a pub in East Street market. We worked out which members of the rival gang were going to be the next victims and we scooped them up and 'Tilburied them' for a couple of weeks. Gave us enough time to find the guns and arrest the murderers."

Dave Driscoll asked, "Didn't they complain when you let them out?"

"Who to?" said Jimmy with a laugh. "If they walked into a police station, nobody would believe them back then and they wouldn't want to lose face by telling their mates Old Bill had kidnapped them and locked them up somewhere for a couple of weeks."

Dave looked stern for a moment and the men in the room held their breath. Had they been too hasty in trusting this young man? Dave's face broke into a smile. "I love it," he said.

Each man's shoulders fell and Peter clapped Dave on the back. "Welcome to the team," he said.

"I think it's safe to assume our old mate from Tilbury Docks is well and truly gone," Terry said. "Anybody got any ideas?"

The men sat in silence for a moment. "Hold on," said Peter, "I knew a guy who was in the Regional Crime Squad. He inherited a smallholding from an uncle down near Dartford in Kent - four or five acres. I was only there once. From what I remember, there's a small lake on it and some blokes stocked it with fish and used it on weekends, although that was years ago. It's in the middle of nowhere and has a good few outbuildings on it, like the Nissen huts from the Second World War. I've no idea what it's like now or if he's still got it. It was a good few years ago. I could get hold of him and ask."

"So," Terry clapped his hands. "That's the first mission - Tilbury, a handful of drug dealers on the estates to stop supply and put the wind-up Ariel Mehmed. The second mission is to deal with Mehmed himself."

Peter blew out of his lips. "So how the hell are we going to do that?"

Before he could answer, the door swung open and Diane appeared with a pot of coffee, six cups, milk and sugar on a tray. They rattled as she placed them on the table. "Are you boys hungry?"

Nicky beamed at being called a boy and said, "Not half."

"I'll do a spread - downstairs in an hour, let's say?" She didn't wait for an answer. "I've got some tinned salmon and tuna for the sandwiches." As she walked away, she said, "Ooo, might have some vol-au-vent cases in the freezer too."

The men laughed and helped themselves to coffee.

"So, Mehmed," said Peter. "We can't Tilbury him, surely?"

Terry shook his head. "Nope. We are talking about a major drug dealer whose henchmen are well-armed."

The men sent each other looks. What were they supposed to do about that?

"Don't worry," said Terry. "I've recruited some help. They'll fly in from Northern Cyprus when we need them."

Dave furrowed his brow. "From outside the police?"

Once again, Terry was concerned that Dave might not be completely on board. "They are not just random guys - they have a stake in the game. Their boss is Mustafa Hassan."

"Brother of Ozzie and Omer?" said John.

"That's right, and Yusuf. Those guys - Mustafa, Ozzie, Omer and Yusuf - ran South London for decades and used to handle most of the drugs that arrived in the UK. For reasons best known to themselves, they did a deal with Mehmed, which ended up with Ozzie Hassan and Omer Hassan getting nicked for the importation of cocaine by Custom and Excise and getting fifteen years each. Which put the Hassan family out of the cocaine business, and Mehmed moved straight in and took over."

John said, "When you think about the power the Hassan brothers wielded in our days, this Mehmed must be some operator to get one over on them."

"Indeed," said Terry. "The family always suspected that Mehmed had a hand in their arrests."

"Oh, so that's why they'll send in some men to help us," said Dave.

Terry liked the 'us.' "Yes, not only that. Mustafa Hassan was an informant of mine for most of the time I was on the Flying Squad. I hadn't spoken to him for years. I rang him in Northern Cyprus before I met with Alan Jones; he still had the same English mobile number we used to use. Once I confirmed for Mustafa that it was, in fact, Mehmed, who had grassed on his brothers to Customs and Excise, he was more than happy to help us."

"So Mehmed is a customs informant, then?" asked Dave Driscoll.

Terry laughed. "Not to my knowledge!"

When the other men had finished chortling, Terry said, "It seemed the right thing to tell Mustafa. I also told him I would arrange for his brothers to get early parole if he helped. That's why I met with the Home Office guy earlier. They're going to transfer the brothers to Belmarsh Prison on Monday morning as a sign of good faith."

Nicky topped up their cups from the coffeepot before Terry said, "Nobody other than Mustafa and us can know about this deal, especially not his brother Yusuf or any of his mob. Do you understand?"

The men nodded.

"In exchange, Mustafa is sending over two of his men, his bodyguard and the bodyguard's brother. He tells me they are as hard as nails and, just as importantly, nobody knows them over here. They'll fly back as soon as we have finished with them." He nodded at John and Jimmy. "You two will work with them."

"Do they speak English?" said Jimmy.

Terry shrugged. "Yes, they do. I want you and John to come with me tomorrow to meet Yusef. Unless he's changed, I don't expect him to be thrilled dealing with us. However, that's his problem."

"I'm not convinced we need outside help," said Jimmy. "Why bring in strangers from abroad? There has got to be plenty of muscle we can call on over here."

"If anything goes wrong, Mehmed will kill anybody helping us. Nobody knows these two and they can be out of the country in a flash."

"What are we telling Yusuf and the two Turks?" asked Jimmy.

"At every place we raid, they keep the cash and we keep any drugs and weapons." He leaned towards John. "It's your job to make sure that happens. I'm not having Yusuf re-circulating the drugs." To Dave Driscoll, he said, "I need you to hand over any drugs and weapons to Mr Jones."

"Of course," said Dave, smiling. It was as though he was watching a show and enjoying every minute.

"Terry?" said Peter. "I've got those phones you asked for. They're already loaded with our numbers."

"Fantastic," Terry said as Peter handed out the mobiles. "From now on, we only contact each other on these."

John picked his phone up as though it was an object from outer-space. It looked tiny in his huge mits.

"I'll talk you through it," Peter whispered to him.

"Right," said Terry, clapping his hands. "Spot of nosh, I think."

CHAPTER SIX

Going downstairs was like stepping out of the past to a none-too-pleasant present. The lights in the downstairs pub shone brightly and the coffee machine was hissing. "Turn that racket off," said Diane to Jake, appearing out of the kitchen. In her arms was a silver foil tray loaded with tuna vol-au-vents and tinned salmon sandwiches not yet curling at the edges. She plonked the tray on a table by the window. "Help yourself, boys." Returning seconds later, she appeared with a pint glass filled with celery stalks and a handful of cherry tomatoes, which she put on the side of the tray saying, triumphantly, "Salad. Can't have you lot getting scurvy."

"Thanks, love," said Terry.

She beamed up at him. "Anything for you boys. Takes me back." She turned her back to Peter for a moment. "Jake, turn those blinking lights down. It's like a school cafeteria here."

Jake pouted. "It's in daytime mode."

She folded her arms.

"Yes, Nan," said Jake.

"Oh!" said Terry, "that's your grandson."

She tugged at his sleeve to bring him closer. "You won't believe this; he's my great-grandson." Terry must have blinked as she continued, "I got married at nineteen and had our Susan at twenty. Her daughter Tracey was fifteen when she fell, so… that great lummox is my great-grandson." She grinned,

"He's lovely really despite that nose ring." She turned to the table, where Nicky already had a paper plate loaded with goodies. "There are more boys. Should you need it?" Then she walked away, much sprightlier than when she'd taken Terry upstairs only two hours earlier.

Terry asked everyone what they wanted to drink. Before Terry could reach the bar, John touched his arm lightly and directed him away from the others. "Thanks for the opportunity, boss," John said. He tugged down the sleeves of his jacket. "I've been struggling a bit recently if I'm honest. Both financially," he paused, "and in myself."

Terry noted the phrase used by John: their generation didn't employ the word depression. "I haven't a clue what you're talking about, John," he said. "You were the first on my list."

John patted his heart. "Thanks, Terry. I appreciate that."

Terry was about to turn to the bar when John said, "From what Nicky has told us, this could get naughty, and you know I'm up for anything that needs doing."

"I've got no doubt about that, John. You were always the man I needed by my side." He squeezed John's shoulder and moved to the bar. Jake worked through the orders. Two bitters (John and Jimmy); two lagers (Terry and Nicky); gin and tonic (Peter) and a lemonade (Dave). Dave appeared at Terry's shoulder. "Want a hand with that?"

"Sure… How are you feeling?"

"Erm…" he gestured to the men. "About this, you mean?"

Terry nodded.

Dave put his elbow on the bar. "My dad used to tell me all these stories and I thought, he was exaggerating. Playing the crowd."

"He could always tell a good story, your dad," said Terry.

"Yes." Dave smiled. "Except it looks like they were true. Makes me miss him even more." He rubbed the bar with his finger. "Wish I'd listened more."

Terry put his hand lightly on Dave's arm. "We're so glad to have you on board, Dave. I want you to understand you are one of us now and I can assure you, we will keep nothing from you."

"That's good to hear. Makes me feel like one of the team."

"Although listen, none of us wants to compromise your position. You have a career, a wife, two kids and a pension to look after." Dave tried to interrupt,

Terry held up his hand. "You will be a party to everything that happens. However, as far as the job's concerned - and in particular Jones - you are merely working as a liaison between the Metropolitan Police and us." Terry leaned closer. "I want him to believe that you hate the role and feel demeaned by us."

"Really?"

"Yep, trust me, if this goes wrong, and it easily could, he'll be looking for a scapegoat and we won't let it be you. Let him believe we are the rogues and you are on the side of his version of law and order."

Dave nodded. "Got it."

"I'm going to ring him later and arrange for you to see him tomorrow at Scotland Yard - wherever that is these days. Is that okay?"

"Sure."

"You'll collect £5000 in cash and two murder case files." Terry then briefed him on what he was to tell Alan Jones about the enquiry and ended by saying, "You're part of the team, so don't let this lot intimidate you."

Just as he said this, there was a loud shout from the table. They turned to see John swearing at a mobile phone in his hand and Peter patiently trying to talk him down. Terry and Dave laughed and wandered over to the table, taking the drinks.

"About time," said Nicky. "I'm as dry as a witch's c-"

"None of that," said Diane, coming over with a tray of sausage rolls.

Nicky blushed and Jimmy said, a twinkle in his eye, "Apparently, they've now got Viagra tea bags. They don't help your sex life, but they stop your biscuits from going soft when you dunk them." Diane rewarded him with a swipe across his shoulder with a tee towel and uproar from the others.

Terry found a seat next to Peter. "Peter, if we are going to scoop up these people to 'Tilbury em', do you have any vehicles that we can use for transport?"

Peter washed down a sandwich with a sip of gin and tonic and said, "Sure. We've got two large and two small unmarked vans we use for surveillance; any of them will be available when we need them." He took another sandwich off the platter and said, "Nothing beats a bit of soft white bread and plenty of butter."

"What the hell!" said Jimmy from across the other side of the table. They looked up to see him staring at his phone.

On Terry's other side, Nicky whispered in his ear: "Do you miss all this?"

Terry glanced at Jimmy and John, still fumbling with their phones, and Peter and Dave trying to help them. "I've missed these clowns, that's for sure. I certainly don't miss the circus, though. Those couple of meetings with Detective Chief Superintendent Jones confirmed everything I believe is going wrong with the police today. If possible, it's even worse than when we left."

"Amazing, isn't it?" said Nicky. "He hates detectives, although insists on using the title Detective Chief Superintendent."

Terry laughed. "You're right, Nicky. I should have pulled him about that."

Nicky then said more seriously, "I know you've got a plan. What if my man doesn't want to play ball? What if he has nothing to do with Mehmed?"

Terry looked around the bar. As it was only four o'clock, the place was half-empty. There was a group of youngsters - students may be - at the far end, chatting loudly, and a couple by the far window holding hands and staring into each other's eyes. It was safe enough to talk.

"Kenny Pierce has been working with most of the top criminals for years: facilitating the route to bring cocaine into the UK. The South Americans have never been keen on Albanians, they don't trust them, and once the Hassan's were out of business, I would think Mehmed turned to Pierce for help."

Nicky reached for another sandwich, stopped himself, and picked up a beer mat instead. He picked at the sides as he said, "What if he won't talk to me? He hasn't been my informant for years?"

Peter leaned into the conversation - Terry hadn't realised he'd been listening - "Kenny Pierce was your informant? My God, no wonder you got so many big arrests."

"Thing is though, Peter, that was years ago. I reckon he just wants to be left in peace now - keep his head down. Wouldn't you?"

Peter looked over at the rowdy exchange between Jimmy and John about who had found the best screensaver. They had nominated Dave as the judge. Peter said, "Maybe the quiet life isn't for everyone."

Terry said, "I'm sure Pierce will do you one last favour, Nicky. And there's the matter of his boys."

"Billy and Bobby? Aren't they banged up somewhere abroad?" said Nicky. "How can… oh, wait, you've got a plan, haven't you?"

"Billy and Bobby are currently languishing in one of Morocco's finest prisons awaiting extradition back here. The thing is, extradition from Morocco takes years. The Home Office has agreed to screw up the extradition procedure when we give them the nod, meaning Kenny's sons would be free to leave Morocco. I told the Home Office they could pick up the boys in another country. I reckon they might simply disappear."

"So…" said Nicky, ripping his beer mat in half. "When we go to see Kenny Pierce tomorrow, we wave a nice fat carrot. Give us Mehmed in return for his sons."

"That's it!"

"Brilliant. He's big on loyalty for family favours. That's how he started informing. His dad was recruiting couriers to smuggle Krugerrands from South Africa. It was all to do with VAT fraud. When we nicked Kenny's dad, Kenny said he'd grass to convict the principal players. He didn't just stop there; he gave me plenty of names throughout the years. I'm under no illusion; I only got put on the Flying Squad because of him."

"Don't put yourself down, Nicky," said Peter, "Handling an informant like him is a skill set very few have. I sure as hell couldn't do it. That's why I got into the tech side."

"We also need to see if Kenny Pierce can give us any information about Harry Baker."

There had been a lull in the conversation (Jimmy having won the screensaver competition) and John piped up, "Harry Baker? I thought he must be dead by now. What the hell has he got to do with all of this?"

Terry looked behind him: the love-struck couple had left and the students were playing a rowdy drinking game. Another group of men was in the far corner, deep in conversation. "The police saw Mehmed and Kenny Pierce at Harry Baker's office in Mayfair on at least twelve occasions," he said.

"Who's Harry Baker?" asked Dave,

"Dodgy solicitor. I'm pretty sure it would have been Pierce who introduced Mehmed to the firm," said Terry.

"Wow," said John, as though the seriousness of their operation had just hit him. This wasn't just going to be a knockabout with some young thugs on the estate. "Baker was a slippery bugger when I was investigating the Brinks-Mat robbery."

"How so?" asked Dave.

"Oh, that man - he could conjure up an alibi witness out of the mist. And sometimes, prosecution witnesses would, how shall I put it?' He made his fingers into quotation marks. "Reconsider their evidence."

"Had the shit put up them," translated Jimmy for Dave.

"Or not turn up at all - mysteriously disappear," said John. "In the eighties, he had clerks at the chambers at Temple in his pocket. Probably still has. Mind you; we almost scuppered him once." He took a glug of bitter. "In 1983, after the Brinks-Mat, we knew he was up to his neck in it because it was mostly his clients that were the prime suspects. We kept a close eye on him, hoping he'd trip up, then… out of nowhere… the law society suspended him for twelve months from practising law."

"Why?" asked Peter.

"We never found out," said John, throwing up his hands. "It wasn't for the want of trying. The Law Society has more secrets than the Magic Circle and the Freemasons put together."

"No shock there," said Peter.

"We had a pretty good idea what he was up to, though. We reckoned that, as he had a pilot's licence and access to a private aircraft at Biggin Hill, he moved some of the bullion to Spain. Honestly, though, he's as slippery as a bar of soap." He shrugged. "I accept it's not part of the remit, Terry, but we'd make many people happy if we could shaft Harry Baker at the same time."

"Cheers to that," said Jimmy, lifting his glass. They all clinked glasses - though most were empty.

"Dave," said Terry. "That's a job for you. Find out what you can about Harry Baker. Be careful, though; I don't want you raising any red flags as I'm sure he's got plenty of friends in high places."

"Your round, Jimmy," said John.

As Jimmy got the round in, Terry thought through the next day: first was to go with Nicky to see Kenny Pierce - convince him to lead them to Mehmed by telling him they could set his sons free. Then in the evening, he, Jimmy, and John were going to meet Yusuf and tell him they needed him to look after the two heavies when his brother sent them over from Northern Cyprus. In the meantime, Dave was going to pick up cash and info from Jones - all the while convincing Jones that he hated the team - and the rest of the team would be searching for old informants. Seemed like a plan.

He sat back and watched his men as they heckled Jimmy, trying to walk back from the bar with too many pints and a bag of crisps under each arm. At first, Terry hadn't been sure he'd be able to pull this off; however, now his confidence had risen. If only I could go home and tell Denise, he thought.

CHAPTER SEVEN

First thing on Friday morning, Dave Driscoll presented himself to the Commissioners' Staff officer at Scotland Yard. Set in the corner of a busy workroom and only separated from the hubbub by plywood and glass, Jones's office didn't seem to keep up with his position. Or the fuss he made about it.

"Ah, Sergeant Driscoll, come in and sit down," said Jones. "How's it going then?"

Dave tried not to smile. "Not great, to be honest, sir. I don't know what I am supposed to be doing - they keep me completely in the dark."

It gratified Dave to see Jones tut and shake his head.

"They told me to come and see you, collect some money and two murder files, and then ring Mr Reid when I've got them. I don't understand why they asked for me. A probationer could do the jobs they're getting me to do."

"Well, you are part of Operation Trident." Jones smiled brightly. "I'm sure they'll start picking your brains soon." His smile switched off. "Where are his offices?"

"Offices? You are joking, sir. They seem to just meet in pubs."

"Typical. What pubs?"

"I've only met them once so far. That was yesterday in The Brockley Jack in Brockley, South London." He lied. "They left me at the bar while they were having a meeting in the corner. When they'd finished, Mr Reid joined me at the bar and told me to come to you this morning."

Jones threw his eyes up to heaven and said, "I suppose they were drunk? I'd left him only a few hours earlier in another pub."

"I only spoke to Mr Reid. The others ignored me."

"Anything else?"

"I'm to research the two murder files you give me and outline the drug connection if there is one. He then wants me to draw up a list of the ten most violent estates in London."

"Who does he think he is? Remember, you work for me, not him."

"I understand, sir."

"I'll give you my email address and mobile number. When you put the list together, send me a copy, and phone me if you find out anything about their plans." Jones handed over two memory sticks and a large envelope of cash. "Everything relating to the murders is there. I recognise it's difficult, Driscoll, nonetheless I want you to keep as close to them as possible and remember anything you hear. Phone me."

"Yes, sir," said Dave.

When Dave was alone in the lift, he let out a huge laugh, which continued down two floors. When he hit the ground floor, the laughter became closer to tears. He couldn't work out why until he remembered his dad saying, "It was the loyalty which was the thing. The loyalty to each other, not the system. Unfortunately, I don't suppose you'll ever know anything like it."

"I do now," thought Dave. "I do now."

~❖~

Just before midday the same morning, Terry and Nicky pulled up at the twelve-foot-high wrought-iron gates of Kenny Pierce's palatial house just outside Westerham in Kent. The heavy gates opened gently and as Terry drove up the long, shingled drive towards the house, he was conscious of the number of CCTV cameras visible: he knew he was being watched.

"You say he's not violent," he said to Nicky.

"No, not himself. He gets others to do his dirty work."

As the drive swept towards the house, Terry noticed a paddock with several horses and outbuildings, which he assumed were stables. Parked outside the double garage next to the house were a black Range Rover Vogue and a black convertible Bentley Continental with the registration plates KP1 and KP2. He chose not to park next to them in his Toyota Prius. Instead, they pulled up at the front of the house. Kenny Pierce emerged from the large oak front door immediately. (Yes, he had tracked them, thought Terry.) He looked fit, tanned, and exceptionally smart in a pink cashmere sweater.

Terry turned off the engine and both he and Nicky stepped onto the gravel at the same time.

"Kenny," Nicky said with a smile, "This is Terry Reid."

Kenny assessed Terry for a moment and then deigned to shake his hand. Terry said nothing because this was not a man who encouraged chit-chat. Kenny led them through a large entrance hall with an enormous crystal chandelier hanging from the ceiling, illuminating the double marble staircases leading to a first-floor landing.

They entered a huge kitchen, which Terry estimated was almost certainly larger than the entire ground floor of his house. On a wall was a forty-inch flat-screen television displaying fifteen different views of the house, outbuildings, and grounds from various CCTV cameras. Terry could now see that, besides the stables, there were other buildings with cars parked outside them. On the other walls were various pictures of two boys at different ages, who Terry assumed were his sons, the ones currently residing in a Moroccan prison.

"Coffee?" asked Kenny.

"No, thanks," said Nicky. "Just had three for breakfast."

Terry smiled and shook his head.

Kenny gestured for them to sit, and they sat down around a large table with the choice of eight chairs.

After sitting in silence for what seemed like minutes, except it was only a few seconds, Kenny said, "I only agreed to meet you, Nicky, out of curiosity. You must have retired from the Old Bill, what, twenty years ago now?"

"You're right, Kenny, over twenty years," said Nicky. "We're here because, unlike me, it seems you haven't retired."

Kenny's face changed. It was a look Terry had seen before: tight lips, reptilian eyes. Surely, Nicky had been wrong when he said Kenny wasn't a violent man. If Terry had been close enough to Nicky, he would have kicked him under the table. Hard.

"What did you say to me?" said Kenny.

Nicky opened his mouth; Terry couldn't risk it. His heart beat hard as he said, "Hear us out, Kenny, and if you don't like what we have to say, we'll go."

Kenny said nothing.

Then Nicky blurted, "Kenny, we're well aware you're in bed with Arian Mehmed and we need your help to get him nicked."

"Fuck off. What do you think I am?"

The swearing was preferable to the cold-killer look. Maybe Nicky knew what he was doing. Terry took a deep breath. "I know exactly what you are. That's why we're here. I think I may have a deal that will be of benefit to you."

Kenny barked out a laugh. "Oh? This should be interesting."

Terry looked him dead in the eye and said, "Your sons."

Kenny turned red with anger and was getting out of his chair when Terry said, "We'll exchange your boy's freedom for Mehmed. That's the deal."

Kenny let out a breath and sat back down.

"We are not interested in you or anyone else, only Mehmed. No matter how this goes, he'll get nicked, and without us, the chances are you will go with him. - You are up to your neck in his business."

Terry ignored the look Nicky flashed at him and said, "If you don't help us, you might even serve your time with your boys when they're eventually extradited from Morocco. A family suite at Belmarsh, perhaps. Won't that be nice? A long stretch, too. You for helping a major drug dealer and your boys for drug importation, then legging it out of the country to escape prosecution. How many years do you reckon, Nicky? Ten to fifteen for each of them?"

"About that."

Kenny narrowed his eyes.

"Listen, it doesn't have to be that way. If you help us, we can ensure your sons won't get extradited from Morocco." He smiled. "Maybe once they release them, they can make their way back home. Under the radar."

Kenny folded his arms. "I don't buy it. You'll stop their extradition. Really?"

Terry knew he almost had him, though it seemed Kenny was unwilling to concede just yet.

"What's stopping me from telling Arian about this conversation as soon as you leave?" he said. "He could just shut up shop and that would be the end of that. If you had any evidence against him, you wouldn't be here. You would have nicked him by now."

"Absolutely," said Terry, spreading his hands. "Nothing is stopping you, and you know him much better than us. However, I reckon he would ask himself why we came to you looking for help, and from what I've been told, he kills first and worries about the answers to questions later."

After a moment of silence, to let Kenny process this, Terry said, "Of course, that still leaves your sons facing a twelve to fifteen prison stretch over here and in the meantime rotting away in Kenitra Prison. Have you seen that place? It's filthy and overcrowded."

Kenny interrupted. "How can I be sure you can stop my son's extradition? This could be just a con."

Terry put his hand on the table between himself and Nicky. "I thought you knew Nicky well enough to know he wouldn't promise anything he couldn't deliver."

Kenny stared at Nicky, who gave him a nod.

"However," Terry continued, "I've arranged for your solicitor to be contacted by the Home Office on Monday morning and told they will delay the extradition papers for another three months. That'll be your proof we have the influence to make the extradition go away - should you help us."

Kenny sat in silence, so Terry continued, "There's a lot to consider, so what I suggest, Kenny, is you think about things over the weekend, wait till your solicitor contacts you on Monday and if you want to deal, ring Nicky." He paused. "I'm going to be straight with you. The deal is only available if you tell us everything about the operation - and I mean everything. Leave anything out and the deal's off. It's only available if the police nick Mehmed."

~❖~

That evening, Terry met with John Olde and Jimmy Smith outside a bookmaker on the Old Kent Road. This wasn't a fancy place like *William Hills,* with floor-to-ceiling glass windows and multiple screens showing dog and horse racing throughout the country and beyond. It looked derelict.–It had one window boarded up, and the other protected by a metal grill. The sign was so dirty it was illegible and the door looked as though people only ever kicked it open.

They stood to the side. "What's Yusuf Hassan like?" asked Jimmy.

"Nothing like his three older brothers. He's a pussy compared to them. Lives off their reputation. He's the only one left to run the family business, with Mustafa, now living back in Northern Cyprus and the other two in prison."

"Family business? "Said Jimmy, looking at the dirty sign. "Not just bookmakers, I presume?"

Terry laughed. "No, they earn the real money from an old-fashioned protection racket and supplying cannabis to all of London. His heavies bully publicans into paying for security; then again, he's careful only to pick on the ones he knows won't fight back. The family has installed their gaming machines or pool tables into almost every pub in South London, whether or not they are wanted."

John nodded. "So, I presume some of his heavies might be here now?"

Jimmy cracked his knuckles. "Of course. Shall we go in?"

They shoved open the door to an empty shop, save for one teller behind plate glass. As soon as he saw the men, he pressed a button under his desk and nodded to a door to their right, which clicked open. They could hardly see as they walked down the stairs. Pushing open the only door, they found themselves in a basement office. It was a small room with paint peeling from the walls. Besides the three men, who stood as they came in, all the room contained was a battered grey metal filing cabinet, a desk with a stash of pornographic magazines shoved under one leg, and two beat-up chairs.

Why the hell did we agree to meet here? Terry thought. He could hardly breathe, squashed against the filing cabinet, with the towering figures of John and Jimmy on either side of him. As big and far uglier were Yusuf's thugs, who stood by the table. Yusuf, himself, was slim and wiry with a face that Terry was sure never smiled.

"We needn't take up much of your time," said Terry. "I'm sure Mustafa has made everything clear."

Yusuf clenched his fists. "Mr Hassan to you."

Terry smiled. "Sure. I rang your brother, Mr Hassan, sorry - and he said that once the two men arrive from Northern Cyprus, you'll house them and we'll get in touch when we need them."

It appeared if Yusuf could have paced, he would have done so. "I don't know what you have got on my brother to make him agree to this. This is a load of bollocks. We don't need any help to sort out Mehmed, especially from ex-old bill. Our family deals with matters ourselves."

"Your brother doesn't agree. Anyway, there should be a nice few quid in it for you," said Terry.

"My brother isn't here. We don't need your money and do you believe turning over some of Mehmed's dealers is going to make any difference to him?" said Yusuf, the veins bulging at the side of his neck.

How much easier it would be to tell him that if he did this small thing, then his brothers in prison would walk free. However, this wasn't a man to be trusted. "This isn't a negotiation, Yusuf," Terry said. "Your brother has already done the deal; I just want to make sure that when his guys fly over, you house them and keep them out of the way. You must keep them out of sight, and I'll contact you when I need them."

"Who are you giving orders to, you cunt?" screamed Yusef.

With a speed that belied his size, Jimmy Smith pounced on Yusef, who was so surprised he jumped back and cracked his head hard against the wall. Jimmy gripped his throat with one massive hand. John Olde was next to react, moving with his back to Jimmy and facing Yusef's men, almost daring them to protect their boss. They both took a step back.

"Listen, you prick, if bullshit was music, you'd be a fucking brass band," said Jimmy. "You've had five years to sort out the man responsible for putting your two brothers in prison.

Except, you've done nothing; you're all piss and wind. Whatever we do will be more than you've done. So, you show some respect to Mr Reid and do as you're told. Nod if you understand," ordered Jimmy.

After a short time, Yusuf nodded.

"Anything else, boss?" Jimmy asked.

"No, I think you've explained everything," replied Terry.

Jimmy let go of Yusef, who sank to the floor, a bright red mark glowing around his neck.

As the ex-detectives were leaving the office, Jimmy turned and said to Yusef, "Next time we meet, you make sure you play nice."

Walking back to their car, Terry found himself shaking. It'd been a long time since he had seen any action. He glanced at Jimmy and John and saw they were both smiling. He said, "It's been a long day. Shall we have a drink?"

He got no arguments from the other two.

Sitting in the Lord Nelson pub in Old Kent Road, nursing a pint of lager, Terry said, "I know it's difficult bringing a couple of strangers onto the team, so I need you two to keep a close eye on them. I'm pretty sure they will be fine, as they've got a good background. However, they have never been out of Northern Cyprus and might need a bit of guidance. I must be mad saying this to you two: I'm depending on you not to let them go over the top. We don't need any dead bodies to deal with."

Jimmy and John smiled. Terry could see they were unsure if what he had said to them was a compliment or an insult.

CHAPTER EIGHT

On Monday morning, Terry's mobile rang. He looked at the screen and recognised the Northern Cyprus international code. On answering, he recognised the gruff south London accent of Mustafa Hassan, who said, "Good morning, Terry."

Terry replied, "Good morning, Mustafa. Is everything all right?"

"I wanted to let you know Ozzie and Omer's move to Belmarsh Prison happened this morning. I understand Yusef has got the raving hump with you and a couple of your blokes. He's not a happy bunny. What did you do to upset him?"

Terry thought again of the red mark on Yusuf's neck. "We had to get a little heavy - had no choice. There's no way we could have told him the full story. We agreed to keep it between ourselves. What have you told Yusef about the move of your brothers to Belmarsh?"

"What you told me to say: I said I'd got a solicitor to put in a moody request, stating that our sister Esma had got cancer and the only way she would ever see them again was if the prison service moved her brothers to London. I've told Omer and Ozzie the same. They believed the story, at the moment."

Terry glanced at the photo of Denise on the wall. "They think their sister has cancer?"

Mustafa laughed. "Sure, why not? Yusef is going to see Ozzie and Omar tomorrow with Esma. Are you sure you can get them both parole?"

"I got them moved to Belmarsh, didn't I? Terry replied. "As long as you keep up your end of the bargain, I'll keep up mine."

"I'm happy to do anything to get the boys out of prison, except I don't see how this will bring that rat Mehmed down. I'm still pissed off with myself for ever getting involved with him. My brothers warned me about getting into bed with that Albanian cunt, and now they are both in prison because of him," Mustafa grumbled.

"You need to trust me; more things are going on at the same time. Your bit is just a part of it. It's obvious how much you want Mehmed put out of business permanently, and I'm doing everything I can to achieve that."

"When do you want my men over there? They're ready to go - you just have to say the word."

"Not yet. I'll let you know. No point in them hanging about over here till they're needed. There's less chance of them being seen. I reckon Yusef will try to shit-stir using them?"

"I don't think you understand, Terry. They're loyal to me and nothing anyone says will change that. Just give me a ring when you want them," replied Mustafa. "When this is all sorted, you must come out and visit me. It's a beautiful sunny day here and I'm having breakfast sitting around the pool. If this all works out, I will owe you a holiday."

They said their goodbyes, and Terry reflected that another piece of the puzzle was now in place. He took out his notes and was working on them when a phone rang. It wasn't the sound of his normal mobile. It wasn't until he located the ringing coming from his jacket pocket in the hall that he remembered it was the phone Peter had given him.

"Hi," he said, breathless.

"Oh, I was just about to ring off," said Nicky. "Kenny wants to meet us this afternoon at four."

Terry punched the air. "That's great. I assume he wants to play ball,"

"I would think so; he didn't say. He wants to meet us at the London Golf Club. He's a member."

"Brilliant. Let's travel together. Shall we meet in the car park of the Rose and Crown pub in Green Street Green near Orpington, say about three p.m.? That will give us plenty of time. And we can go together. "

Having met as arranged and travelled deeper into Kent, they arrived fifteen minutes early and waited in the golf club car park surrounded by Rolls Royces, Bentleys, Mercedes Benz and every make of four-wheel-drive vehicle known to man. Despite the obvious wealth of the members, it shocked Terry when Nicky told him the joining fee for this golf club would cost around £20,000 plus the annual fees - no wonder it was so exclusive. He felt pleased he had never caught the golf bug, unlike so many other ex-police officers, including Nicky.

"Is that how much yours costs?" he asked Nicky.

"Don't be daft."

They stared out of the windscreen, watching the well-heeled golfers entering and leaving the clubhouse, some of them swaying as they left. Terry said, "Just as well, their motors are keyless entry. I think a few of them would have a problem finding the lock with a key."

Nicky laughed. "We should tell the local nick. It would bump up their statistics if they sat at the entrance with breathalysers."

"Too much paperwork."

Nicky said, "I never asked before, how did you get Mustafa Hassan working as an informant for you?"

"It was a bit of luck. I used to see him in the pubs and clubs we all used in those days. He'd send a drink over to me and I'd send one back. It was just a nodding acquaintance. One day, out of the blue, I got a message asking if I could meet him at lunchtime in a restaurant on the Old Kent Road. When I got there, he told me a story about his nephew, on his wife's side, who was the first of their family to go to university. He got nicked in Canterbury, in Kent. He'd been in a nightclub with a group of his mates when it all kicked off. The doormen got them all outside; unfortunately, a kid in the opposite mob lost an eye during the fight. The police had already got the CCTV from inside and outside the club and they charged his nephew and the others with affray. Not knowing anybody in Kent Constabulary, he turned to me looking for help."

Two stunningly beautiful women wearing shorts, golf shirts and sun visors walked toward them. In close pursuit was a young man carrying two golf bags, which he dispatched into the boot of a new Rolls Royce Ghost parked next to them. The women drove off, but not before taking a long hard look at Terry and Nicky, two elderly men sitting in an elderly Toyota Prius.

"So what happened?" asked Nicky.

"Back then, Kent Constabulary used to send their junior detectives to the ten-week Metropolitan Police Detective Training School Course at Hendon. I struck up a friendship with one of them on my course, as we both played rugby, and we kept in touch over the years. By then they had promoted him to Detective Superintendent based in Maidstone. I met him for a bit of lunch and it transpired that Mustafa's nephew and another kid were right on the periphery of the fight and the police in Canterbury together with their prosecution service had already decided to offer no evidence against either of them at the next court appearance. I had another meeting with Mustafa and told him I had arranged for the charges to be dropped against his nephew and, for appearance's sake, they'd drop charges against another kid."

Nicky laughed in admiration.

"He didn't ask questions, and I didn't offer any explanation. He wanted to compensate me for my time and effort, which I refused. I knew then I had him. As a matter of honour, he would have to repay the favour. About three months later, a team of armed robbers was hitting the high-end jewellers in Knightsbridge and Mayfair. We had intelligence; they were a south London team, so I asked Mustafa for help and that sealed our relationship."

Nicky paused before saying, "There's something you need to know about Kenny Pierce. Everyone thinks he's a bit of a gentleman thief. There's a dark side to him."

Terry moved in his seat, so he was facing Nicky.

"He started his criminal career, like his dad, involved in a VAT fraud, in a big way. He roped in a straight businessman called Joe Brown. Brown was a family man in his fifties with five kids, including twin sons aged eighteen and three younger daughters. Brown got nicked by the Fraud Squad and did a deal by agreeing to give evidence against Kenny and the others." Nicky took a deep breath before saying, "Shortly after, police found the bodies of Brown's twin sons in a burnt-out car in Herne Bay. They had shot both of them in the head. Nobody could prove Kenny Pierce's involvement; in fact, he was in Spain when the murders occurred. Brown retracted his statement and Pierce was in the clear. A few months later, while awaiting trial, Joe Brown hung himself in his cell."

"I see," said Terry.

Nicky looked at the clock on the dashboard. "Time?"

"Time," Terry agreed.

They walked into The London Golf Club. Looking around, Terry felt the entrance area was like a lobby of a five-star hotel rather than a golf clubhouse. Although a modern building, it had a cathedral ceiling with wood beams and panelled walls. Two attractive women in uniform attended the large reception desk. Kenny Pierce was sitting alone at a table in the adjoining bar. Terry didn't know if Pierce was any good at golf, or if he just dressed like a professional. He was wearing lime green trousers with a matching polo shirt.

Terry thought about remarking on Kenny's outfit when they arrived at the table. He decided against it. Kenny smiled, stood up, and shook their hands. How different from their first meeting, thought Terry.

"They do a nice burgundy here. I'll order us a glass each, see if you like it," Kenny said, raising his hand for a server. When they arrived, the glasses shone on a silver platter; the wine was blood red and tasted expensive.

"I'm thinking about investing in the vineyard," said Kenny, and the men smiled politely.

"So," said Kenny, "My brief got the message from the Home Office informing him they are delaying the service of the extradition documents to return Billy and Bobby for up to three months." He laughed. "He's fuming. He says they're well out of order for the delay."

"I assume you said nothing to him," said Terry.

"Of course not." He took a sip of his wine. "What happens now?"

Although the tables were wide and separated far from each other by expanses of soft blue carpet, Terry leaned forward and lowered his voice. "You tell us everything about the operation, leaving nothing out, and once we nick Mehmed, we'll make sure they release your sons."

"Don't take offence. I need to know how that will happen."

Terry understood his apprehension. This was about his son's freedom. He nodded and said, "In short, the Director of Public Prosecutions will serve extradition documents on your solicitor. He'll find a discrepancy in the paperwork, enough to get the application thrown out. I can't tell you any more than that. You've known Nicky a long time and I guess you must trust him; otherwise, we wouldn't be sitting here now."

Terry had chosen not to mention the solicitor, Harry Baker, to this point; he assumed he was representing his sons. He wanted to hold this piece of information back in case he needed to use it to test if Kenny Pierce was being honest with them.

Kenny ordered them more wine and sat up in his seat. This was going to be a long story. He started by saying, "I trust you, Nicky, but you both know that if this ever gets back to Mehmed, I'm a dead man. Please don't let me down. My sons couldn't do bird for that many years over here."

"How are they doing in that Moroccan prison?" asked Terry.

"It's a shit hole. I've spread a lot of money about over there. That doesn't stop it from being a rat-infested dump. Prisoners die every week from the diseases they catch there."

Kenny took a long drink of wine.

Nicky reassured him: "As long as you're straight with us, Kenny, we'll be straight with you. Leave one thing out or tell one lie and the deal is off."

Kenny nodded. "In the late seventies and early eighties, things were getting hot in London because of super grasses. A good few of the boys legged it down to Spain and started buying properties in and around the Marbella area. Some of them had brought their wives, whilst most of them enjoyed the regular supply of girls on holiday or others they flew over. It was like their own private club in the sun. The bonus was, it was before any extradition between Spain and England." He took a sip of his wine and continued. "After a while though, some guys just got bored while others were running low on funds. Seeing as they were so close to Morocco, they set up routes to get cannabis into England." he hesitated before continuing. "They needed someone over in England who they could trust, and they turned to me. I started flying back and forward to Spain and arranging for their money to be delivered to them. It was a lot easier back then as nobody questioned cash, and they could even buy properties with it, especially in Spain."

Kenny waved at the server, who replaced the drinks on the table with a bottle of the wine they were drinking and fresh glasses. They sat in silence until the waiter left them. He then said, "After a few years, everyone realised that the big money was in cocaine: you could deliver far smaller parcels, which were easier to conceal for a much larger profit. Over a few months, they had meetings with a Columbian syndicate, and they agreed to a deal. They found alternative routes and everything was going well. From time to time, police or customs intercepted loads and people got arrested. That went with the territory. About seven or eight years ago, Arian Mehmed turned up on the scene, looking to do deals. He was spending a lot of time in Spain. He even flew down to Columbia. Unfortunately for him, the Columbians didn't trust him.

In London, I was dealing with one family who was distributing everything that landed in England. Mehmed got involved with them and shortly after, Customs and Excise were all over the place and a group of them, including family members, got captured with a load of cocaine."

"Would that be the Hassan brothers you're talking about?" asked Terry.

Kenny nodded

"Didn't Omer and Ozzie Hassan get fifteen years each?" said Nicky.

"That's right. The boys in Spain wanted nothing more to do with Mehmed after that, and anyway, by now, they all had enough money to retire. Mehmed took over the entire operation. I knew the Columbians wouldn't deal with him directly, so when Mehmed came to me, I agreed to be the middleman between him and them for the deliveries."

"I assume the boys in Spain thought Mehmed grassed on the Hassans, so why would you get involved with him?"

"Simple. Without me, Mehmed was out of business. He owes me big time. No one would work with him. He had the network, although he couldn't do a thing unless I was on board, so I felt safe. Anyway, I kept myself away from the deliveries. That's where nearly everyone gets nicked."

Terry said, "Kenny, you're telling us nothing we don't already know or couldn't work out, so let's cut to the chase. How does Mehmed get delivery of the cocaine and how does he make payments?"

"OK, I'm getting there," insisted Kenny. He had finished his drink and poured out another. Terry and Nicky held their hands over their glasses. "I told you the Columbians don't trust him, so he always has to pay upfront. When he gets a delivery, a courier is there, and Mehmed puts in his next order and pays the courier in advance."

"What size of delivery does he get?" Asked Nicky.

"Anything over fifty kilos. It's always around a hundred kilos."

"And what does he pay?" asked Nicky.

"£16,500 a kilo, which includes delivery; it's top quality and pure, so I assume he cuts it before moving it on."

Terry asked, "What do you get?"

"£1000 a kilo out of the Columbians' end."

Nicky blew air out of his lips. No wonder he can afford the fees here, thought Terry.

"Are you at the drop?" asked Terry

"No, I told you, I'm just the middleman,"

"So tell me when and where the drop is and where the courier delivers the money," said Terry.

"I get told by the Columbians in advance when it's arriving in the country, and I tell Mehmed. He's got four different warehouses, and he tells me which one he wants to use. On the day of the delivery, I get a call telling me what time it will be at the drop. I pass that on to Mehmed."

"I assume you don't have these conversations on the phone, so how do you do

it?"

Pierce hesitated. Terry could see him calculating: he'd grassed-up plenty of people in the past through Nicky. He probably hadn't liked any of them. Mehmed was in that same category. He would know this was going to be the end of a very lucrative arrangement. However, his sons were more important to him than money.

Terry sensed he was struggling and said, "If you're worried about Harry Baker getting nicked, I've already told you we are only interested in Mehmed. You're still tight with Harry. Is his firm dealing with the extradition?"

Kenny blinked, then smiled. "Of course - you know about Harry Baker. I wouldn't want him… he's been good to me over the years."

"And that's where you meet Mehmed - at Harry's office."

Kenny nodded.

"And where does the money from the courier go?" asked Terry.

"The courier takes it by motorbike to Harry, who sends my corner to an off-shore account. He's never told me what he does with the rest of the money for the Columbians."

"Does Harry Baker work for Mehmed as well?" asked Nicky.

"No way, he's proper scared of him and anyway, Mehmed thinks it's just a safe place to meet, he hasn't a clue Harry knows anything about the operation or his involvement with the Columbians,"

"So, what happens when the courier tips up at Harry Baker's office with a bag full of cash?" asked Terry.

"I've only been there once, and that was the first time. Mehmed had to pay upfront for his first-ever load. He ordered a minimum of fifty kilos. I had to introduce the courier to him and he handed over a bag with £825,000 in it. I then took the courier to Harry's office and introduced them."

"What did he do with the money?"

Shaking his head, Kenny said, "He made the courier wait until he counted every penny; it took forever and then he wrote it down in a book and made the courier sign it; typical solicitor, he probably got Repetitive Strain Injury from counting - mind you he told me he has got a money counting machine since then."

Terry asked, "Then what happened?"

"What do you mean?"

"What happened to the money?"

"When the courier left, Harry put the money and the book back in the safe," answered Kenny.

Terry looked at Nicky and smiled.

"What, a safe in his office?" asked Terry.

"Don't get me started on that; he's got an antique safe he inherited when he moved into the office; it's his pride and joy; he had it restored; it cost an absolute bundle because they had to do all the work in his office, it was too heavy to move. He's on the third floor; god knows how they got it up there all those years ago. I suppose they built it there." He chuckled and said, "He never stops going on about it. They built it in 1920 and he uses it to keep his drinks decanters and glasses on as a centrepiece for his clients." Shaking his head, he continued, "He loves showing it off, and he gets the right hump if you don't remark how beautiful it is."

"I don't suppose you know the make?" asked Terry.

"I do," said Kenny. "It's got 'Ratner' on a plate on the front; I remember because I made the mistake of taking the piss one day and said it must have come out of one of those cheap jeweller's shops. Anyway, he gave me a right lecture on 'Ratner' being the top safe makers who fitted out Harrods Safe Deposit Vault and how his safe was rare because it came with two original keys."

"Why did you get Harry Baker involved?" asked Nicky.

"He already was. About the time we changed over to cocaine from cannabis, the cash was too much to take to them in Spain, and even here, it was getting difficult to use large amounts of cash. I spoke to the boys in Spain, who all knew Harry, I came to an arrangement with him and he set up offshore accounts for everyone and dealt with the money. Mind you; he charges a lumpy commission to straighten the money up. It just seemed natural to keep using him when Mehmed got involved," replied Kenny.

"So," asked Terry. When is the next delivery due?"

Kenny drained another glass of wine. "The Columbians should contact me in the next ten days. They then give me about a week's notice for the delivery."

"How much is the next delivery?"

"One hundred Kilo."

"Okay," said Terry, "I need you to phone Nicky when the Columbians contact you, and you have arranged a meeting with Mehmed."

With that agreed, Kenny wanted to order them another bottle, but Terry declined, and they left him to get drunk alone.

~❖~

As they were walking back to the car, Terry looked at his watch and realised they had been with Kenny Pierce for nearly three hours. He yawned; even his bones felt tired. He wanted to sleep, though he needed to process the information they had received and formulate a plan.

Just as they pulled into the Rose and Crown car park, he said to Nicky, "Tomorrow morning, would you call the troops and arrange a meeting at eleven o'clock? We need to crack on with these dealers."

Nicky nodded. "There's been two more stabbings since Isaac Okoro died. It's all over the news."

"I've seen it," said Terry. "We have to get these drug dealers on the back foot, not knowing who's going to be hit next."

~❖~

Once he had dropped Nicky back to his car and, after long delays getting through the Dartford tunnel, Terry arrived home to a dark, empty house. He had arranged for a neighbour to look after his dog while he was working.

Getting a bottle of lager from the fridge and his favourite Stella Artois glass from the adjoining freezer, he settled into the sofa and took a long gulp of the ice-cold drink. Terry was only too aware of the distinction between being alone and being lonely. It was at times like this he realised just how lonely he was. He missed his wife more than words could express. He never sat on her favourite sofa and still slept on the right-hand side of their king-size bed. Denise's clothes remained in her wardrobe; despite kind offers of help from her close friends, he gained comfort from their presence. During the night, he would constantly wake and expect to see her next to him. He resented the fact Arian Mehmed was now constantly on his mind, occupying the space that should be reserved for Denise.

He couldn't contemplate failure. Of course, not every job was successful when he was in the police; however, then he moved on to the next case. That wasn't available to him now. The fear of failure was more powerful than the joy of success, and the idea of letting the team down by a wrong decision overwhelmed him. The sleepless nights were now piling on his chest like concrete blocks. Despite this, he drifted off into a deep sleep, fully dressed, on the sofa.

CHAPTER NINE

The visiting area at Belmarsh Prison in South East London was large and grubby, with tables and chairs secured to the floor. Each table had enough room for one prisoner and a maximum of two visitors at a time. Except Ozzie and Omer Hassan had different treatment - they always did. The prison officer showed them to an area tucked into the corner, away from other prisoners and their visitors. As they reached the table, Ozzie and Omar made no show of welcome to their brother and sister - Yusuf and Esma - they simply sat and lifted their chins.

Having his back to the wall, Ozzie could see other prisoners in the room, looking at them and whispering to their visitors. He knew his family would be the topic of conversation on the landings as soon as visiting was over: their notoriety was something he was aware of, lived with, and used to his advantage.

He flexed his chest a little under his shirt, hoping either Yusuf or Esma would tell him he was looking good. They didn't - it wasn't that type of family - nor did they tell Omer that he was fatter than ever. They simply stared, waiting for Ozzie to start the conversation. He said, "Mustafa has played a right blinder here. I take it you're all right, sis? You're not sick or anything?"

Esma rolled her eyes. "No, I'm great. I've got the raving hump, though. I've had to turn up here wearing no make-up, trying to look as if I'm ill and dying. It's a right pain."

Ozzie and Omer smiled.

Yusuf frowned. "I don't know what's going on. Mustafa has wrapped himself around some ex-old bill, and that can't be a coincidence. On top of that, he's sending Ali and Elgin over from Northern Cyprus to help them. They're supposed to be going after Mehmed." He balled his hands into fists. "I've told them we don't need any help, especially from any ex-old bill."

Ozzie leaned over the table and hissed, "Keep your voice down." He sat back, pleased that his younger brother had cowered. Yusuf had always been a weed. "Look, you're out there. We're in here. Omer and I have both been in shit prisons miles from home. We hardly see our families. Now look at us…" he spread his hands, "We're sharing a cell and our families are a stone's throw away. I don't care what Mustafa is doing."

"Yes," growled Omer. "Mustafa is your older brother, so show him some respect."

Yusuf turned to Esme. "Cut that out!"

She threw up her hands. "What?"

"Waving at the other prisoners. They've got their wives with them."

She shrugged and Omer and Ozzie grinned. "It should be her you tell to have some respect," Yusuf said to Omer.

"Such a fucking baby," said Omer to Ozzie.

Yusuf shrank back in his seat.

"A baby," said Ozzie, "Who can't run a business." He turned to Yusuf. "Why is my wife having to chase you for money every month? I've been speaking to Omer, whose family has the same problems. What the fuck are you playing at?"

Yusuf bit his nails before saying, "I've been very busy and sometimes I haven't always got time to run around dropping off money."

Ozzie turned red. His eyes bulged and his body shook as he rose from his chair. "You're too fucking busy?" he screamed, saying each word slowly.

The entire room looked in their direction, although the guards didn't attempt to control the situation. Omer gripped his brother's muscled arm and pulled him back into his chair with every ounce of strength he possessed. Ozzie was still shaking when he said, "Make time. Do you hear me, Yusuf? Make fucking time.

Omer said calmly, "Everything you've got is because of us. I promise you, even from here, it would be easy to take it all away. Do you understand?"

Yusef nodded, "I'm sorry, it won't happen again."

"It better not," said Ozzie.

A loud bell rang, signalling visiting was over. Ozzie, not wanting to take liberties on their first day, nudged Omer and they got up to return to their cell. As they parted company, Esma said, "Mustafa has said I need to keep up the pretence. I've got to keep coming to see you. I'll share the visitor orders with your wives and children." Yusuf promised to visit them again. Seeing as this was his first visit since their convictions, they all knew that this was a lie. They wouldn't see him again until they had completed their sentences.

CHAPTER TEN

It was warm in the office above the Peacock, and the vinegar smell of decades of beer soaked into the carpet was permeating the room. The sooner we are out of here, the better, thought Terry, as he ran his eyes down his notes. They were just waiting for Nicky.

When he arrived, he was wearing a tatty tweed coat. "Fuck me, Nicky," Jimmy said. "That jacket looks older than you. Have you just come off your allotment?"

"I'll have you know this was an expensive jacket when I bought it."

"Really? When was that? You look like an extra from Family at War."

Everyone laughed.

John looked at Dave. "I'm not sure what you're laughing about. Did you think it was fancy dress today?"

Dave was wearing a black t-shirt combined with a pair of faded jeans with tears on both legs. As Dave smoothed the sides of his hair with the palm of his hands, John continued, "You off to Glastonbury when we're finished here?

"I doubt it," said Jimmy. "It's not raining today, and it always rains at Glastonbury.

Terry wrapped his knuckle on the table. "So," he said. "Let's all catch each other up on where we are. You go first, Nicky."

Nicky grinned. "Looks like Kenny Pierce is completely on board. He's going to tell us where and when the Columbians are going to drop the cocaine."

The men clapped.

Terry held up his hand. "Don't let's get ahead of ourselves. We're not working on our own - there's the tricky issue of putting this together in such a way that even Detective Chief Superintendent Jones can't screw it up. The problem is that we'll lose control of the shipment as soon as he knows about it."

"He'll tell the press too," said Dave.

"Right," said Terry. "Listen. We've got a couple of weeks to work something out, so for the time being, we'll keep this amongst ourselves."

Terry then outlined the full content of the meeting with Kenny Pierce. Nicky chipped in with any additional details.

"There was some more good news from Kenny," said Nicky. "He told us the make of the safe where all Harry Baker's documents are."

Terry knew the answer but said to the group. "Do we have anyone who can get in it for us?"

They looked at each other before John said, "Well, the best Peterman back in the day was Monkey Gregory. An old safe like that would be right up his street."

They all agreed except Dave, who stayed silent and shook his head.

Terry said, "Does anyone have a way to get hold of him, even if he's still alive? Didn't you know him, Jimmy?"

Jimmy flexed the beefy fingers of his right hand and let them make a fist before sniffing and saying, "Police-wise, I didn't. We both were at the same school, Sir John Cass, in Stepney. He's a year older than me. When I first started boxing at the Repton, he used to go down there. He wasn't interested in boxing, only knocking out hooky gear he always had wrapped around him. The coaches soon cottoned on, kicked him out, and barred him. The last time I saw him was maybe twenty-five years ago. I was out running and I bumped into him. It turned out he was renting a flat about half a mile from where I lived in Ilford. I went for a drink with him a good few times near his flat. He was on bail waiting for trial, for a safe-breaking in Epsom."

"So, he was still grafting, then?" said John

"Not really," replied Jimmy. "I got his full life story every time we met. Don't laugh; I felt sorry for him. He had realised that safe-breaking was dying out; companies just didn't keep big lumps of cash in safes anymore. They were using night safes or even security van collections. During one of his stretches, he did a carpentry course and when he got out, he got a job at a locksmith in Soho to learn the trade properly."

"A safebreaker was working for a locksmith," Terry said. "You've got to be joking with me."

Jimmy said, "The guy who owned the shop was a cousin of Monkey's wife; besides, he's old school and wouldn't dream of touching a customer. Anyway, after a while, he branched out on his own, fitting security doors and locks and was doing all right until this firm asked him to do a job in Epsom. He told me he hadn't fancied it and, instead of asking them for a percentage like normal, he asked them for a big, upfront fee, thinking it would put them off. That way, he wouldn't have to lose face. To his surprise, they agreed and paid him. Everything was fine on his end until one of them got nicked flashing money about and then stuck Monkey up to the police. They arrested him and he was awaiting trial. That was the last I saw of him; I'm pretty sure somebody told me he got eight years. He must have been out years ago."

John said, "I've got to ask. Why is he called Monkey?"

"It started at school. He had a flat face like someone had hit it with a shovel, and one day a girl said he looked like a monkey and it stuck for the rest of his life."

Terry grinned, got up, and opened the second sash cord window, a pointless exercise as all it did was let in warm air.

"Dave," he said, "another job for you. Monkey must collect his old-age pension by now; see if you can get an address for him - his date of birth will be on his criminal record. What's his first name?"

"Phil," said Jimmy, "Philip Gregory."

There was a knock at the door and Diane entered carrying a tray with two large jugs of orange squash and six glasses. The welcoming sound of ice clinking against the jugs caught their attention.

"Thought you might prefer this to coffee today."

"Hope there's a good splash of vodka in it," said John.

"Are you taking the piss?" replied Diane.

"Thanks, Diane, that's great. Take no notice of him; he's only winding you up," said Peter as she left the room muttering under her breath.

"Right," said Terry. "More immediately, how are we doing with these estates? The body count keeps getting higher every day."

Peter Rhodes looked over his shoulder to confirm Diane had left before saying. "I went down to look at that smallholding near Dartford. It's been left unused for years. Parts of it are so overgrown it's impossible to see much, which suits us. Two of the Nissen huts are usable; the others are rusty and not secure. The two we can use will need a bit of work on the doors and new locks; other than that, they're perfect. If you give me the go-ahead, I'll get them sorted."

"Is it isolated, Peter?" Asked Terry.

"I'd say so. It's definitely not on any sat-nav. I had a hell of a job finding it and I've been there before."

"Well done, Peter. If you could get on with that and arrange supplies, we're looking at two, maybe three weeks' worth. I found a firm that will supply heavy-duty door openers. Can you get two of them for us? If you see me after the meeting, I'll give you the details and some cash. What about informants? How are we doing with them?"

"We've got a couple of things going and hopefully, we'll have something concrete by the end of the week," replied Peter.

"OK, keep on it. We need to see some progress by next week. I want Dave to explain to us how these drug gangs on the estates operate. The more we find about them, the better prepared we'll be."

Jimmy replenished their glasses with orange juice.

Dave cleared his throat, took out a folder, and said, "Okay, if I run through the rank structure of the drug gangs, and how it works?"

"Sure," said Terry. Dave was already passing out pieces of paper.

"You're organised," said Jimmy, reaching for his glasses in his inside pocket.

"It starts with Teenies," said Dave, "who are normally under ten because they are under the age of criminal responsibility; they're used to move weapons or drugs between older members."

"Bloody hell," said John, "I've got shoes three times their age."

"Right," said Dave. "Then there are the Runners or Shotters: they're up to fifteen and work the street corners selling drugs or in 'trap houses'. After them, you have the Youngers who are under eighteen. They have some authority over Teenies and Shotters. They set up trap houses, recruit Teenies,

Runners and Shotters and report to the Elders." He turned to John. "The Elders are generally over eighteen, but not by much."

John blew out his lips. "Jesus."

"The Elders run street operations and trap houses. They deal with large amounts of drugs and facilitate the purchase of firearms and other weapons. They have authority over street dealers and Youngers. At the top of the chain are the Faces or Olders, who have limited contact with street-level operations; the street-level members may not even know who the Olders are. They run the entire system on a combination of respect and fear."

"Just like the Mafia, only younger and with different titles," said Jimmy.

"Exactly," said Dave. "Terry and Nicky have told me how much Mehmed is paying for his cocaine. It's important to remember every kilo of pure coke he receives, he cuts with something like benzocaine, which he buys for around £15 a kilo. The street dealers cut it again. As you can see, the profit margin is vast, and even without cutting, Mehmed could sell a single kilo for between £40000 and £60000 to his friends up North."

Terry asked, "Why are there so many stabbings and killings? It must draw the attention of police and can't be good for business?"

"The press would have you believe it's all about a postcode war," Dave replied. "There is a bit of that, although it's also to do with money being owed, robberies from the Teenies and Shotters and revenge for those robberies. However, many of them are pointless stabbings of innocents committed by the younger kids trying to gain a reputation for themselves. They want to be noticed by the Elders. These kids see the trappings of wealth around the Elders and look at it as their way out. The Elders encourage this by giving away pairs of top-end trainers or some designer clothes to them, as rewards for jobs done."

The men sat in silence for a while. These were the streets they grew up in. Yes, petty crime had always been a thing, not this violence; not the ruining of young lives through the greed of a few anonymous men. And had they been young now, would they have been Teenies and Runners? Not one of them could have put their hands on their heart and said no. Each one knew the shame of old clothes, and the pinched faces of their parents trying to make ends meet.

"Well, Terry said, "I think that's enough for today. "We'll meet up on Friday morning for updates on any progress with the informants." He sat forward in his chair. "I can't emphasise enough that time is of the essence. Before concentrating on Mehmed, I want the estate issues tied up and dealt with. Any delay is going to be a problem for us."

~❖~

They retired to the bar, which was quiet, before the lunchtime rush. Dave and Peter sat at a table and divvied out the work required to trace past informants.

"Of course, some of them may be dead," said Peter, "Or moved away."

Dave looked at the list and furrowed his brow. "I'm not sure how many will be on the council list, either. There are not as many council houses as there used to be."

Peter waved his hand and told Dave the other methods he had to trace people. As Dave sat open-mouthed, Peter, explained to him about his contacts within Royal Mail, BT, Sky and most of the mobile phone companies, together with his researchers who could infiltrate most websites.

"My God," said Dave. "Why the hell did you leave the force?

Peter didn't like to tell him the circumstances of his leaving, and even now, the question annoyed him. "It's better this way," he said. "We play by our own rules and get results."

CHAPTER ELEVEN

John Olde walked in the shadow of one of the concrete tower blocks on the Brandon Estate in Kennington. Once a utopian dream in which planners imagined children would play in the large grass areas around the eighteen-storey brutalist blocks, at the time the tallest in London. Since the original construction, lower maisonettes had appeared, interspersed within the high-rise flats. The entire estate was now a no-go zone for the police. Even the ambulance and fire crews were at risk when attending calls. And here he was, John Olde-by-name and now pretty old in age, wandering unprotected. He held his head high, rolled his shoulders and ignored the stares of groups of young kids wearing hoodies. They were like swarms of ants, some on foot, with others on bikes, aimlessly hanging about. It appeared attending school in this area wasn't a priority. Debris covered the little greenery that now existed, including supermarket trolleys, mattresses, and car tyres. John mused that few future premiership footballers would get much practice or hone their skills on this estate. John had escaped from a rough estate in Peckham to join the police. He thought it wasn't as bad as this place on its worse day.

To the side of one maisonette, he saw bunches of flowers and teddy bears and though he did not stop; he knew it was where the brutal murder of Isaac Okoro had occurred. Raised a Catholic, he made a brief cross sign and entered a tower block. Via a graffiti-ridden, stinking lift, he found his way to a third-floor flat, where Peter and Dave had traced Jilly Jones. Ex-model, ex-informant, ex-lover and former wife of Jimmy Jones, a prolific armed robber from the early eighties.

He felt nervous as he reached for the doorbell. He hadn't seen Jilly for many years and their relationship ended suddenly.

~❖~

As she opened the door, he took a step back. He had thought the years might have taken their toll on Jilly, but she still looked fantastic. She had obviously invested in a boob job since he had last seen her. He knew she was fifteen years younger than him, but even so.

"You look incredible," he said and leaned in to kiss her on the cheek. She was too quick and slapped him with considerable force across the face. John pulled back, rubbed his cheek and said, "I always loved it when you were feisty".

"Feisty? Fucking feisty? You screwed me so you could screw over my old man and once he got a lump of bird, you fucked off," she screamed.

"Can I come in or do you want all the neighbours to know your business?"

She looked both ways along the third-floor landing before leading him into the living room. He couldn't help but notice how smart the room was. The walls and carpet were fashionably grey and there were two plush black crushed velvet sofas. On either side of the sofas stood mirrored tables and lamps with black shades. None of this surprised John. Jilly was always classy.

"Look, Jilly," John said, rubbing his cheek, which still smarted, "we both know the reason your old man got nicked was that you found out that he had two other women on the go. So, you used me."

"Hold on a second. It was you who told me about the birds."

"So I did you a favour in the long run. Anyway, I didn't just disappear; I had some problems and had to leave the police force in a bit of a hurry. When I got myself settled, you'd moved, changed your number and I didn't have the facilities of the police to trace you."

Jilly sat on the sofa, all energy spent, and said, "So how did you find me now?"

"Friends," he said, vaguely. "I like that lampshade."

"Listen, what do you want?"

John smiled. "Always to the point. I'd just want to find out how you are and what's been happening to you over the years."

"Bullshit. What's the angle?"

He took a seat. "No angle; I'm genuinely interested if you are alright and how life has treated you."

She settled her back against the deep velvet sofa. Relenting, she said, "When Jimmy got his fifteen years, he still didn't have a clue how he and the others got nicked for the robbery, so he told me where I could get my hands on the money he'd stashed. I only took half, mind," she made clear. "And then I got this place from the council. I invested the money from Jimmy into a launderette close to here and now I've got three. It's all cash, so it's a good living."

"What about your house in Camberwell?"

"I bought that before I met Jimmy, with my money from modelling. He never knew it was mine. As my mum and dad were living there, he always thought they rented it. When they both passed away, Camberwell had become right upmarket, so I had it done up and I rent it out. It's a good earner. Last year, an estate agent said it's worth a right few quid now, well over a million."

This impressed Olde. Although he couldn't understand why on earth was she living in this shit-hole. "Good for you," he said. "What about Jimmy?"

"You know what it's like in prison; the others were trying to convince him I was the grass. Every time I visited him, it always ended up in a row. He thought I was too stupid to grass on him. Then I heard one of his other birds was visiting him and that he'd set her up in a flat on the same estate we were living on and he had a kid with her. I can tell you, I stopped feeling guilty about grassing him up after that." She grinned. "I visited him in prison for one last time, threw his wedding ring at him and told him to keep his new bird as I was moving on."

John laughed. He loved her lack of shame.

"He must have come out years ago now. He never got in touch. Which was just as well. I'm not sure if he's dead or alive, in the country or abroad." She folded her arms. "Look, John, I've no regrets about what I did. That piece of shit treated me like dirt. Once we were married, he made me give up modelling and treated me like his trophy. He would go missing for days. One time, he went on the missing list for two weeks. When he came back with a suntan, he told me he'd been away on business in Spain. It was one reason I got hooked up with you."

John smiled and said, "That, plus my charm and good looks."

"You were always full of yourself."

"So, you were glad to see the back of him,"

"Let me tell you; my prison sentence ended when his prison sentence began."

John cracked his knuckles. "Have you got a new man in your life?" He looked away as though to seem disinterested in the answer.

"No, if I've discovered anything in life, it's that men are like tights; no matter how well you look after them, they always end up running,"

John smiled: she must have some stories. He hoped to hear them all at a later date.

"Your flat is beautiful. This estate is a nightmare. Why do you stay here if business is so good?" he asked.

"I don't know. At first, it was handy for the launderette that's nearby." She looked towards the window, which was framed by expensive-looking grey curtains. Outside, all that was on view were the tops of the maisonettes and the blue sky. "Believe it or not," she said, "this used to be a nice place to live. Even that poet, John Betjeman said so."

John nodded. He'd never heard of him.

Jilly continued, "Now the drug gangs are making everyone's life a misery. I'm going to have to move out soon, anyway. They've killed the business in my local launderette. The bastards use it to sell from and nobody will go near the place or any of the shops nearby. It has graffiti everywhere: there's more paint on it than in the Tate Gallery. I'm going to have to close it down soon." She sighed. "You heard about young Isaak Okoro, right?"

John nodded.

She tutted. "Doing nothing wrong, just cutting through the estate on his way home from school. Butchered to death." She threw up her hands. "I know my brothers and his mates were a right handful when they were kids; they were nothing like this lot, though."

John took a moment and said, "I think I might be able to help you out."

"What, you offering to paint the launderette for me?"

"Put the kettle on, love. I think you're going to like this."

After three cups of tea and a lot of note-taking, John had everything he needed to start working on the source of Jilly's problems: The McCullen brothers, who supplied all the drugs on the estate.

"You're a star," he said.

She winked. "You're not so bad yourself."

As she saw him to the door, Jilly said, "It grieves me to say this, you're still a good-looking bastard, John Olde."

As Olde walked back to his car, he had a smile on his face, a spring in his step and a date with Jilly the next day.

CHAPTER TWELVE

Rory "Dreads" McCullen and his brother, Gerald "Bumpy" McCullen, sat in the living room of the semi-detached house they had bought for their mother in Eltham, each balancing a cup of tea and a plate of homemade cakes. The crockery was her best china, the thought of damaging them petrified the brothers. As usual, Rory and Gerald had chosen the same clothes this morning: both wore black Armani tracksuits and black Yeezy trainers; both had their hair styled with short cornrows. Rory liked how people often mistook them for twins. Somehow it made them more powerful: double the trouble.

Mrs McCullen peered at them from over her teacup and asked the same question she always asked. "Have you heard from your father?"

Rory shot a look at Gerald and tried not to roll his eyes. They had stopped lying to their mother about their father a long time ago. He said, "Mum, you know he's gone, and he isn't coming back. He told everyone he was going back to Jamaica. The police seem to think he was in America. It doesn't matter. He's wanted for three murders over here, so there's no way he's coming back voluntarily."

"You can't say that. I thought he might get in touch."

Rory wanted to comfort his mum. He knew she couldn't accept her husband had left them in a flat on the Brandon Estate years before his disappearance. While he lived in luxury in a penthouse apartment in Mayfair, they had lived in squalor and poverty. What could Rory say? There was no way he could change the sins of his father.

He nudged his brother to let him be the one to change the subject.

Putting his cup and saucer on a side table, Gerald said, "Have you got everything you need, mum?"

She flashed him a crooked smile. "Since you showed me how to do that online shopping, I don't even need to leave the house. It's wonderful."

"What about the cleaner?" Rory said. "Are you happy with her?"

"She's lovely. The minister from my church recommended her. She's the best thing I've done and she won't take any money."

"That's very kind of her," replied Gerald, while Rory tried not to smile. She would never discover that her sons had arranged and paid for the cleaner, together with a healthy donation to the minister and his church.

"And you two?" she said. "You're keeping out of trouble?"

They nodded.

"Maybe you'll show your face in church soon?"

"Yes, mum," said the boys together. Rory stood. "We need to go mum; we've got some business to take care of."

"See you tomorrow," Gerald said as they kissed her goodbye and headed for the Elephant and Castle."

As Gerald drove his red Audi TT, Rory turned to him and said, "There's an auction in Mitcham tomorrow. The property agent has marked off four houses he thinks would work for us. Do you fancy going?"

"How many will that be if we get them?"

Rory did the maths. "Twenty-five, not counting Mum's."

Gerald blared his horn at a driver who tried to cut them up. Casually, he turned to Rory.

"Do they need much work?"

"He said one needs a new kitchen and bathroom. The others only need paint jobs. At this rate, we'll hit our target of forty before the end of the year," said Rory.

After they'd parked the car, Rory stood to one side while Gerald retrieved his favourite toy from the boot.

~❖~

In a lockup under the railway arches in Elephant and Castle sat Prince Boateng, a tough enforcer their father had employed many years before his sons began in the business. On either side of him stood two of Rory and Gerald's recruits. They may not have looked as intimidating as Prince; however, they were eminently more violent. Rory and Gerald entered the sparse and dimly lit lock-up just as the noise from a train rumbling overhead faded. "What's this all about?" demanded Prince.

"You're stealing from us," said Rory, as though they were passing the time of day. He'd learned over the years that the calmer he was, the more intimidated people were.

A trickle of sweat ran down Prince's brow.

"I've never stolen from you. I worked for your father for years and he never accused me of stealing."

"That's because he never caught you," said Gerald, unzipping his jacket and pulling out a machete. In one motion, he sliced a gaping cavity in Prince Boateng's face, who immediately put his hand to the wound. The next blow took the tops of three of his fingers off. As he collapsed to the floor, the brothers turned to walk away. Over his shoulder, Rory ordered, "Get rid of him, and make sure he's not found."

On returning to the car, Gerald put his now blood-stained favourite toy back in the boot.

As they drove home, Rory said, "That Prince was the last of the old man's workforce. They were totally out of touch with the real world."

"Yeah," said Gerald. "They didn't know how to function, once Mehmed was on the scene. Back in their day, it was all about selling cannabis to Rastas and hippies."

As Rory buckled himself into the passenger seat, he remembered the first meeting with Mehmed all those years ago. When their father left suddenly, they had all his workforce and contacts but no product. It had taken balls to persuade Mehmed to supply them. Maybe he'd seen something in the brothers not long out of school. They'd shown him guts, that's for sure. Eventually, Mehmed agreed to a deal with them. The McCullens would buy only from him and supply all of Kennington, Camberwell, Walworth and Dulwich. They left the meeting to celebrate, with Mehmed's last words ringing in their ears.

"Fuck up, and it will be a slow, painful death for both of you."

Rory's thoughts were cut short as Gerald stopped at a set of traffic lights on Walworth Road and a police car pulled alongside. Gerald and Rory ignored the stares of the occupants of the vehicle. Once the lights changed to green, Gerald pulled away, being careful to keep below the thirty miles an hour speed limit.

~❖~

On arriving back at the Brandon Estate, the McCullen brothers made their way to one of their flats on the third-floor, where they stood over three youths sitting on a battered old sofa. The boys were fidgeting, although none of the three had an ounce of fear in their eyes, only total defiance. It impressed Rory. He could see a lot of himself and his brother in these boys. However, he barked, "You three pricks have cost us bundles of money. Stabbing up, that kid has brought police all over the estate for weeks. Today is the first day we've been able to get back to normal. You owe us big time, we now own you, and you'll do what we want when we want - do you understand?"

The boys stared at him, and Rory could see the resentment in their eyes. He guessed their actions had been to enhance their reputation with the other crew members and to put fear into any outsider trying to invade their territory.

Gerald said, "If you're going to stab and kill people, make sure it's for a reason, not just some random kid walking through the estate on his way home from school. People will give you respect if you kill for a purpose. Do you get it?"

They nodded, too in awe to talk back to either of the McCullens.

"Now get the fuck out of here and start earning back some of the money you've lost us."

The three youths jumped to their feet and ran out the door without looking back.

Gerald laughed and said to Rory. "They've got plenty of bottle them boys; we need to keep them working; there's a future for them."

"Just what I was thinking."

"What happened to the weapons they used?"

"I got rid of them and all the clothes they were wearing. They're brothers and tough boys. Nothing frightens them. They're raw and very wild - homeless. Dad has disappeared and their mum's in the nick."

"I'll get one of the crew to give them fifty quid each and watch out for them," said Gerald. He yawned. "It's been a busy day, bruv. I fancy getting home and having a cup of tea."

Rory clapped him on the back. "I'm with you there. After the auction tomorrow, we can take mum for a bit of lunch to celebrate."

CHAPTER THIRTEEN

Jimmy Smith sat in a café in Chrisp Street Market, East London, waiting to meet Jerome Campbell, whom he had last seen many years ago as a child. He hadn't planned on meeting Jerome; only when he had tried to ring his old and most productive informant, Winston Campbell, it was the young man who had picked up. He thought about it now as the shoppers streamed past the window and he could hear the muffled shouts of hawkers selling their goods.

"Hi," Jimmy had said, "Is Winston about?"

"Who's this?"

"My name is Jimmy Smith. I'm an old friend of Winston. Is he there?"

"You haven't heard then? Dad was murdered nearly two years ago. I'm his son, Jerome."

Even though Jimmy was an unemotional person, he'd felt, for no good reason, guilty. He should have known of Winston's murder long ago. It was this guilt that found him sitting in a café in Chrisp Street market, waiting to meet Jerome Campbell.

He looked up, interrupted by the chat of the owner, who was keeping several conversations going with more than one table. The customers seemed to be mostly market traders there for the fifth mug of tea of the day. Jimmy couldn't help thinking that the owner might be wise to invest some of his earnings in dental work: he had more tattoos than teeth and those he had were mostly black and looked like a row of

condemned houses.

He turned back to his thoughts, remembering his first meeting with Winston in the Repton Boxing Club back when they were fifteen. They'd become firm friends, although their friendship didn't dampen their competitiveness when sparring. Winston was the son of a Windrush family and living as a black boy in London's East End had been tough. He had dealt with it using humour and sometimes violence.

Look what happened when they left school. Jimmy supposed the police wasn't an option for a boy like Winston back in the day: With unemployment rife and cut off from legitimate ways of making money, Winston had supported himself with petty crime, which led, as it usually did, to stints in jail.

They'd met again when Jimmy was in the Flying Squad. A policeman had caught Winston with a gun, and he was certain to be sent down for a long time. It wasn't even his gun - he'd been doing a favour for a frightened kid who a local gangster had bullied into delivering the weapon to him. Winston said he'd take the gun himself, then got caught with it, on his way to the drop-off. After he reached out to Jimmy, Jimmy organised things with the arresting officer to hand the case over to him. He then got Winston to deliver the gun as planned, and uniformed officers stopped the gangster when he returned to his car and arrested him for possession of the weapon. Winston got to walk free.

Jimmy chuckled to himself. Today, it would have needed a full risk assessment report and an armed response unit to do that stop. The café door opened, Jimmy looked up, and it was only two more market traders being greeted by their counterparts.

Winston's gratitude rekindled their friendship, and their relationship continued for years as informant and handler. The criminal fraternity considered Winston trustworthy, and his information was so prolific Jimmy had to pass much of it on to other teams. As Winston got older and the villains younger, his information slowed down and once Jimmy left the police, they drifted apart and lost contact with each other. I was such a fool, thought Jimmy. He wasn't just an informant. He was my friend.

Looking up, he saw a large, good-looking black man in front of him. Standing up, he offered his hand, noting that Jerome was about the same height as him, slim and muscular, with his father's deep brown eyes. They'd only met once when the boy was a nipper. How old was Jerome now? Thirty? Thirty-five? Jesus, I'm old, thought Jimmy.

Jerome ordered some tea from Toothless Wonder and sat down. "I remember you," he said, "coming around our flat when I was a kid. Didn't you and dad box together?"

"We did a long time ago. I'm sorry to hear about your dad. How's your mum dealing with it?"

Jerome sighed. "She'll never get over it. She spends all her time at the church now, and she doesn't even speak about him." He leaned back and folded his arms. "You know, they say the murder involved a drug deal that went wrong. That's nonsense. My Dad was a thief, but he hated drug dealers."

Jimmy nodded. The day before, just after the phone call, he'd rung Dave and demanded all the files relating to Winston's murder.

After reading every document, starting with the crime scene, the lacklustre house-to-house enquiries through to the post-mortem and then to the less than thorough investigation, it became obvious it had been a sloppy enquiry. There appeared to be no witnesses or suspects, and they had made the easy and lazy conclusion that it was a drug deal gone wrong. Although he hadn't seen Winston for a good few years, Jimmy, like Jerome, knew that wasn't possible.

Jimmy looked him in the eye. "What do you think happened?"

"I know what happened; Dad was walking back from meeting one of his mates. He had cut through the market here and came across a lad from the estate, getting a beating from Monty Johnston and a couple of his boys. It seems the kid owed them some money. Dad jumped in to help. He could still have a row." He stopped and his eyes filmed over. "They stabbed him six times. Then left him to die in the gutter before the ambulance got there."

Jimmy shook his head. "Terrible, terrible."

They sat for a moment in silence and then, softly, Jimmy asked, "Who's Monty Johnston?"

Jerome made a face as though he wanted to spit. "He runs all the drugs on the Brownfield Estate and rules it through violence." He tapped the table with the flats of his hands. "That's why we have had so many stabbings and shootings on the estate over the last few years. The police know all this, and they do nothing!"

Jimmy looked around; afraid others could hear the outburst. Luckily the street traders were arguing about some horse race with the Toothless Wonder.

"I can't remember the last time I saw a police officer around here," said Jerome, quieter now. "I wanted to go after Johnston myself. My Mum made me promise not to get involved."

"She was right. Your dad didn't want you caught up with crime or criminals. He wanted you to get a proper education and a good job."

Jerome gave a weak smile. "I know, and I have done that. I work for a large insurance company in the City and now run my own division."

"That's fantastic. Well done," said Jimmy, and then, afraid he'd overstepped his boundaries, said, "Your dad would have been so proud."

"He was."

A scream of, "For fuck's sake," from the cafe owner, who'd dropped a load of dirty crockery, interrupted their conversation. Every head in the café swung towards the noise, relieved the sound was only crockery.

Jimmy turned back to Jerome and said, "Why haven't you moved away from here?"

"I did. Got a nice little flat in Aldgate. I'm letting it out now. I moved back in with Mum after what happened to Dad." He took a sip of tea. "The council offered her a move away from the area; she wouldn't go. She didn't want to be away from Poplar Baptist Church. It's her life. Mum's there every day; she helps the pastor and his wife run things. She's involved in feeding the homeless around the area. It's her life now."

Two men at the table behind them started arguing loudly about West Ham Football Club.

"They've been playing shit football ever since they moved from Upton Park," said one.

"How would you know? You don't even go to the games."

"You're right, I was a season ticket holder for twenty-two years and I ain't going to that new shit-hole."

Raising his voice slightly, Jerome asked, "Anyway, why were you trying to get in touch with dad? He'd told me all about how he had worked with you when you were in the police. He liked you,"

"I liked your dad - we had a lot of fun when we were youngsters. It doesn't matter now; a few of us are looking into the gangs peddling drugs on the estates and I wanted to ask your dad if he could help."

"Let me help," Jerome said. "I know everything that's happening on the Brownfield. They talk openly in front of me. I'm known as 'Holy Joe' because of my mum and the church. Look, they even told me how they killed Dad."

Jimmy stared at him: could he use him? He shook his head. "Sorry mate, your old man would turn in his grave if I even thought about letting you get invol

"Please, Jimmy, I can't bear the guilt of letting Monty Johnston get away with killing Dad. Surely you can understand that? I see him walking about the estate every day like he owns the place." Jerome gripped his hands together as if praying.

Jimmy sat back and contemplated the young man. Why not give Jerome the chance to avenge his father's murder? And who was better placed?

"Okay," he said. "If there's any inkling at all that you are in danger, you tell me and we'll get you out." He took out his notebook. "Tell me everything about Monty Johnston. How did he get started?"

"His best mate, Wesley Coombe, supplied all the drugs on the estate. They were at school together. Monty worked for Wesley as his enforcer. Everyone hated him. Wesley got shot and killed in a drive-by shooting, and most people think it was Monty who shot him. Mind you; nobody says that out loud. After Wesley died, Monty just took over the entire operation."

Jimmy ordered them more teas and a bacon sandwich each: sitting with empty cups would draw attention to them.

"Red or brown sauce?" said Toothless Wonder.

"HP or Daddy's?" asked Jimmy - partly to wind him up.

Toothless Wonder narrowed his eyes. "Red or Brown, mate."

Jimmy smiled. "Brown would be perfect."

Jerome waited until Toothless Wonder was behind the counter and started again, "When Monty took over, everything changed. He told everyone Wesley had been too soft. He started handing out beatings for late payments; for every perceived wrongdoing, he devised a suitable punishment."

Jimmy considered asking for the details but he didn't. He'd find out soon enough.

"Who are his customers?"

"He supplies the offices in Canary Wharf during the day and the new flats on the Wharf at night. He's got an army of kids running cocaine for him; I mean dozens of them."

"Does he work with anyone?"

"He's got a cokehead, Tony Mitchell, running the kids for him. He must know Tony samples the product. I imagine he sees him as a fall guy if anything goes wrong. The kids pick up the cocaine from Tony's flat before dropping it off at the Wharf. "

Their sandwiches and cups of tea arrived and again, they waited to talk. "Do you know who supplies Monty?"

"No, I think he said he's Albanian."

Jimmy suppressed a smile.

"It's the same guy who supplied Wesley," Jerome continued. "Monty says he hates him. That doesn't mean much; he hates everyone."

Jimmy nodded and tapped his pencil on the notebook. "Anything else?"

"I heard another gang have been looking to muscle in on Canary Wharf, trying to undercut prices. Monty's seen them off for the moment. He boasted recently, he's moving over five kilos of cocaine a week."

It seemed to Jimmy that Monty Johnston was running the equivalent of a sandwich delivery business only using cocaine and violence.

"Here," he said, scribbling his number on a corner of his pad, ripping it off and giving it to Jerome, who, within seconds, pinged his number onto Jimmy's phone.

"You're a good lad." He was going to say that Winston would have been proud of him again, but then he remembered Winston would have hated Jerome working with Jimmy. He'd worked hard keeping the young man off the streets and now Jimmy was putting him right back in the firing line.

He turned to tell Jerome he'd changed his mind; however, he'd already left. He was on his way back to the estate: back to the trouble, he'd spent most of his life trying to avoid.

CHAPTER FOURTEEN

After chatting with Diane for a few minutes, Terry made his way upstairs to The Peacock's office. The others were already there, deep in conversation about what they had discovered. The mood was sombre and business-like, with no quips or jokes. Although the windows were partially open, the room was stifling. Terry undid his top button and listened to John recount what he'd learned from Jilly.

"Two brothers run all the drugs on the Brandon Estate: Gerald and Rory McCullen. They are supplying their area and all the other local dealers have to buy from them for their customers."

"Sorry," interrupted Terry. "Are you saying the other estates buy from the McCullens and not directly from Mehmed?"

"That's right, they've done some sort of deal with Mehmed, and the other gangs have to come to them," replied John. "The Brandon Estate is a staging post for South London cocaine distribution."

"Wait a minute," said Jimmy, rubbing the back of his neck. "Does that mean if we take out these two, we knock out the supply to a whole lump of South East London?"

"Looks like it."

Jimmy slapped John's back. "Tell us more."

"Ow, you big bastard." He grinned. "So, the brothers use one of the tower blocks as their base and have two flats, the third-floor one being the 'Trap

House' where they sell from. The fifth-floor flat is where they both live and where the drugs are most likely kept before going downstairs."

"Imagine living on the fourth floor," said Peter.

"That's right," said John. "Not the best neighbours. They don't trust anybody except each other. Nobody gets near them: they're as close as ticks on a cat, which means the complete operation should grind to a halt as long as we take both of them out."

"Fantastic," said Jimmy, rubbing his hands.

"Don't get too excited," said John. "The downside is they are not likely to come easily. They're supposed to be vicious bastards and there is every chance they are both tooled up." He sat back in his seat as though exhausted. "I don't suppose Diane has got a fan? It's bloody hot."

He said to nobody in particular.

"Are you going through menopause?" Said Jimmy, who stood and opened the windows fully; it was noticeable the back of his shirt was dark with sweat.

"Dave," said Terry, "Have you got more on the McCullens?"

Dave pulled a notebook out of his trouser pocket. This time, he had discarded his ripped jeans for a pair of Levi's and a white polo shirt. "This is what I've got so far. Gerald McCullen has a street name of Bumpy and is twenty-nine.

"Bumpy?" Said Peter.

Dave ignored him. "He's got form for grievous bodily harm and affray. His brother Rory is thirty and has the street name of..." Dave turned to Peter, "... Dreads."

Peter nodded, as though if he had to choose one of those names, he'd pick 'Dreads'.

"Dread's previous convictions are for possession of an offensive weapon - a machete - and grievous bodily harm. Neither of them has done any bird other than a bit on remand."

Jimmy shook his head. "What the hell does it take these days?"

Dave rushed on. "Fortunately, Operation Trident did some work on them last year, so I've got good up-to-date surveillance photographs of them. From the Trident logs, it doesn't look as though they socialise much or have any haunts they use. Other than visiting their mum in Eltham, they spend most of their time at home. John's right when he says they only trust each other; they're always together. They have some right nasty hoodlums working for them, although, unlike other gangs, there is no inner circle, just them. As John says, there is every chance we will find these two armed."

Terry had been making notes throughout. He put down his pen and said, "Thank you, Dave. Have you had much communication with Detective Chief Superintendent Jones?"

"Only every day," joked Dave. "Some days, he phones twice. It's getting right up his nose that you're treating me so badly."

"Poor you," said John.

Smiling, Dave continued. "I've just stuck to the party line and assured him that as soon as you tell me anything, I'll tell him."

"After this meeting, give him a ring and tell him I've got you doing background checks on a couple of estates," and said, tapping his nose, "just not the ones we're talking about today. That might keep him off your back for a few days." He turned to John. "How far are we away from moving on, these brothers?"

"If we were looking to build up evidence against them for court, well, there would be a lot of work to do. Seeing as we're not, we can go when you like."

"Let's get it on," said Jimmy in a poor American accent.

"And I'll keep on top of the informant in case there are any changes," added John.

As everyone knew, John's informant was Jilly Jones, the men hooted. "You're a martyr, John," said Jimmy, "a fucking martyr."

When they had settled down, Terry turned to Jimmy. "I was sorry to hear about Winston. I remember meeting him with you when he put up that fur job in the city. He was a right character; I liked him. Where are we up to with his son?"

"His information is all about Balfron House on the Brownfield Estate, Poplar, near Chrisp Street Market, East London. The main dealers most likely stabbed Winston on the estate, called Monty Johnson. He has a right-hand man, Tony Mitchell. We've got addresses for both of them. Any big money we believe will be in Johnston's flat and the drugs will be in Mitchell's. They're moving shit loads of cocaine to Canary Wharf, where more than a hundred thousand people are working."

He turned to Dave. "You're sorting out their photographs, right?"

Dave nodded.

"And I still want to double-check their home addresses and watch them for a couple of days," said Jimmy. "Just like John said, if we were looking for evidence, we're miles away; as that's not an issue, we're nearly there."

"You'll keep an eye on Jerome?" said Terry. "He won't know the game like his dad, and the last thing we need is him getting too involved."

The smile fell from Jimmy's face. "I get what you mean. The problem is, he knows it was Johnston who murdered his dad, and he's desperate to get revenge…" He tapped the table. "He's a bright bloke and I'll do everything I can to keep him under control."

Terry nodded. Jimmy's change in tone affected the entire group. For a moment there, with the talk of disrupting the entire supply to South East London, East London and the Canary Wharf, the thing had seemed easy - or at least possible. However, there were risks. There were drugs and guns and men bent on revenge. And who were they? A group of tired old men and one young detective.

"To get this to work, we need Detective Chief Superintendent Jones involved," said Terry.

Although the men groaned, he could see they agreed. "Jimmy and John, I need you both to find venues near your plots where we can get him to muster his troops." He held up his hand. "Near enough to be handy, mind, but not so close that they're in the way."

"Got it," said John.

Terry thought about what else they could do to protect themselves. "I'll ring Mustafa today and arrange for his men to get over here now. Nicky has heard nothing from Kenny Pierce yet. I think we should deal with these two jobs first, then concentrate on Mehmed." After all, they could deal with the Big Guns once they disabled the supply and 'Tilburied' the culprits. Which reminded him… "Peter, what's happening in Dartford?"

Dartford."

Peter smiled. "All done. We've got two Nissen huts that are secure with new doors and padlocks. I've picked up the supplies we need for them: boxes of crisps, cases of water, buckets, torches and batteries. The vans are on standby, and I'm picking up the door openers tomorrow."

"Great." Terry scratched his chin. "Considering what John and Dave have just said about the reception we might get, I need you to get some additional equipment for us." The men looked up, interested. "We can talk after this meeting, Peter," said Terry. "Let's crack on. Dave, tell us about Harry Baker and Monkey Gregory."

Dave turned the pages of his notebook and said, "You all probably guessed Harry Baker had a few quid; I couldn't believe the extent of his wealth. I didn't realise solicitors, bent or otherwise, earned that much money."

"Ha!" said John, "All those buggers are rolling in it."

"I think this guy might earn more than just his wage," said Dave. "He lives in Frimley Hall, a palatial eight-bedroom listed estate on the River Thames, just outside Windsor. According to Zoopla, it sits on fifty acres of land and is valued at twenty million pounds."

"Mortgage?" asked Peter.

"Nope," said Dave. "A check with the Land Registry shows there is no charge on the property, meaning he's paid it off or never needed one. He even opens the gardens and maze to members of the Royal Horticultural Society a couple of weekends a year. His annual Spring Ball, held in the Great Hall for charity, is legendary and an invitation is much sought after in the local high society."

"La-di-da," said John.

"He owns fifty-one per cent of Baker, Radcliffe and Wright Solicitors and has a chauffeur who drives him to and from his offices in Upper Brook Street, Mayfair, in his brand-new Rolls Royce Phantom. He's a bigwig in the Law Society and a past president. For every function they organise, Harry Baker is always on the top table. Besides the Rolls Royce, he also owns a vintage nineteen sixty-one E-Type Jaguar Coupe, and he's got a regular column in the magazine Vintage Jaguar World."

Jimmy sniffed loudly, clearing his nose, saying, "I wish I'd studied harder at school instead of boxing."

"Nobody coming out of Sir John Cass School was ever going to be a solicitor," said John. "Anyway, you would have needed more than your O level in woodwork."

Turning the pages in his book, Dave said, "As for Philip 'Monkey' Gregory, he lives in a caravan in an over-fifty residential park near Littlehampton, a seaside town in West Sussex. He moved there not long after completing his last prison sentence. It was that eight years bird Jimmy was talking about, and it appears he's stayed out of trouble since his release from prison. He's not paying taxes, so is living off his pension or cash-in-hand jobs. The local police have never heard of him and don't even know he lives on their patch. He may well be going straight."

Terry continued to take notes throughout the conversations.

"Jimmy, will you and Nicky go and see him? Find out if he's interested in opening the safe for us. We just want all the documents photographed and put back; anything else in there is down to him. I'll give you a couple of grand upfront money for him if he's willing to do it," said Terry.

Peter said, "Shall I have a look at Baker's premises in Upper Brook Street and see what the security is like? Monkey might get into the safe; however, we need to get him into the building first."

"Good idea," said Terry. "Do you want any backup?"

"No, it's fine. I'll go this afternoon,"

"You're not still using that 'looking for a job routine, are you?" asked Terry.

"If it works," he said, "why change it?"

Why indeed, thought Terry. The old methods did work - or at least he hoped they would if everything went to plan. Not long now, he mused, and they'd get to see whether his methods or Jones' were the ones to get results. "Right," he said. "Anyone fancy a nice cold beer?"

CHAPTER FIFTEEN

At four fifty-five p.m., Peter was in Upper Brook Street, Mayfair, which ran between Grosvenor Square and Park Lane. He looked up at the elegant Georgian building with five floors and a basement. The shining gold plaque had the engraved name Baker, Radcliffe and Wright Solicitors, and a smear of pink polish was visible around one screw. He walked up the four steps that led to the highly glossed black front door and into the ground floor, which housed a reception desk and a large high-ceiling reception room with a stunning crystal chandelier as a focal point. At the reception desk sat a man in his mid-fifties with a military bearing. On seeing Peter, he sat to attention and said, "Good afternoon, sir; how can I help you?"

Peter smiled. "I haven't got an appointment. It's you. I want to speak to you. Are you ex-military?"

"Yes, sir, Scots Guards, nineteen years," he replied and, if possible, sat even more bolt upright in his chair.

"That's wonderful," Peter said. "Thank you for your service."

"It was a pleasure to serve." The men stared at each other for a moment. "And how can I help you?"

"Well," said Peter. "I hate to take your time up like this; I'm a retired police officer and... well, I'm looking for security work. I think I'd be good at it but really, I don't know the first thing. Rather than go to some gimcrack agency, I thought I'd ask someone who was actually doing the job." He looked around the marble hall. "Someone who is, well... at the top of their game."

"It's not as easy as it looks."

"I'm sure."

"And you are lucky you caught me." He rolled his eyes. "Many other security guards are civvies. A lot of them are foreigners."

Peter shook his head. "The way of the world now. Listen, when you knock off, can I buy you a pint? If you haven't got time, I understand."

The guard made a show of looking at his watch. "Sure, why not? I'll meet you in the Marlborough Head. It's just around the corner. I'll see you in about half an hour."

Walking to the pub, Peter ran through what he had already discovered: the front door was a heavy-duty Victorian with the original antique lock bolstered by two sophisticated Chubb deadlocks. There were no CCTV cameras, and the alarm was a very basic contact system on the front door only. The problem was going to be the door

locks.

After a short while, the ex-soldier arrived at the pub and introduced himself as Bob Pope. Peter got him a pint and sat back to listen to Bob's life story.

"I come from a military background. Before I joined, my father was a Regimental Sergeant Major in the Scot's Guards. Even as a child, I was destined to join both the army and my father's regiment. I travelled with my wife and daughter all around the world and I saw active service in three conflicts." He suddenly stopped speaking before adding, "Unfortunately, some good friends never made it back."

Peter bought them another round of drinks and changed the subject to Bob Pope's present occupation.

"I will not lie. It's been difficult adjusting to civvy street, especially when you're used to the discipline and structure of army life. I think it's been tough on my family. I've been a right moody bugger," explained Bob.

"Are the solicitors good to work for?" enquired Peter. "Not really. Security is very slack and there's no proper control over who comes and goes. Don't get me started on securing the premises at night. That's a minefield."

Bob then outlined every detail of the security systems inside Baker, Radcliffe, and Wright. Although he was after information, Peter enjoyed the company of the ex-soldier and his dry sense of humour, including his impersonations of the staff at Baker, Radcliffe and Wright.

On leaving Bob in the pub, Peter returned to Upper Brook Street and, using his phone, photographed the locks on the ground floor door and the basement door. As he walked towards the Marble Arch station, he was looking around for street CCTV cameras. He also now had the security company address that might help him with a job similar to Bob Pope's. Funnily enough, he owned it.

CHAPTER SIXTEEN

Jimmy and Nicky pulled into the car park of Sea View Over-Fifty Residential Mobile Home Site in Littlehampton. Sea View seemed a bit of a stretch, seeing as it was at least two and a half miles from the seafront, although there was a row of seagulls on top of the unmanned and unkempt administration building. Looking around the rows of caravans of every size, colour, and condition, Jimmy thought this place may not have been the end of the world, although they probably both had the same postcode.

Jimmy said as they left the car and walked towards Monkey's caravan, "Monkey loves to talk. We should let him talk himself out before mentioning the job. Ah, here it is."

It was a grubby two-bedroom mobile home, no better or worse than its companions. Two steps made of four paving slabs led to the front door. Jimmy knocked. It shocked him when Monkey opened it and looked precisely the same as when he'd last seen him twenty-five years ago in the pub in Ilford.

Monkey looked equally shocked and stood with his mouth open. Suddenly, a smile spread over his face. "Oh, my word, if it isn't Jimmy Smith! Come in, come in."

Inside the dimly lit mobile home, Jimmy introduced Nicky. Monkey shook his hand vigorously. "Any friend of Jimmy's is a friend of mine."

Poor bloke thought Jimmy; he obviously didn't have many visitors.

"Can't believe you've ended up down here," said Jimmy, trying not to look at the holes in the lino and the small, sad belongings of an old man who has spent too much time alone. "I always thought you were an East End boy through and through. How did you find yourself in this place?"

"How did you find me, more like?" He laughed and slapped Jimmy on the shoulder, "Never mind. You'll tell me soon enough. Cup of tea?"

Jimmy wasn't sure he should take his provisions; then again, he didn't want to refuse the kindness. "Yes, lovely. Two sugars for me. None for Nicky." He moved a pile of racing papers off the banquette and placed them next to an overflowing ashtray. "Alright, if we sit?" he said, sitting down.

"Make yourselves at home."

As Monkey pottered around switching on the Calor gas and lighting the stove, he said, "That last lump of bird was tough going, and I realised I had to get out of the game, as long as I was living in the same area, there was always the temptation to go back to work." He filled a kettle with a bottle of water. "Near the end of my sentence, they sent me to Ford Open Prison, near here, and I liked the area. We used to be allowed out during the day and I realised this was where I wanted to be."

"The seafront is lovely," said Jimmy, who hadn't been there.

"What about your wife and daughter?"

Monkey busied himself with cups. It was obvious Jimmy had touched a raw nerve. Monkey squashed a tea bag against the side of a cup and said, "The wife divorced me during that last stretch. She turned up at the prison with the papers for me to sign and I haven't seen either of them since. Even my daughter." He blinked a few times and the tip of his nose turned red. "A good few summers ago, I met an old mate from back in the east end. He was down here on holiday staying in a bed-and-breakfast. He told me I had a granddaughter called Linda. She's probably a teenager now. She may even have brothers and sisters. I'll probably never find out." Monkey had difficulty getting the last words out as his eyes welled up with tears. Getting up, he took some kitchen rolls and wiped his eyes. "Sorry about that," he said.

Nicky held up his hand. "No, don't apologise."

There was a moment's silence: respect for Monkey's sadness, then Jimmy asked, "Are you working?"

Monkey smiled, as though grateful to change the subject. "I do some carpentry and change a few locks for a locksmith in Littlehampton. It's cash in hand and with my pension." He lifted his chin. "I'm all right. "

"What about the rest of the community here? What's the social life like?"

"Not bad. Over the years, I've made some good friends here; unfortunately, they keep dying off on me. I get invited to a lot more funerals than weddings, that's for sure."

"Don't we all?" said Jimmy

Nicky looked at the corner of the room as though considering this.

"It'll come to you too, whippersnapper," said Monkey.

"I'm the same age as you!" said Nicky.

Jimmy laughed. "Oh, Monkey. I've missed you."

Monkey didn't respond as Jimmy expected. He shook his head, solemn. "I've done everything to put the past behind me and even you calling me Monkey seems strange. Everyone down here knows me as Phil. Not one of them knows what I can do."

"In the end," said Jimmy, "it must have been difficult for you to keep up with all these new digital safes, not like in your day. People like you are a dying breed."

"Listen, Jimmy," said Monkey, sitting up straight, "These digital safes are useless. You might as well use a locked drawer - you can open one of them in five minutes."

"The big safes need blowing or cutting, don't they?" said Nicky.

"Ha! Shows how much you know." He turned to Jimmy. "Trouble is, people haven't got a clue; you've got to know your safe before trying to open it. If you don't and you try to blow or cut most safes, the heat is going to destroy the contents. So, what's the point? Kids these days learn how to use a torch, cutting up motors in car breakers yards and then think they can get into any safe. The best methods are still, lock manipulation or drilling; again, you need the skills because if you don't know your safe, you won't have a clue where to drill and you certainly won't be able to get a lock opened."

Jimmy cradled his mug of tea and said, "What about a Ratner safe?"

"Now you're talking: a beautiful piece of engineering, depending on the year of manufacture, of course." A faraway look settled over his face. "They were beautiful locks. You won't see many of those nowadays."

"What about a nineteen-twenty Ratner?"

"As long as it's the original mechanism, then that will be the Ratner Change Key Safe Lock."

"How would you open one of them?"

Monkey slapped his leg. "I knew you were here for a reason." His face fell. "Coming straight to my door, acting all friendly."

Jimmy sighed. "It's true, Monkey, we want something from you only because you are the best." He cleared his throat. "And it's good to see you. It is."

Monkey stared at him for a moment and then his face broke into a smile. "I was the best, wasn't I?"

"I bet you still are."

"Mate, I've told you I'm out of the game now. I'm going straight,"

"Look, Monkey," said Jimmy, "the safe belongs to a right arsehole and there's paperwork in it we need to have a look at. We just want them photographed and put back. Anything else in the safe is yours." He reached into his jacket pocket, took out a fat envelope, and laid it on the table. "There's a couple of grand here if you'll help us out and there could be a good few quid in the safe as well; of course, I can't promise that."

Monkey stared at the envelope. "I'm not sure, Jimmy. They'll throw the key away if I get nicked again. I can't do any more bird."

They sat in silence for what seemed like ages, and then Jimmy said, "If it helps, I'll be with you every step of the way to make sure it goes smoothly,"

Nicky shot him a glance: this wasn't part of the deal. Still, he'd said it now.

After a moment, Monkey said, "Jimmy, you were good to me while I was waiting for trial on that last job. You just listened to me. I must have bored you to tears. I've never forgotten that. Okay, I'll do it."

Nicky continued to stare at Jimmy.

"We need to get into the building before we can get to the safe," said Jimmy.

Peter had briefed them on the security at Upper Brook Street, and Nicky produced the photograph of the basement door they had received from him.

Monkey put on his glasses and studied the photograph, and his face lit up. "That old lock is a Shaw Lock. Arthur Shaw from Willenhall produced them. The company started way back in the eighteen hundreds, great locks well before their time."

"Can you open it?" asked Jimmy.

"Yes, no problem. The Chubb lock in the picture could be a lot trickier. I mean, I can open it eventually. It will take a good bit of time."

"They don't lock that one," said Nicky.

"Serves them right then. I've got no sympathy for people who don't use the security they've got."

It was a long time before they could leave the caravan after that. Monkey rambled on in deep engineering and historical detail about each safe he'd unlocked. Jimmy had to nudge Nicky to keep him awake. "Oh, Monkey," Jimmy said as Monkey paused midsentence. "It's been so good to see you. We have to go now. I'll keep in touch and I'll see you soon."

"It'll be like the old days," said Monkey.

"Only this time, we're on the same side."

Monkey puffed up. "I hadn't thought of it like that."

As they climbed into the car, still waving at Monkey standing on his step, Nicky said, "You going on the job with him wasn't part of the plan."

"I get it," said Jimmy, switching on the engine. "He wouldn't have done it otherwise. You could see that, and then what would we have done?"

Just as they pulled into the street, Nicky left it for a moment and said, "I don't understand why you're taking such a chance. We're not in the police now. If you get caught, you'll get bird."

Jimmy felt his stomach tense. "If we plan this carefully, there is no chance of getting caught," he said. "You heard, Peter, there is no CCTV and a minimal alarm system."

"If Terry finds out, he will do his nut and put a stop to it," said Nicky.

Jimmy gave him a sidelong glance. "Well, I won't tell him if you don't."

The rest of the journey was in silence.

CHAPTER SEVENTEEN

As Terry made his way to the back office of Yusef Hassan's bookmakers that Sunday evening, he clenched his jaw. How was Yusuf going to be this time? Coming here again wasn't ideal, but their guests from Northern Cyprus needed to be kept under wraps. If Mehmed got wind of the Hassan family's involvement, there would be a bloodbath.

He looked over his shoulder to make sure Jimmy and John were following close behind, then knocked on the plywood door. Yusuf greeted them with something resembling a smile and shook their hands. Why? Thought Terry. The last time Jimmy had touched Yusef, it was with a hand around his throat. Most likely, he didn't want to risk humiliation in front of his brother's men.

"Good evening," said Yusuf. "This is Ali and Elgin."

The six of them barely fitted in the room. Ali was an enormous man, with massive hands. He looked immensely strong, and Terry bit down on a smile when he saw even John and Jimmy looked impressed. Elgin was slightly smaller, with an athletic physique. Terry found it hard to believe they were brothers. As impressive as Ali was, it was Elgin who drew Terry's attention. He stood in silence, his deep-set eyes suggesting he was even more dangerous than his brother.

Yusuf indicated with his head that he and Terry should talk outside the room. They stood in the dank corridor smelling of dampness and decay.

"Where are they staying?" Terry asked.

"There is a flat upstairs," Yusuf said, pointing to the flaking ceiling. "It's not great; it will do. The good thing is they don't need to go through the bookmakers: there are stairs in the backyard that get you straight up to it. How long do you think they will be here?" be here."

Terry scratched his chin. "Probably about two weeks; it may be longer. Is that going to be a problem?"

"No, I've put a telly in there for them, just thinking they'll go stir crazy if banged up for too long."

"Have they got a phone?"

"Yeah, a burner. I'll give you the number before you go. When do you think you will need them? Let me know and I'll sort out transport," said Yusef.

Terry didn't want to upset Yusuf's new conciliatory mood, but he didn't want him anywhere near what was going to happen. "Thanks, Yusef, but Mustafa doesn't want you or your boys to be seen with them."

When they walked back into the room, the others were discussing boxing. Ali had his fists up, describing a fight he'd watched and the knockout punch that finished it - all in almost perfect English - while Elgin watched his brother with a slight smile. John and Jimmy laughed as Ali came to the end of his story. It was great. The four of them were hitting it off. Terry needed them to work as a team. For the operation to succeed, they needed to trust each other. Just looking at them convinced Terry they would have little difficulty dealing with the physical side of the tasks at hand, but what about under pressure?

When he, John and Jimmy stepped into the warm evening outside the bookmakers, there was a strong smell of fried chicken from bins left in the sun too long. A group of lads swarmed past them, some without shirts and cans of beer in their fists.

"So," said Terry, "what do you reckon about our new friends?

"I think they could both be a right handful," John said. "I reckon Elgin could be a nasty piece of work. Not that I'm complaining. That might come in handy."

Jimmy nodded.

Terry shook their hands, and they each left to find their cars on the crowded street. Terry settled into the driver's seat and took out his phone.

"Nicky, it's me." He told him about Ali and Elgin. "Will you tell Peter and Dave we'll meet at the Peacock tomorrow morning?"

CHAPTER EIGHTEEN

Diane wasn't in the following morning, and Terry had to do without the usual chitchat. He was glad of it: his stomach was tense and his mind was full of plans and doubts. Everything had moved so fast and now, right now, they were ready to spring into action. He entered the upstairs room and found Peter, Nicky, and Dave already waiting. They'd been so silent, he'd presumed the room had been empty. Moments later, John and Jimmy joined them.

As he sat down, he said a brief silent prayer to Denise for strength. Despite his Catholic upbringing, he wasn't a religious man; only sometimes, in fact, this was the only way to calm him. Denise had been his rock.

"Right," he said and surprised himself to find his voice as steady as ever. "We will go after the McCullens on Wednesday."

"Wednesday?" said Nicky, bringing up his thumb and forefinger to count the two days until the operation started.

"Strike while the iron's hot," said Terry. "Let's go through it carefully and iron out any problems. First CCTV cameras. Is that going to be a problem?"

"No," said Peter, "they vandalised all the cameras on the estate a long time ago."

Terry turned to Dave. "Have you checked that?"

Dave nodded. "And I checked if there are any police operations in the area and there are none. Despite that last murder, they've withdrawn from the estate."

"What about gaining entry to the block?"

"The security doors on all the entrances on the estate are fucked, and the doors left open," John said. "Just in case, the informant has given me the code."

"What time are we sure to get the McCullens in?"

"According to the informant, these two do very little and are normally home every night by ten. The Trident surveillance logs confirm that other than meeting their lieutenants and visiting their mum in Eltham, they conduct all their business in their flat on the fifth floor. For the element of surprise, though, I would think between four and six a.m. would be good," said John.

Dave distributed photographs of the McCullen brothers, together with plans of the estate and floor plans of the flats. They all took time to study their copies.

"What about the flat doors? Will the openers do the job?" said Terry.

"They're so full of themselves they've not bothered with any extra security on the doors," said John. "They're just bog-standard council ones, so the openers will be perfect."

"Great," said Terry. "Any idea who we should expect in the flats?"

John put his fingers on one of the floor plans. "In the third-floor flat, we won't know till we get there. It would normally be two or three kids; they won't be a problem if we hit it hard."

He moved his fingers over to the next floor plan. "On the fifth floor, it will be the McCullen brothers in the two bedrooms. They may have women with them as well. Who knows?"

Nicky asked. "What else are we expecting to find in the flats?"

"In the fifth-floor flat, I expect money and possibly weapons," said John. "Downstairs should be the bulk of the cocaine, although it's difficult to tell."

Throughout the conversation, Terry's stomach had not stopped fluttering. He stood and put both hands on the table. The others looked up, eyes wide.

"Ok, none of us gets hurt," Terry said. "That's what Ali and Elgin are here for."

"We know, Boss," said Nicky softly. "We'll be careful."

Terry sat and, under the table, wiped his sweaty palms on his trousers. "Peter has got us two stun guns, isn't that right?"

"Top of the range. Unlike what you see on the telly, they'll give us a couple of minutes to get them secured," said Peter.

Dave opened his mouth and then shut it again. That's a good lad, thought Terry. We have to be protected, no matter how illegal it might be. "I want these two incapacitated as soon as we confront them," he said. "We're taking no chances. We hit them hard and fast."

"What about the workers in the third-floor flat?" asked Nicky.

"We'll just scare the shit out of them and let them go. Only once we've got the McCullens in the van and out of there. Got it?"

The others nodded and Nicky gave him a thumbs up.

"What about what's in the flat?" asked John.

"Any drugs, weapons and phones in the flats we take. Any money and valuables will be down to Yusuf." John, I need you to take control of everything we seize."

John nodded.

"Peter, Nicky and I will do the third floor," said Terry, "leaving John, Jimmy, Ali and Elgin to do the fifth floor."

"Don't you want Ali or Elgin with you?" asked John.

Terry tried a smile. "I think we've still got it in us. Besides, you are going to need them to help with the brothers. The McCullens are the dangerous ones."

"Fair do's."

"We'll hit both addresses at five A.M."

There was a moment of silence and in it, Terry could see it wasn't just him who felt the pressure. Of course, they could do the legwork; of course, they were masters at relationships with informants; but this? Did they still have it in them?

"John, give Ali and Elgin a ring and arrange for you and Jimmy to pick them up early. You can brief them on the way," said Terry. "Dave, I need you to be with

Jones."

Dave's face fell.

"It's not ideal for you, but honestly, it's a really important role."

"He'd have the press all over us in a flash, getting in our way, if we're not careful," said Nicky.

Terry nodded. "You need to see him this morning and give him just enough time to have some officers close by."

"Where?" asked Dave

John stepped in. "How about the old Camberwell Police Station? It's been closed for years, but I'm sure they can use the yard at the back. Someone must have a key."

"Great," said Terry,

John added. "And we could meet down the side of Camberwell Bus Garage. It's as good as anywhere that early in the morning."

With that settled, it felt as though they were ready and yet, there was still more to do. "What's the story with Baker's office?" asked Terry.

Peter opened his MacBook Pro in front of him and said, "The Building is over five floors plus a basement. Baker, Radcliffe and Wright occupy all other than the top floor. The ground floor is a reception area with a waiting room and clients' toilets, the first and second floors are the offices for the solicitors and their secretaries, and the third floor is where the partners have their offices together with a conference room. The basement is the engine room. It's where they have the post room, typing pool and storage for current and historical cases. It's a mess and like the top floor, they didn't update it when they refurbished the building eighteen years ago." As he started pressing keys on his laptop, he said. "Being a listed building, they had to submit plans to Westminster Council Planning Department. I got copies and had them put on my computer." They gathered around and what confronted them was a series of 3D images of the building. Peter took them on a virtual tour from the basement to the top floor.

"You got this from Westminster Planning Department?" asked Jimmy.

"No, I printed out the plans and one of the guys in my office transferred them into this format."

"Bloody marvellous."

"The interesting thing is the top floor. It's apparently in shit condition, and it's occupied by Tanner Accountants. The only person who works for them is Geoffrey Tanner. According to the receptionist, he has no nameplate on the door and no clients, as nobody ever rings for him, nor does he have any appointments. Dave has done some research and the only Geoffrey Tanner he can find, as an accountant, did seven years in prison in 2000, for embezzlement of several million pounds. I'd hazard a guess he's the one laundering the Columbian cartel money for Baker."

"That's brilliant, Peter. Can we get someone in the building?" said Terry.

"Those who work in the basement have to enter and leave the building through the basement door and lock the Chubb locks on leaving, but they never do. They only ever use the original antique lock. I sent photographs to Nicky before they saw Gregory."

"What about alarms and cameras?" asked Terry.

"There's no CCTV and only a limited alarm system on the ground floor main door. I've checked the area and there is a way to get in and out of Upper Brook Street, avoiding all street CCTV."

"What about Monkey? Is he game?"

Before Nicky could answer, Jimmy said, "Yes, he's up for it. It won't be a problem for him, and we'll brief him on all the information beforehand."

He paused. "Seeing as we're tight on time with everything else happening, I was thinking maybe this Saturday."

Terry thought for a moment. By the end of the week, this could all be over. "Ok," he said. "What do you need?"

"Peter has already sorted out one of his vans and a camera to take the photographs. John said he'll be there to do the driving. I don't think we need anything else. I'll ring Monkey and arrange to meet him," replied Jimmy.

"That's settled then," said Terry. "Let's hope they don't lock the basement door this weekend for the first time. Tell Monkey to be careful." He knew it wasn't just Monkey that was going to have to be careful: it was all of them. One wrong step and they could be in jail, with the real criminals still at large.

CHAPTER NINETEEN

Later that morning, Dave walked into the Commissioner's staff officers' office and handed Jones a buff file.

"What's this?"

"Briefing document, Sir."

Jones tutted and flipped it open. As he read, his mouth tightened. On the last page, his face turned red. He slammed the file shut. "I can't believe he thinks he can get away with this. I knew it was a mistake, getting that gang of has-beens involved."

Dave bit his tongue and said, "They seem to know what they're doing, sir."

"Really. How would you know? I thought they told you nothing."

Dave opened his mouth to reply, but Jones jumped in. "They can't just give me a couple of days to pull this together. Never mind expecting the council to fix CCTV, clean up graffiti and board up addresses with little or no notice."

"They seem to think you could pull it off, Sir."

Jones stared at Dave as if trying to work out if he was being facetious. Dave smiled.

"And what's to say if that gimcrack group of old men do clear the estate of the drug dealers, they won't be back again the next day?"

The word 'Tilbury' ran through Dave's head. "Mr Reid said they wouldn't be back," he said, "and the police will have enough time to re-establish themselves on the estate."

"I told him we need at least a week's notice," said Jones. "How am I meant to package this up for the Commissioner?"

Dave understood this was a rhetorical question and kept quiet. Jones looked up. "I expect you to be at my side, you know? In fact, you can brief the team. I will be busy with the press."

"The press, Sir?"

Jones narrowed his eyes. "Yes, the bloody press. It's our duty as civil servants to keep the public informed. I tell you what, though, this better work out. I'm not falling on my sword for anyone."

"Yes, sir."

"Now, get out and I'll see you on Wednesday morning at 6 o'clock at Camberwell Police Station."

CHAPTER TWENTY

John crunched the gears in Peter's transit van. Damn this thing, he thought. He knew it wasn't the van's fault - it was a new Mercedes - it was him being on edge. It was Wednesday, the day of the raid. When all they had been talking about was finally put into action.

He looked in the mirror to check on traffic; his three huge passengers, Jimmy, Ali and Elgin, obscured his view. Each of the brothers nursed large holdalls. John chuckled to himself: the brothers must expect to find bundles of cash. He slowed for a red light and then stopped.

Turning to the back, he saw that Jimmy had spread out the floor plans of the flat and the McCullen's pictures on seats beside the brothers. "Remember, they might have guns," said Jimmy. The brothers shrugged. John's stomach flipped again.

"Put those away now," he said to Jimmy. "We're nearly at the bus station."

Two minutes later, they were there. Peter waved and walked over. Before they could get out of the van, he handed them the kit he'd got: cable ties, two heavy-duty door openers, gloves, plastic sacks and two stun guns. "The stun guns will give you a couple of minutes to secure the McCullens that should be enough time." Silently, John handed Jimmy his spring-loaded baton they'd stored under the passenger seat. John slipped his own under his belt.

A few yards from their van was another van also supplied by Peter. Outside it stood Nicky and Peter. Nicky was finishing a sausage roll and Terry was drawing fiercely on a cigarette. He greeted them with a nod of his head.

~❖~

Terry put out his cigarette and pulled out another. Overnight, he had reconsidered the makeup of the teams and now, seeing John with a baton in his belt and a grim look on his face, he knew he was right to change plans. Because of his relationship with Jilly, John was far too invested in making sure the McCullen brothers were put out of business - permanently. Fair enough; however, Terry didn't want either of the McCullens to be seriously injured. The idea was to whisk them off to the lock-up quickly and quietly, not to an Accident and Emergency Unit.

"Hey John," he said softly. "I've been thinking about things and I'm concerned we don't know what to expect in the third-floor flat. We will swap places. I'd feel more comfortable if you were with Nicky and Peter, in case there is any resistance. I still want you to take the McCullens down to Dartford."

John looked into the far distance as though considering this and then gave a brief nod. Good, thought Terry. Now the only wild cards were Ali and Elgin. He glanced at them standing by the depot wall: quiet and watchful. Could he trust them? He was going to have to.

Calling the men together, Terry ran through the plan. He surprised himself with how calm he sounded. "That clear?" he asked. "John, Nicky and Peter to take the third floor where they sell the drugs; and me, Jimmy, Ali and Elgin to capture the McCullen brothers on the fifth."

They got into the two vans and headed to the Brandon Estate.

The block's front door was open as expected, and they made their way up the stairs. Nicky, John, and Peter stopped on the third floor. John watched Terry, Jimmy, Elgin and Ali disappear up to the fifth floor and felt a little hurt. He wanted to be the one to catch the McCullen brothers; he wanted to go to Jilly that night and tell her, casually, over a deep red wine, how he'd made them squeal.

Nicky's vibrating phone interrupted his thoughts: it was their signal. John swung back his door opener, the weight satisfying in his hands, and crashed through the flimsy plywood door. There had hardly been any recoil. He threw down the door opener and charged in, Nicky and Peter close on his heels. The plans had been simple enough and John made his way to the living room, knowing that Nicky and Peter were taking the bedrooms. It had only been a second since he smashed the door and he caught the horror on the faces of the two kids, still with PlayStation consoles in their hands. One of them threw his.... at him. He missed and John ran at them, taking his baton out of his belt and flicking it open in one motion. He hit one across the shoulder and the other across his legs. They both fell to the floor, squealing–he smiled as he knew he hadn't hurt them. Not as much as he would have liked to. He stood over them, his spring-loaded baton resting on his shoulder, hoping at least one of them would try to make a run for it.

"Bedrooms are clear," said Nicky, coming into the living room. He was breathless and red in the face.

"Bog, too," said Peter, leaning against the door frame. "Okay with these two while we do a thorough search?"

John gave a lazy smile. "Sure."

~❖~

At the same time as John had broken down the door on the third floor, Jimmy had used the opener on the fifth. Terry ran in after him, expecting Ali and Elgin to follow him. When they didn't, he had no choice other than to continue, cursing that he ever thought bringing two strangers into the mix was a good plan. What the hell are they doing? Thought Terry as he ran to the living room. Nothing there but a telly the size of the wall and a sofa with the stuffing coming out. He heard the footsteps of Ali and Elgin coming in - thank God - and made his way to the kitchen. He bumped into Jimmy in the narrow hallway.

"Bathrooms clear, boss."

"Bedrooms."

Jimmy set off towards one bedroom; Terry to the other. The door was wide open and as he ran in, he found Ali holding a shotgun against Gerald McCullen's spine. What the hell?

So that was what was in the holdalls. Terry felt a little shaky as he took out his taser. He held it to Gerald's neck and fired.

"Bastard!" Gerald said.

He fired again and this time, Gerald passed out.

Terry let out a breath he hadn't realised he'd been holding. He held up his hands. "Gun down, Ali."

He lowered it reluctantly.

"Find a tracksuit or something to dress him and get the cable ties on him," Terry told Ali, running into the next bedroom to see if Jimmy had subdued Rory. He had and next to him on the bed was a blond girl who looked barely sixteen and was holding a sheet up tight to her neck. Although Rory was unconscious, Elgin was still holding a

shotgun close to his head.

Terry said to the girl. "Get your clothes on."

She jumped out of the bed naked and headed for a chair with clothes scattered over it. Terry turned his back to her and gestured to Elgin to dress Rory with a bundle of clothes on the floor next to him. As the girl dressed, she said, "I only met him last

night."

Once she dressed, Terry asked. "How old are you? And tell me the truth."

"I'm nearly fifteen," she said, shaking with fear.

"So, you're fourteen." He shook his head. "Go on, get out of here and keep away from men like this. For God's sake, get out of this shithole."

She stared at him wide-eyed, then ran for the door, carrying her shoes.

Terry and Jimmy searched the flat as Ali and Elgin dressed and watched over the McCullens, who groaned and griped as they slowly came around.

The McCullen brothers had set up the living room like a factory with different stations for different stages of cutting and bagging cocaine. At least a kilo of the stuff was in a plastic bowl; it was difficult to tell if it was pure or cut. At the other end were at least a hundred small bags of cocaine and, in between, were scales, cutting agents, and hundreds of empty plastic bags.

"Boss, look at this!"

Under the kitchen sink, Jimmy had found a loaded handgun and three-kilo slabs of cocaine. Terry recognised the gun as a Glock 17. He made it safe by removing the magazine containing ten rounds of ammunition and checking to ensure the chamber was clear.

Jimmy scrambled around in the cupboard and found a further thirty bullets in a plastic bag. They moved to the bedrooms, where Ali and Elgin had raised their guns and were pointing them at the bound McCullen brothers once more. Terry said nothing and searched in drawers and wardrobes, pulling out bundles of cash. A quick tally showed the money, which they had individually wrapped in one-thousand-pound wraps, and then tied together in ten-thousand-pound bundles amounted to more than a hundred thousand pounds.

Jimmy's muscles bulged as he pulled out the wardrobe and whistled as he uncovered a mass of gold and diamond jewellery and ten high-end watches. Next to him, Ali grinned. It was the first time Jimmy had seen him smile.

Meanwhile, on the third floor, John, Peter and Nicky had discovered dozens of bags of cocaine, a mountain of cash, two large knives, an axe, and four mobile phones. They placed

them on the coffee table in front of the two young would-be gangsters, who were still sitting on the floor nursing their wounds facing the blank television.

John barked, "Where's the rest of the cocaine?"

"That's it," said one, his voice breaking. "I promise there's no more here."

John stared at him. He believed him, except it was no fun to let him know that.

"Honestly!"

Peter scooped up everything in a black bag and was just wrapping the blade of the axe in a thick wad of bags when John's phone rang.

"I'm wanted upstairs," he said.

"You get going; we've got it," said Nicky.

John charged up the stairs three at a time, meeting the others in the doorway as they manhandled the McCullens out into the hall. A woman poked her head from a flat opposite and quickly disappeared as she saw the McCullens with black plastic bags over their heads being dragged from their flat.

Terry tipped his head towards the McCullen's flat. "Go collect the spoils," He said to John. John scooped up the cash, cocaine and jewellery and then added to his heavy load by calling in at the third-floor flat and taking the contraband from there. He was breathless when he opened the back of the van and put the bags in with the McCullen brothers. Ali and Elgin reminded the McCullens of the presence of guns by ramming the butts of the weapons in their chests.

"Take them now," said Terry. "Good work."

~❖~

Terry walked down to the third-floor flat. The two boys were still quivering on the floor. He stood over them. "Fuck off and keep your mouths shut." Not realising that was their cue to go, they just sat there until Terry nodded his head towards the door. They jumped up and ran out, all injuries forgotten.

CHAPTER TWENTY ONE

In the yard at the back of Camberwell Police Station, Dave looked over at the crowd and regretted not being with Terry and the rest of the crew. After all, they should have had one police officer with them. That Ali and Elgin seemed wild cards… and John and Jimmy were not much better. What if…?

Another question from a reporter, directed at Mr Jones, interrupted his train of thought. This time louder and more agitated than the rest.

"If you can't tell us what this is all about, then perhaps you can explain why the crime stats relating to knife crime and murder have been so bad these last two years?"

Jones gave a tight smile and looked as though he was about to speak when the four German Shepherds started barking in unison. There didn't seem any reason for it and their handlers snapped them tight on their leashes. The four van loads of Territorial Support Group officers, who had been standing to attention, now fussed with their body armour, pulling out their collars for a bit of breeze against the heat, checking truncheon and handcuffs. The news crew from ITN and another from the BBC jostled for space with the many print journalists and photographers from the national newspapers, along with the crime reporter from the South London Press. It was all getting out of hand.

Jones turned to Dave and hissed, "When is he going to ring you? This is ridiculous."

"I don't know, sir. From the briefing, he said he would ring me with the location as soon as they cleared the dealers' from the estate. I assume they are still working on that."

"Well, ring him and find out how long he is going to be."

"I have," lied Dave, "and there is no reply."

When Dave's phone finally rang, he had to work hard not to giggle, as the crowd hushed and stared at him in silent anticipation. He walked away from them, as best as he could, and stood in a dank corner where ferns were poking out from the crumbling red brick wall.

"Hi, mate," said Terry. "Tell Jonesy-boy that we confiscated a shit-load of coke plus a gun with ammunition and other weapons."

"Everyone okay?" Dave said. He meant anyone injured or dead.

"Oh, yes. The lads are now off to a nice little bijou cottage in the countryside. Though don't tell Jones that."

"Of course not."

"Oh, and meet us at the Peacock after the circus is over."

In the stilted formal language, Dave wrote what Terry had said.

Jones snatched the notebook out of his hand when he returned.

"This morning," he announced, "we disrupted one of the largest drug suppliers in South London. We have seized a substantial amount of drugs and a loaded firearm together with other weapons. The presence of this gang has been responsible for beatings, stabbings and murders in an area near here. We will now retake the estate, board up the premises they have been using, reinstate CCTV cameras and give the residents of the Brandon Estate their lives back. We will head there now if you want to follow the police vehicles."

Jones, ignoring Dave, got in the back of his car and drove off. Dave considered following him to the Brandon Estate. How the hell was Jones going to answer questions from the television and press relating to the seizures? Instead, he decided he had heard enough bullshit for one day and headed to the Peacock.

~❖~

The convoy snaked its way along Camberwell New Road towards the Brandon Estate: police vehicles in front followed by television vans, press reporters and then two council vehicles. In the back of his car, Jones was rehearsing his full press briefing and how he would break the news to the Commissioner and the Home Secretary. The question about the crime stats had stung. Now, he'd show them. Perhaps involving Terry and his gang hadn't been such a bad idea after all.

When he arrived, Jones stood to the side of his car and watched as the Territorial Support Group stormed past, dust kicking from their heels and surprised residents throwing themselves to the side, eyes wide open. He followed them at a brisk pace to one of the empty flats with its front door hanging from the hinges.

"Sir," called one of the police officers, "it's safe to enter."

He squeezed past two officers on the door and entered the dingy flat. Looking around the ransacked property, the amount of damage astonished him. There wasn't an item of soft furnishing that wasn't slashed open, including mattresses and pillows. The kitchen cupboards lay on the floor, ripped from the walls and the bases of wardrobes broken open. Terry and his gang knew their stuff. Not a hiding place left.

Next, Jones checked the police had formed the inner and outer ring he'd asked for and gave orders for the council employees to seal the flats with metal doors, fix the CCTV cameras throughout the estate and clean the graffiti. "Make it nice," he told them. After all, this estate was to be the symbol of his success.

He walked out of the block of flats to see film crews attempting to interview some of the crowd of residents gathered to watch the excitement. Most refused to talk, other than one old man who said, "We were prisoners in our homes because of them." Then a woman, presumably his daughter, ushered him away.

Never mind. A soundbite was enough. Jones was sure it would be on the television news channels today and headlines in the printed press tomorrow morning. It couldn't have gone better.

"Mr Jones!" The reporters had spotted him and rushed over.

"Could you give us some more details?"

"The whole matter is now sub judice," he said. "However, I'm happy for you to take photos." He placed himself out of the block of flats' shadow and ensured the sun was shining on his face.

CHAPTER TWENTY-TWO

As Peter drove along Shooters Hill towards Dartford, he could hear a commotion in the back of the van. Thumps, groans and protests.

"Is everything alright back there?" he shouted.

"Everything's fine," Jimmy told him. "Ali is just explaining to these two the rights and wrongs of shagging a fourteen-year-old girl."

"We need them alive! Calm it down."

Jimmy laughed. "No worries, mate." And the sound ceased.

Peter glanced at the sat nav. They'd be there in twenty minutes. For some reason, Terry had given last-minute instructions that when they arrived in Dartford, he was to telephone him, away from Ali and Elgin. What was that all about? Never mind, he'd soon find out. First, they had to lock up the McCullens.

Turning off the A.2, he carried on along a country road till he came to the metal gate. Getting out, he opened the new padlock and drove through, then locked the gate behind the van. He called out, "Hang on to something," as he bumped along the unmade, overgrown path that brought them to a yard with sheds and huts all around it. Perfect, he thought.

He got out and stood for a moment in the sun. Sure, the place looked neglected; crickets chirped in the long grass and hovering over one outbuilding was a bird who sang sweetly. Was it a lark? He wanted to think so, but he didn't have a clue. The only thing he was sure of it wasn't a pigeon.

A thumping noise came from the back of the van, which snapped him back into his mission. Peter headed over to one hut, unlocked the bolt, and opened it. In one corner were boxes of crisps, crates of water, a torch and batteries. In the other corner were two buckets and some toilet paper. Peter picked up the torch and swept it along the walls to check for any escape routes. There were none: they weren't digging out of the concrete floors nor busting through these corrugated iron walls. They were going to need the water though: it was hot in here.

Peter retraced his steps and opened the back of the van. As Ali and Elgin pulled Gerald and Rory McCullen out, he stood to the side. The two gangsters started pleading for their lives. I was right to stop that beating, Peter thought. Plastic bags still covered their heads. Peter ran his eyes across their bodies to see how badly injured they were. Simpering on the floor, they seemed in a lot of pain, although he couldn't see anything seriously wrong with them.

"Take them in," he said and almost added "Carefully" as Jimmy and John dragged one of them by their ankles into the shed across gravel, and Ali and Elgin took the other. He turned away so the men wouldn't see him wincing. He never could bear the violent part of his old job, which was why he loved the clean tech side.

When the brothers were safely in the shed, he stood by the door and watched Jimmy cutting off their cable ties and taking the sacks off their heads. Both of the brothers' noses had blood clots around them and Rory had a cut above his right eye which bled down his face. That probably needs a few stitches, Peter thought.

John stood over the brothers and said, "I thought you two were tough bastards."

They stared at him but didn't reply. John grabbed Rory, pulled him back to his feet, and slammed him against the wall. "Not so tough on your own, are you? How much do you owe Mehmed? He's going to have the raving hump with you when he discovers you've done a runner. How long do you think it will be before he sends people after you?"

"Fuck off," said Rory, suddenly defiant.

The words had barely passed his lips when John hit him on the jaw. Rory fell backwards and landed on his brother, who jumped up.

Jimmy moved effortlessly forward, stood in front of Gerald, and said, "Are you sure you want to do this?" When Gerald hesitated, he said, "you're not very brave when you haven't got your gang to back you up, are you? Now sit down with your brother." Jimmy pushed Gerald to the floor.

Ali and Elgin looked on, impressed. Peter was afraid they were about to join in. He called out, "Let's leave them to think about what they have done."

The four men stood still for a moment and then sauntered out. Peter put the padlock on and checked it was secure.

"Look!" said Jimmy, pointing to the far end of the small holding where a jumble of farm machinery, old caravans and cars stood, rusting and ivy-clad. "I think that's an old Vauxhall Victor; my dad used to have one of those. I remember when service manuals showed you how to change the oil, spark plugs and fan belts. Now they warn you not to drink the battery acid."

Peter let the others go and wandered over to the body of water behind the huts. It was bigger than a pond, thought Peter, however not as big as a lake. Many times he'd seriously considered moving into the country and never got around to it. It's too late now, he thought. On the water were some skinny black and white duck-like things. He smiled as the two of them dipped in tandem, bums up in the air. When they righted themselves, he made his phone call to Terry.

"The boys settled in?" asked Terry.

He considered telling Terry about the beatings and decided against it, knowing the only thing Terry cared about at the moment was getting the job done. "All the mod cons," he said. "It's lovely here." He was serious.

"Listen," said Terry. "I want you, Jimmy and John to bring Ali and Elgin to KwikKash Metals - you know, the scrap metal yard in Deptford?"

Peter watched a rat swim out from the reeds. "I know it."

"I want John to divvy out the spoils. We're keeping the weapons, phones and drugs,"

"The rest goes to Ali and Elgin?" said Peter

"Yeah, that was part of the deal."

"Is that right? They had two shotguns?"

Terry was silent for a moment. Peter could hear the faint sound of laughter from the men on the other side of the smallholding. "When you get here, tell them to come into the office, where I'll be waiting. I want you to park the van up and take the shotguns and get rid of them," said Terry finally.

"No problem,"

He walked back to find John and Jimmy chatting about buying the land and concreting it over. "Bet you could get a couple of hundred houses on this site."

"Probably can't get planning permission," said Jimmy. "They prefer it to sit here growing wild."

"What a waste," said John. "Mind you; there's bugger all to do out here."

"Let's sort out the booty," Peter said. "Better to get it into separate bags here rather than in South London.

Standing at the back of the van, John divided the spoils from the two flats into bin bags. He moved the money, watches, and jewellery into one bag and the drugs, telephones, weapons, handgun and ammunition into the other. Peter looked back only once: not at the hut where the brothers were, but to the lake and the sky above.

CHAPTER TWENTY-THREE

Once they heard the van start up and drive off, the McCullen brothers put their shoulders to the door, slamming it again and again. It was no good, and their wounds throbbed with each impact.

Although there were some shafts of light through small slits in the corrugated metal roof, the Nissen hut was too dark to see. They felt their way around the walls looking for anything that could force open the door until they came across the supplies left for them, including a torch. Gerald switched it on and the beam of light hit the boxes of crisps and cartons of water.

"If they were going to kill us, why would they leave this stuff?" Rory said.

Gerald scratched his head, wincing when he found a bump. "I can't work out what it's all about. It has to be something to do with Mehmed. Maybe they're trying to push him out."

"Snatching us up won't put Mehmed out of business."

Gerald stood for a moment, his light playing on the water. "Who do you think they are?"

"Don't know," said Rory, "it's a weird setup. Two look like they are Turks; the others are white boomers. I don't get it."

They slumped against the wall, deep in thought. After about ten minutes of silence, Gerald said, "I know we've talked about it before; we need to think about getting out of this business. We've got plenty of money and the houses will keep the money coming in. What do you think?"

"I've told you, bruv, I've wanted us out for ages. If you're serious, I'm with you all the way. We don't need this shit anymore."

Gerald picked at a weed growing up through the crack in the concrete. "Shit!" he said, suddenly. "What about Mum? She's going to lose her nut if we don't turn up today."

They made another rush at the door and paced the hut, looking for a weak place in the metal where they could peel it back; however, it was no good. They were stuck.

"Cheese and onion?" said Rory, pointing to the box of crisps.

Gerald shrugged. "Might as well."

~❖~

Jimmy tapped his legs on the drive back and began singing Summer Holiday.

"Mate!" said Peter, "I'm trying to drive here.

"Alright, grump," said Jimmy. He kept the song in his head. Today couldn't have gone better. Two low-lives locked up. The old dogs still have it in them, after all! He gave a mock one-two on the dashboard and laughed. Then, noticing Peter turned off Lower Road said, "Where are we off to now?"

"We're meeting Terry and Nicky at KwikKash Metals." He glanced in the rear-view mirror to see Ali and Elgin deep in conversation with John. "They're going to hand over some of the gear to the brothers."

They drove through a high metal gate and bumped over the uneven tarmac to a portable office. On either side of them were cars waiting to be scrapped.

"Jeez," said Jimmy, pointing to a Ferrari, which was crumpled to half its size. "Bet that cost a pretty penny."

"Probably cost a life too," said Peter.

"You really know how to put a damper on things."

"Jump out," said Peter, turning his head to John, Ali and Elgin. "You too, Jimmy. I'm going to park up."

Glad to be away from Peter's buzz-kill, Jimmy leapt out. The yard was noisy with the sound of the metal crusher on full whack. He walked into the Portakabin office ahead of Ali, Elgin, with John at the rear carrying the stash in sacks. "Wey Hey, lads," he said to Terry and Nicky. "We did it!"

He attempted to give Terry a high five. Terry ignored him. "It's not over yet," He said. Another buzz-kill. Still, John grinned at him and Ali and Elgin broke into the first smiles he'd seen from them when Terry, after inspecting the bags, handed them a sizable amount of cash together with the watches and jewellery.

"That's for Yusuf," Terry said. He glanced out of the window, "And it's in exchange for the two sawn-off shotguns that Peter is taking from the van right now."

The smiles dropped from their faces.

"You can tell Yusuf you guys don't need shooters."

"Big men like you," said Jimmy, slapping Ali on the shoulder.

Ali bristled.

"I mean it. You did a fantastic job. Great work. Both of you."

Jimmy sweated as Ali eyed him. Then it appeared he believed him and gave a small nod.

"The last thing we want is someone getting shot," said Terry, "especially as we are supposed to be preventing shootings and stabbings. Do you understand?" They both nodded; their facial expressions gave nothing away. "Peter will drop you off. We may not need you till next week. Thanks for your help today. You did great. It couldn't have gone better."

All the men left the building. Peter wasn't in the van. They searched the scrap yard and found him next to the metal crusher. At once, they understood where the guns were. Ali held his hand over his heart as though in mourning.

CHAPTER TWENTY FOUR

"Hello, my lovelies," said Diane as Terry, Nicky, John, and Jimmy walked into the Peacock. "All of London's a-twitter about what you did."

"What you mean?" said Terry with a grin.

"I may be old. I've still got eyes and ears, young man. Haven't I Jake?" she called to her great-grandson, who was pulling a pint. "Once I saw that buffoon on telly taking credit for a raid on an estate, I thought, 'That's not your doing, fella-me-lad, that's my boys did that!'" She sighed. "Though expect that means you won't be coming

much anymore."

"We've not finished yet," said John.

"Ooo, fancy!" said Diane. "And here I am offering you all a farewell pint."

She cocked her head at Jake, who lifted a tray with six pints of lager on it. Terry was glad to see she hadn't forgotten Peter and Dave, who were heading over soon.

"Cheers, love," said Jimmy, lifting his pint. "Here's to a bloody successful day!"

As the others grabbed their pints, Terry said to Diane, "Not that we had anything to do with the raid."

"Ha!" she replied. "Who are you kidding, Mister? Ah," she said, spotting Peter and Dave coming in, "Here are the other two musketeers. Drinks on the house, my darlings!"

The men took their pints and retired to the room upstairs. It was as muggy as ever and despite not wanting a drink before they sorted out the next part of their plan, Terry knocked back his lager. "Well done, lads," he said, lifting his empty glass.

"Piece of piss," said Jimmy.

"Yeah," said John. "Those McCullen brothers are pussies. How the hell they got to reign over South London is beyond me."

Dave sipped his lager. "Most of their reputation comes because they are willing to both order and use extreme violence when required. And they've got a gang of followers ready to inflict that violence.

John said, "They may give out orders, but they can't hold their hands up and have a row, can they?"

"I get what you're saying," said Dave. "This is a different world now. Guns and knives dictate who the toughest is."

"Yeah," said Jimmy, "Look at Putin. He's a pint pot."

Before they could solve the world's problems, Terry called order and gave Dave instructions to take the drugs and weapons, including the handgun and ammunition to Jones. "Oh, and tell us about what happened at Camberwell Police Station."

"It was a right farce," said Dave. "He led them all there and took credit as though he'd stormed the building single-handed. He is so into the publicity side of things it's sad."

"There have always been senior officers like that in the job, even in our time," said Terry. "Let's hope it doesn't turn and bite him on the arse - in which case we're all in for it."

There was a moment's silence and, realising he shouldn't have brought the mood so low; Terry asked John to tell them what Jilly had said on the phone on the way over.

"Oh, it was fantastic," said John. "She reckoned within a matter of hours; there was a completely different atmosphere on the estate. People were out of their flats talking and laughing when previously they rarely saw each other. One old boy compared it to VE Day."

The men laughed and John and Jimmy clinked empty glasses.

"What did she say the police are doing now?" Terry said.

"They've set up a roadblock, so there is now only one way to get in and out of the Brandon Estate. They monitor that entrance twenty-four hours a day, checking everyone entering the estate. The police are now patrolling the estate and counsel workers are reinstating CCTV cameras without being molested. The two flats used by the McCullens are now boarded up."

The men sat back in their seats. Terry was proud of them and what they achieved, though he realised the next step was going to be just as testing, and when they were targeting Mehmed directly, it would be far more dangerous.

~❖~

Jones put down his phone after a very pleasing conversation with the Commissioner followed by an equally heart-warming chat with the Home Secretary. On the computer in front of him, tabs were open at all the major newspapers that had reported the raid in glowing terms. The only thing now was to count the booty. He made his way to the evidence room. Dave was waiting there, slouching against a metal shelf scrolling through his phone.

Jones cleared his throat.

Dave snapped upright. "Sorry, sir, just looking through the news reports."

"Rather good, aren't they? We did well."

Dave raised his eyebrows, and Jones had the impression that he was waiting for something. He couldn't think what.

"OK, show me what we've got."

Dave heaved one of the large holdalls, confiscated from Ali and Elgin, onto the metal evidence desk and unzipped it.

"Good God," said Jones. "Wait here! The Commissioner simply has to see this." Rather than phone, he ran from the room and up two flights of stairs, returning more sedately with the Commissioner.

After passing the gun between them several times, the Commissioner asked, "Has someone made it safe?"

Jones was almost sure he caught an eye-roll as Dave said, "Yes sir… and it's likely they wiped it, so no need to worry about fingerprints."

The Commissioner dropped it quickly back in the bag as Jones narrowed his eyes at Dave.

"Did all these drugs and weapons come from one address?" asked the Commissioner.

Dave hesitated before responding. "I believe it was two addresses, Sir."

Why the hesitation? Thought Jones.

"And do we have the perpetrators?"

Jones cleared his throat. This was one aspect he wasn't sure about. "We are working on that, Sir. My best men are on it."

Dave made a strange sound, which turned into a cough. Jones ignored him. "I've arranged for all the drugs to be taken to the laboratory in Lambeth for analysis and weighing," he said to the Commissioner. "We will then have a valuation available for the press by this afternoon."

"Have you any idea what else we can expect? Do you know what's next?"

Jones threw a glance at Dave; his face was straight now, giving nothing away. "It's all under control, Sir. They are working on something and as soon as they've firmed the plans up, I'll let Mr Jones know."

"Well, convey my thanks and gratitude. You can tell Mr Reid that he has impressed the Home Secretary and me with the speed and accuracy of his information and the outcome. He shouldn't hesitate to ask if he requires any other resources."

He marched away, leaving Jones and Dave in the evidence room. Dave had that look on his face again. "Well, what is it?"

"Nothing, sir. I just thought they did well."

Jones stared at him for a moment. "A bit more notice would have been handy; however, yes, a reasonable job was done."

CHAPTER TWENTY-FIVE

Terry was sitting in the kitchen early the next morning when Nicky called him.

"Kenny Pierce just rang," he said. "The Columbians have contacted him with the date of the delivery. He's meeting Mehmed at Harry Baker's office this afternoon. It's a bit of a rush, as he's flying to Morocco this evening."

"No rest for the wicked," said Terry.

"Do you mean Kenny or us?"

"Both."

"So, do you think we should cover the meeting?"

Terry looked at the picture of Denise while he thought. "I'm not sure we have the manpower or enough surveillance equipment."

Nicky paused. "I think we can trust Kenny," he said. "He wouldn't have rung me otherwise. I'm sure he'll be straight with us about what is happening."

When Terry put down the phone, he said to Denise. "Who can you trust, though? The only one I trusted was you." Then he realised that wasn't true. He trusted his men and if Nicky believed in Kenny, then so should too.

~❖~

As soon as Kenny walked into the plush office, Harry Baker sprang from his chair. "Mehmed is in the conference room and he's in a foul mood."

"Good afternoon to you too," said Kenny and brushed past him into the conference room. There sat Arian Mehmed, larger than life and twice as ugly. On either side of him stood two bodyguards, legs wide, hands clasped by their crotches - the usual gangster stance. Kenny's stomach flipped at the thought of what he'd promised Terry. Despite this, he strode over, his hand outstretched. He'd always been able to bluff. And who better to turn in than this monster in front of him?

Mehmed ignored his hand. "You're late," he snarled.

Kenny smiled and checked his Rolex. "It's exactly two o'clock,"

Ignoring this, Mehmed said, "You know everyone in South London. Are you aware of who is trying to muscle me out? Old blokes your age."

"You're joking," said Kenny. "Who's going to try to muscle you out?"

"Do I look like I'm fucking joking?" he exploded. "Not only have they nicked a good lump of my gear, but my two main guys have also disappeared off the face of the earth owing me money. The police are now everywhere on the estate."

Kenny made his face into a mask of surprise and concern. "God, that's awful. I didn't know. I've been in Morocco and I'm going again…" He checked his watch again "… as soon as we're done."

"It's all over the fucking television and newspapers."

Kenny tutted. "That's terrible."

Mehmed narrowed his eyes. "You taking the piss?"

Kenny glanced over Mehmed's head at the piece of abstract art which adorned the wall. It was a mess of blood red and white, blobbed out of an oil tube. "No, Mehmed, my friend, of course not," he said. "What is bad for your business is bad for mine. Airfares aren't cheap."

Mehmed slumped in his seat. He looked out of place here in this swish office, even, in his expensive suit: its seams straining over muscles. He should be street fighting in some back alley for a handful of Albanian lek. Still, you had to hand it to the man. There were brains inside that thick skull. He'd come from nothing and made an empire. An empire Kenny was about to destroy.

Kenny cleared his throat. "Your next load is arriving on the seventeenth of June. Where do you want it?"

Mehmed looked up. "I like you, Kenny," he said, and Kenny's stomach clenched. This was never a good start. Mehmed's next words put him at ease. "You are all about the business. I am all about the business, too." He picked up a pen and clicked it a few times. "I want the next load dropped at the Woolwich Yard." Mehmed stood. "You'll ring with a time?" He didn't wait for an answer and swept out, followed by the two goons.

Kenny returned to Harry Baker's office, where Harry was standing by the door watching Mehmed's back as he walked away. He came in and shut the door. "That man scares the life out of me," said Harry. "He even frightens the staff, and they never speak to him."

"I'd like to say he's a teddy bear," said Kenny. "But I'd be lying. He's as evil as he looks."

Harry shuddered.

"We've got brains on our side," said Kenny. Looking straight into Harry's eyes. "The trick is knowing when to get out, mate." He wondered if it was true what they said about loyalty between thieves. In his books, Harry was okay. However, he realised that despite what Terry and Nicky had told him, Harry would probably go down with Mehmed, but he was glad he'd given him a hint. Not that he seemed to have taken it. Instead, he picked up a file and held it out to Kenny. "What do you want me to do about this delay in serving your boy's extradition papers from the Home Office?" he said. "I don't understand what they're playing at. Maybe they think the boys will come back voluntarily if they hang it out. I could fight it, but they would probably tie us up in red tape."

Should Kenny tell Harry how the police were letting the boys free? No, he'd given him a hint, and as much as he liked and respected Harry, he daren't trust him with the entire story. Once the police arrested Mehmed, both their lucrative income streams would cease and Kenny was aware Harry wouldn't give that up by choice.

"I'm flying out to Morocco to see the boys this afternoon. I'll catch up with you when I get back."

When he left Harry's office, he returned home first, collected his bag, and rang Nicky on his way to the airport. He felt a little sick as he told Nicky the date and place of the drop. He felt better when thinking he was doing it for the good of his sons. They'd be free, and he'd be free. This last job was the last time he would ever help the drug dealers or the police. When this was over, he'd be nothing but a family man.

CHAPTER TWENTY-SIX

Kenny sat in the Escape VIP lounge at Stansted Airport, scrolling through his phone. Oh, that was a good one - the boys jumping into the pool: proper action shot. And there was Bobby, the same height as that old Alsatian they'd had - poor Buster, the boys, had teased him mercilessly; Billy, with ice cream all over his face, was next. God, he missed those days. When he'd come home and they'd climb all over him. Mind you; they'd been right tearaways even before they were out of nappies. Trish would tell him stories about what they'd been up to before he'd scarcely got time to take his jacket off. And as they'd grown, it was no longer neighbours they had to apologise to or the parents of a kid at the boys' school but other more dangerous types. The job had shifted from Trish to him. Apparently, he was now meant to be the expert in this world.

A smiling uniformed waitress placing a large glass of red wine and a dish of mixed nuts in front of him and clearing the empty glass from the table interrupted his thoughts. Being a regular traveller and a heavy tipper meant Kenny didn't need to serve himself like other travellers. Looking at his watch, he realised there were forty-five minutes away from boarding. After he took a sip of his wine, Kenny admitted to himself that letting the boys have control of his Oakfield Properties business, when they were not long out of school had been a mistake.

Trish had thought being trusted employees would give the boys some purpose, something to work towards. He couldn't blame her. She always thought the best of them; mums always do. He and this was something he rarely admitted to himself, saw in the boys the worst of himself - untampered by age or circumstance. He'd given them everything - a house, a pool, a private school education, money for whatever they wanted, hoping it would protect them from the darkness he had: that desire for money because money was power. And once that itch was in you, it was hard to disobey.

He brought his hands up to his eyes to stop the image of Joe Brown, which came unbidden. The ghost of him and his twin sons came only rarely now and mostly at night; there he was - his once partner in crime. It was others who convinced him that killing Joe's twin sons was a sure way to get him to retract the statement he had made implicating Kenny and others, but he had made the final decision. For appearance's sake, he had flown back from Spain for the boy's funeral. He remembered standing around the grave and glancing at Joe, who stood handcuffed between two prison officers. He could see no anger in his eyes, only sadness. Billy and Bobby are the same age Joe's twins were when they so brutally lost their lives, Kenny mused. No wonder Joe Brown took his own life in prison.

Kenny grabbed his wine and lifted his hand for another. Thinking better of it, he picked up his hand luggage and walked through the concourse until Joe Brown had disappeared and his plane was ready to depart.

As the tarmac disappeared and the wings cut through clouds, he sipped at another red wine and nodded off. He awoke only when they landed and walked through the hot, stale air of the airport. The sweat on his neck cooled as he stepped into the air-conditioned car. He did not need to tell the driver where he was going - it was always the same one and he didn't need directions.

He looked out of the window at the now familiar adverts which lined the road, the mess of people, some without shoes and thought - why did I send my boys here? Having taken the money from Oakfield Properties' account to start a drug business, why had they chosen some random blokes to deal for them? - Men who squealed at the first sign of trouble? Hadn't they learned anything from him? Once he discovered the police had an informant telling them everything relating to his boy's involvement, he needed somewhere for them to lie low while he tried to get to the source of that information. Morocco seemed perfect, with all his old contacts from his cannabis years still in place. He accepted now he should have factored in how stupid his sons were.

As he passed the neon lights of a nightclub, he realised he should've sent them to a desert island. This place was too full of excitement for two young bucks - two men willing to fight over some fly-by-night girls and get arrested. Why hadn't they just stayed in the hotel like he'd asked them to when he'd sent them here? It was the least they could have done. It wasn't like he'd just bought them a ticket: no, he'd had to fly them out from Biggin Hill Airport in the dead of night to France; he'd booked their bus tickets from Paris to Malaga and a ferry to Tangier. It had been a bloody nightmare. However, he thought nothing like this, looking up at Kenitra Prison's walls. Thanking the driver, he stepped out of the car. It was like walking into an oven: an oven filled with sewage.

He walked into the reception with its dirt floor. Recognising Kenny, the guard smiled, took out his keys and let him through. A group of cells was close to the prison's main office, separate from the main population. The cells were large - normally accommodating twenty prisoners. Kenny had ensured that the boys had one all to themselves. He'd had to. There was no way these two could mix with the rest of the prisoners.

"Dad!" they said and wrapped themselves around him. It was good to feel the solidity of their bodies - no longer boys, they were now men - still, the stain of his thoughts was on him: how much trouble they had caused, how it was because of them he was working with Terry and Nicky - putting his own life in danger.

"How have you been?" he asked.

"Not so bad, Dad," said Billy, throwing himself on one of the bunks. Bobby sat next to Billy and punched him in the leg just for the hell of it. Bobby punched him right back.

Kenny tried not to grimace - tried to be grateful to spend time with his healthy young men. Both were wearing smart Under Armour sportswear and Nike trainers and looked well-fed, unlike the rest of the prison population. Kenny's money bought them anything they needed, including alcohol, in a Muslim country.

"When can we get out, Dad?" said Billy.

He shrugged his shoulders. He wasn't about to tell them about their imminent release. They hadn't got a brain cell between them and would no doubt blab about it, putting the whole thing in jeopardy. There was another reason too. For the first time, he wanted them to feel the consequences of their actions.

"Can Mum come next time?" said Bobby.

"Son," said Kenny, looking him straight in the eye, "that's not going to happen. It would break her heart to see you here in this place."

As he left his sons, the call for prayers sounded, a low mournful noise, and seconds after, he heard loud rap music from the boys' cell. It echoed down the corridor, drowning out the muezzin.

CHAPTER TWENTY-SEVEN

Nicky waved at Diane and charged up the stairs at The Peacock before she could embroil him in conversation. He had work to do. In the room upstairs, Terry was waiting.

"Nicky, you're here at last."

"Sorry, boss, traffic, and…" he grinned, "a phone call from Kenny about his meeting with Mehmed." He caught his breath. "He's given me the address of the warehouse the cocaine is being delivered to. It's in Woolwich, and he's confirmed the date."

"That's brilliant!" said Terry. "We can start working on that. Anything else?"

"Mehmed was ranting about two of his dealers going missing and the money they owe him. He wanted to know if Kenny had any idea who had kidnapped them."

Terry tapped the table: a little drum roll of celebration. "Good to hear it's winding him up. Wait till the next lot go on the missing list,"

They both laughed and Nicky said," He was on his way to the airport to fly to Morocco. I told him we would meet him when he comes back and if he hears anything while he's away, to give me a ring."

They now had the date and location of the drop.

"Are you going to tell Jones?" asked Nicky.

"No way. This has to be watertight first before we hand anything over."

Nicky nodded. He'd rather they didn't tell Jones anything.

"I want you and Peter working on this full-time. We need to watch this place in Woolwich where they are going to do the drop-off. Try to find premises somewhere nearby that we can use for surveillance. If not, we might have to resort to using the back of one of Peter's vans and at our age, that's not the most comfortable option."

Nicky imagined himself cramped in the back of a van with a flask of tea and a bottle to relieve himself in and shuddered.

~❖~

Nicky contacted Peter, and they met in Greenwich before heading off to Woolwich Docks. They drove around the industrial estates' general locality, ensuring they identified every way in and out. Nicky said, "These were working docks when I was a kid. They used to be important naval dockyards, where they built ships from the early sixteenth century." He sighed and pointed to an ugly block of flats rising from the ground, still unfinished. "Look at that. There's nothing other than warehouses and apartments now." They turned down Mill Side and back up Dockyard, looking for somewhere they could leave cars and survey the drop. It was like a rabbit warren.

Peter turned left, and they found themselves at a dead end. As he did a three-point turn, he said, "I'll need to get some up-to-date plans for the area - if they exist. We'll need something for briefings."

"Yeah," said Nicky, "It's hard to get your head around it. Shall we go see the site of the drop now?"

On arrival, they both swore. The location was a major problem, as it was on one of the new estates and was one of eight identical warehouses. It had a yard with double metal gates. Inside the gates and against the fence was a grey BMW 3 series and through the yard was the warehouse, large enough to contain two or even three HGVs. Two sliding doors secured the warehouse, both were open.

"Drive up a bit. Go slow," said Nicky.

Peter drove as slowly as he could without bringing attention to himself as Nicky peered into the warehouse. There was one man inside on a forklift truck. Nicky twisted in his seat to watch as the forklift drove into a sliver of sunlight just inside the door. The man was probably in his mid-fifties and looked Turkish or Albanian.

As they moved away, Nicky said, "Shit, out of the eight warehouses, that one is the only one occupied. There's no way we can park a surveillance van anywhere near it, it would stick out like a sore thumb. If Mehmed is having a hundred kilos of cocaine delivered, then he's going to be hypersensitive to anything out of the ordinary, and a van parked up on an empty street is out of the question."

"Anyway, none of the other warehouses has windows overlooking it," said Peter.

Nicky fished a sausage roll out of his pocket and wolfed it down in three gulps. There were still bits of flaky pastry down his front as he rang Terry to give him the news. Terry's disappointment matched his own. "We'll talk about it tomorrow," said Terry.

"I've had an idea," said Peter, through his open window, as he dropped Nicky off.

"What?" said Nicky. Peter drove away without answering.

Nicky shook his head. Peter sure loved a secret: working in surveillance had made him wary of saying a single thing to anybody. It must have driven his wife mad.

He pondered on what the idea might be over a dinner of sausage and mash and went to bed, still thinking about it.

The next morning, he woke late, rushed his breakfast and drove over to The Peacock as fast as he could. The men were already in the room upstairs. Without waiting for any of them to acknowledge him, he flung open his arms. "So, what was this idea, Peter?"

"Good morning to you, too," said Terry.

"No, he said he had an idea about the warehouse. There's no way we can be there incognito in our vans. There aren't even any bushes!"

The men laughed. "Come on, Peter," said John, "Spill the beans before Nicky has a stroke."

"Fine," said Peter. "When we were down there, I noticed a CCTV camera on the side of the warehouse aimed at the front gate of the yard. After I got back to my office, I got one of my guys to hack into the camera." He opened up the Apple Mac in front of him and showed them a clear black-and-white picture of the yard and gate.

Nicky felt his mouth drop open. "That's scary and brilliant," said Jimmy.

"This is the only camera they have," said Peter, "which is good; however, I think it's safe to assume they will unload inside the warehouse and not the yard. This morning I got the plans for the empty unit next door, and as I thought, being new, they rent them as shells. It's down to the occupants to build internally for whatever suits their needs. I've got to get a look at the interior of Mehmed's warehouse so I can work out what sort of kit I would need, but I'm pretty sure I could set up a camera inside his warehouse. Also, although I'm fairly confident there is no alarm system, I want to make sure."

"Good work," said Terry. "Even if you can have a look inside, how are you going to get in long enough to set up a camera?"

"I returned late last night."

"What?" said Nicky. "I could've come with you."

Peter ignored him. "Around the back is a single-glazed toilet window. It doesn't look very secure and we might get it open, showing no damage. If not, the glass style is 'Flemish', I've measured it and got one of my guys to get a piece cut to fit. If all fails, we can take the old glass out and replace it with the new one when finished."

"Genius," said Jimmy.

"Yeah," said Peter, "Only thing is…" He turned to Terry. "I know you would prefer to keep everything in-house; nevertheless, I'll have to use one of my blokes to fit the camera. There's no way I could get in and out of that small window."

"Perhaps Nicky could try?" said Jimmy.

The men hooted with laughter.

"Oy!" said Nicky, looking down at his belly.

Terry kept his face straight. "And we can trust your guys, right?"

"Absolutely. Most are ex-Old Bill."

"That's fair enough," said Terry. "I'll leave it to you. We haven't got a lot of time. You and Nicky keep at it, and tell me if you need any help."

Nicky raised his eyebrows at Peter. "Oh, it's you *and* Nicky. Apparently, it wasn't you and Nicky last night."

Peter clapped him on the shoulder. "Sorry, mate, I just wanted to see if it would work before sharing. I won't do it again."

Nicky nodded, and Terry turned to John and Jimmy. "I want you to pick up Ali and Elgin to check out what's happening down in Dartford."

"Really? Those guys?" said Jimmy, "I mean, they were good at-"

"I'm sure you don't need them," said Terry. "I just want to keep them involved. It shows good faith." He took a sip of coffee. "I also need you to concentrate on the Brownfield Estate. We've heard how pissed off Mehmed is about the McCullens. It would be good to take the other dealers sooner rather than later. That should certainly get up his nose."

Jimmy rolled his neck and sniffed before saying, "Mitchell and Johnstone have got two flats like the McCullen brothers. It looks like the Mitchell flat is where the kids pick up the cocaine from and the Johnstone flat is where all the money is." He took a sip of coffee. "The Mitchell flat is in constant use: young kids coming and going dozens of times a day, back and forth to Canary Wharf." He shook his head. "I can't even imagine how much cocaine they are moving."

"Bankers and politicians are where the money's at for those guys," said John.

"Right," said Jimmy, "And it looks like they store the money at Johnstone's flat. The kids drop the takings off there regularly all day - only stay a minute and they're out."

"So, we have Mitchell in the drug flat and Johnstone in the money flat," said Terry.

"No," said Jimmy, "It's not as simple as that. At about ten A.M. every day, two youngsters tip up to Mitchell's flat. He leaves and goes to Johnston's flat, where he stays till about ten P.M. before returning to his place."

"So we can get them both in one fell swoop?" said Terry.

"Possibly." Jimmy exchanged glances with John. "Mitchell's flat is easy. It's just a basic standard council door. Johnston has replaced his door with a solid, secure one with a reinforced metal door frame, and we don't even know what the locks or bolts on the inside are like. We have to assume our door openers won't get us in quickly.

"How the hell are we going to get in?" asked Nicky.

"Well," said Jimmy with a smile. "We're going to use the old Trojan Horse method."

CHAPTER TWENTY-EIGHT

In his car on the way to pick up Ali and Elgin, Jimmy could tell something was troubling John. "What's the matter with you? You've been in a shit mood all day."

"Nothing, I'm fine," replied John

"Bullshit. I'm not going to let it go, so you might as well tell me."

John slumped down in the passenger seat. "If you must know, it's Jilly. Since the police have cleared her estate, the McCullen gang members have moved just down the road and now are permanently hanging about the row of shops where her launderette is."

"Why? They've got no drugs to sell now, have they?"

"No, don't worry." He pulled his seatbelt away from his neck. "It's just that they like hanging out there. And everyone is shit-scared of them, so no one's going in the launderette. She thought helping to get rid of the McCullens was going to solve all her problems and it hasn't."

"That's crap," said Jimmy, and it was. What was the point of all that hard work if the dealers were still terrorising the neighbourhood? And it certainly wasn't fair on Jilly. The McCullens would still be dealing at the Brandon Estate if it hadn't been for her information.

"I'm really worried about her," said John. "She's talking about selling up. Who's going to buy it now?"

Not only that thought Jimmy. What if she moved away altogether, out of John's life? Aside from this grumpy moment, John was the happiest he'd seen him in a long-time. Lost in this train of thought, he almost missed his turning. He swerved the corner to a barrage of horns and saw Ali and Elgin standing outside the bookmaker shop.

"Get in, lads," he shouted through his open window and then, scowling at a driver who was holding up his middle finger, drove quickly away.

"We are going for a trip to the country again, yes?" said Elgin.

"That's right," said John. "We are going to check on the McCullens."

Jimmy thought about what state their prisoners might be in as he drove. He hoped Rory's head had healed because the last thing they wanted was some kind of medical emergency.

Down at the smallholding, Jimmy held his breath as he took the bolt off the door and opened it. Standing with his feet firmly planted on the ground, he prepared himself for a charge from the brothers. None came, although he almost keeled over from the smell. He opened the door wide to let some air in and saw the two brothers huddled in a corner. "The hard men of South London," John quipped. "Wonder what your gangster friends would make of you now."

The two Turkish men looked on, shaking their heads.

"Real men would fight back," said Ali.

The McCullen brothers didn't even lift their heads.

Jimmy got them to stand on their feet and empty their bucket. Followed by Ali and Elgin, they trudged outside carrying the bucket and an empty crisp box, shielding their eyes from the sunlight. Once they returned, they sat down in silence.

"Let's try again," said John. "Tell us what you know about Arian Mehmed?"

Rory lifted his head. "We're not grasses. Anyway, we never see Mehmed; his men deal with everything. We met him once in a café in Tottenham and that's it."

"How do you get your cocaine, then?" asked John.

Rory glanced at Gerald, who gave him a brief nod and said, "When they do a drop-off, there's a piece of paper with a telephone number. It's different every time. Your phone on a Monday and just say the amount you want; they deliver on Thursday and you pay for the previous gear you've had. He's going to be screaming for the money we owe him."

John towered over him. "Have you any idea of the misery you cause people, not just your punters but also the poor sods who have the misfortune to live on the estate?"

"And what about the families of the kids who've been stabbed and killed?" said Jimmy.

"I don't see why you kidnapped us. It won't stop anything," Rory then turned to John and said, "I've been thinking, haven't I seen you around the estate?"

"First, being kidnapped means someone will pay a ransom for the return of that person," said John. "Well, let me make it clear, nobody would pay for you two and anyway, we have no intention of letting you back on that estate. Second, just in case you do ever get kidnapped, never let your captor know you might identify them, as that's a guaranteed way to get yourself killed."

The McCullens sat in silence. Not that it mattered, they had all the information they needed from them. Saying nothing else to the brothers, John and Jimmy checked they still had boxes of crisps and water. Jimmy then re-attached the padlock to the door, and they left.

~❖~

On the way back, they stopped off at a pub and Jimmy explained the plan for the Brownfield Estate, "We're going to do the same as we did to the McCullen's, only on an estate on the other side of the River Thames in East London."

He then gave the details of what they expected of them. The brothers asked no questions; Jimmy was sure this was just the sort of task Ali and Elgin enjoyed, and they would look forward to the call.

Changing the subject, John said, "None of us like the idea of the McCullens shagging young girls. You two went to town on them. What was that all about?"

There followed a terse conversation in Turkish between the brothers. Ali paused as he appeared to be considering his answer.

"Some years ago, three men from a nearby village raped our fifteen-year-old sister. One of them was the son of a gangster from that village. Elgin and I found them and killed them slowly and painfully. Even their mothers couldn't recognise them." Jimmy could hear the venom in his voice and see it in his eyes.

"That certainly explains things," said John.

"How did you meet Mustafa Hassan?" asked Jimmy

"Mr Hassan was visiting his parents. They had moved back to our village, where they were born. It was common knowledge what had happened to our sister, and he heard our mother feared revenge. He offered our family his protection from any reprisals. He fixed it with the families of the rapists and we remain indebted to him."

How is your sister now?"

"She was terrible for a very long time until Mr Hassan gave her a job running the house he had built, and she is fine now."

Although John tried in vain to interrupt him, Jimmy told Ali and Elgin of the concerns relating to Jilly Jones's business. Without hesitation, they volunteered to help resolve the issue. Cobbling together a plan, they headed back to the Brandon Estate.

At the Brandon Estate, the three brothers who had butchered Issac Okoro were holding court with five other members of McCullens' gang. Their status was now enhanced since the murder. They were standing in the doorway of Jilly's launderette 'Bubbles', the middle premises, adjoined by a Spar Supermarket, a newsagent, a ladies' hairdresser and a betting shop. Loud grime music was blaring from a large stereo system. A woman in her late seventies pulling a shopping basket left the Spar Supermarket and attempted to walk past the youths. They purposely blocked her path and thwarted every effort to get around them. "Get out of my way, you fucking toe rags," she pleaded as one of them grabbed her handbag and attempted to wrestle it from her grip. She wouldn't let go and toppled forward face-first onto the pavement. From nowhere, two Turks carrying baseball bats and two ex-detectives carrying spring-loaded batons descended on the thugs. They set about the gang members with vicious intent, and the youths lay cut, bruised, bloody and some semi-conscious in a short time.

As he lay on the ground with a gaping wound on his forehead, one of them blubbered, "What have we done?"

Jimmy said, "Some days you're the dog, and other days you're the lamppost. Today you're the fucking lamppost."

John screamed at them. "If you ever, I mean ever, come anywhere near these shops again, I swear we'll come back and fucking kill you." He finished the conversation by smashing their stereo system to pieces. As they helped each other away, cheers and applause came from the tenants hanging out of the windows of the flats above the shops, together with the shopkeepers of the adjoining premises.

Two women from the hairdressers took the elderly lady back to their shop. Despite her ordeal, she had a beaming smile on her face.

John and Jimmy dropped Ali and Elgin off at the bookmakers on the Old Kent Road and put them on standby for a call. Without words, there was an understanding between them that the evening's events wouldn't be a topic of conversation with the rest of the team. Heading back, John said, "That Elgin is a bit tasty. I thought he was going to kill that tall kid with the dreadlocks,"

"That lad certainly made a right ricket, giving Elgin lip and thinking he could get away with it. I don't see any of them going anywhere near those shops again," said Jimmy. "I'm going to have to take a long soak in the bath when I get home. I'm already stiffening up. We're getting a bit too old for this lark." John smiled, smelling the sweat from his exertions. He realised he had blood splattered all over his clothes and needed a shower and change before spending the evening with Jilly.

~❖~

When Jilly opened the door for John, she had a huge smile on her face. He could see her excitement was overflowing.

He said, "I didn't think you'd be this excited to see me."

Ignoring the comment, she said, "You're not going to believe what happened."

"What?"

"Some geezers battered the crap out of a bunch of McCullen blokes down at the shops."

"Really? When?"

"A couple of hours ago. The entire estate is buzzing about it. Do you think they will fuck off now?"

"Hope so, babe. I bought a couple of bottles of wine. Maybe I should have got champagne."

He opened a bottle and poured generous measures of Chianti into two wine glasses.

"I don't want to count my chickens before they're hatched, but if they have fucked off forever, business could be good again. Mohamed from the Spar rang. He reckons he's had his best evening in months. People are coming off the estate and into his shop. Nobody ever dreamed of coming out once it got dark."

Throughout dinner, Jilly couldn't contain her excitement. Having opened the second bottle of wine and several glasses later, she suddenly stopped talking and after a moment of silence, said, "Did this have anything to do with you?"

Innocently, John replied, "What?"

"Don't give me that. You know what I mean. Tell me the truth."

John smiled.

That was all Jilly needed. She jumped out of her chair and hugged him tightly, blurting out, "I love you, John Olde."

"If I'd known giving a group of arseholes a good hiding would return this result, I would have done it ages ago," said John.

CHAPTER TWENTY-NINE

On Saturday evening, John and Jimmy waited at the concourse of Victoria Station for Monkey Gregory.

"There he is," said Jimmy, catching sight of him through the crowd. Framed by a group of Scandinavian backpackers, Monkey seemed smaller and more bent over than ever. He was huffing as he reached the men, although his train had arrived on Platform 1 and he hadn't far to walk. I hope the old man is up to this, thought Jimmy, as he took Monkey's bag from him and showed him to the van.

John dropped them at the back of the Dorchester Hotel in Park Lane and Jimmy led Monkey through the route Peter had planned to avoid any CCTV cameras. Late evening, it wasn't quite dark yet; there were few people around. When they arrived outside the building on Upper Brook Street, Jimmy stood against the railings. Below him, down a flight of concrete steps, was the basement with two Buxus trees in ornate pots on either side of the door. Monkey slipped down the stairs while Jimmy kept watching. Within thirty seconds, Monkey whistled and beckoned for Jimmy to join him. The door to the basement was open.

Boy was that Monkey quick, thought Jimmy as he took one more look over his shoulder and joined him. Having memorised the plan Peter had given him, Jimmy led the way. Monkey tapped him on the shoulder and, as he turned, produced a pair of latex gloves from his bag and handed them to him, Monkey was already wearing a pair.

"Are you sure nobody's on the premises over the weekend, Jimmy?" asked Monkey.

"I'm sure," Jimmy reassured him.

They made their way up the stairs and although the basement had been dingy with fluorescent light fittings adorning the ceilings, the restoration on each floor above was beautiful, with lights and furnishing of the Victorian and Edwardian eras. Having crept through the ground and first floor, they ascended the stairs to the second floor, which seemed to creak at every step. As an enormous grandfather clock on the second-floor landing struck nine, they both jumped. Monkey put his hand on his heart and Jimmy stifled a giggle.

Arriving on the third floor, they found the door with the gold plate announcing Harry Baker LLB. Inside the imposing office, the restoration included walls clad in dark oak panelling with crystal glass wall lights and an impressive chandelier that hung from an elaborate rose in the middle of the ceiling. As Jimmy had been told, the Ratner safe was in a prime position under a window. On the safe was a large silver tray containing two cut-glass decanters, four matching whisky glasses and four matching brandy glasses. Monkey mimed having a drink, and Jimmy grinned at him and shook his head.

Jimmy watched as Monkey knelt by the safe, which, to Jimmy's eyes, was a thing of beauty. He knew though that Monkey didn't care a bit about the cosmetics of the safe: the engineering of the lock was his concern - no, more than that, his passion and joy. Beaming, Monkey got straight to work with tools from his bag while Jimmy rummaged through Baker's desk and removed several sheets of personalised headed paper. All the time, listening to the soft clicks Monkey was making.

The noise stopped, and Jimmy turned to find the safe already open. He patted Monkey on the back and gave him a thumbs up. Inside were two thick folders and bundles of banknotes, all bound in bank seals. Monkey passed over the two folders, one blue and one green, and continued examining the contents of the safe. Using Baker's desk, Jimmy laid out the documents from the blue folder and photographed them one at a time. There were pages of handwritten figures and even with a cursory look, it was obvious they referred to millions of pounds. He took great care to return them in the order he had found them. Jimmy then opened the green folder and found individual files containing sheets of handwritten notes; each sheet had a name on the head, then a series of dates, times and comments together with photographs and reports. His mouth fell open. What he was seeing was astounding, except there was no time to think about it. He photographed each page carefully and returned them to the folder in the correct order. When Monkey placed the folders back in the safe and transferred the money into his bag, he mimed if Jimmy wanted it open or closed.

"Closed," Jimmy mouthed.

Once Monkey had locked the safe, and after checking the desk was exactly as they had found it, Jimmy signed for Monkey to wait where he was and he ascended the stairs to the top floor offices of Tanner Accountants. He got as far as the first landing, where the presence of a locked heavy-duty fire door stopped his progress. None of this was on the plans Peter had supplied, and there was no signage to hint at what was beyond the door. Should he get Monkey to unlock it for him? There might be an alarm if it was a new introduction to the building. He decided not to risk it and returned to Baker's office, where Monkey was sitting at the desk, eyeing the brandy in the decanter.

Jimmy checked out the adjoining door that led to a lavish conference room with a large antique table surrounded by eighteen antique chairs. Jesus thought Jimmy; Baker must rake it in to pay for all this splendour. Crime does pay.

Back in Baker's office, Jimmy once again checked that everything was as they had found it and they made their way back downstairs to the basement. Monkey locked the basement door on leaving and they headed back on the same route that had taken them there. Jimmy made a call and John picked them up where he had dropped them off in the van.

Pleased to speak, Jimmy finally turned to Monkey and asked, "Are you happy?"

"Definitely, there must have been between fifteen and twenty grand in that safe. Do you boys want a bit out of it?"

"No, you're alright mate," replied Jimmy. "We'll take you back to Victoria Station. You can buy us a couple of pints on the way."

"No problem, Jimmy. I'm going to give you back the two grand you gave me upfront. It's only fair."

John headed to the less salubrious area of Pimlico, close to Victoria Station. They stopped at The Warwick Arms on Warwick Street. Over a couple of pints and several games of pool, Monkey explained that although he had enjoyed his brief spell out of retirement, this was him finished with the game forever. "I'll be honest with you. My nerves are gone. If you hadn't been with me, Jimmy, I couldn't have done it."

"I would never have noticed," said Jimmy, thinking of Monkey sitting at the desk. "You were so quick. Genius talent."

Monkey looked glumly at his pint. "Last time I'll ever use it, I suppose."

"Good to go out like this, though?"

Monkey grinned. "Yes," he said. "I don't like to boast, but I am pretty good, aren't I?"

At the station, Jimmy shook Monkey's hand and said, "You get back to Littlehampton and back to being Phil Gregory."

"I will, Jimmy, I will," Monkey said as he walked away, happy and a lot richer.

It was dark as Jimmy and John drove to Peter's office. He'd been expecting them and the lights were all on. Jimmy handed him the camera and Peter downloaded the contents and printed out copies. John and Jimmy loomed over the computer, watching him touch-type an email to Terry. "When will he get it?" asked John.

Peter grinned and Jimmy could tell he thought he and John were Luddites. They all had unique talents, though; that was what made the group so special.

"Right away," said Peter. "Though we'll give him some time to read through. Drink?"

Just like Baker, Peter had drinks in his office, although hidden away in a neat cupboard which looked like part of the wall. He pressed on the panel and a door slowly opened. "Whisky? Lager?" They all settled for a lager - Jimmy and John not bothering with the crystal glass proffered. Twenty minutes later, Peter picked up his phone and put the speaker on.

"Have you had a look at them, Terry?"

"I've just had a glance through them," came Terry's voice, sounding a little strange and echoey. "There's a lot of stuff in there, and Mehmed's name is all over them, as is Tanner Accountants,"

"I know," said Jimmy, leaning close to the phone. "We haven't got the calculator out yet. I'm sure we're talking millions of pounds having gone through Baker and the accountant."

"Sorry, Jimmy, I didn't realise you were there. Fantastic work. Did everything go alright with Monkey?"

"No problems. That Monkey is a real old pro. He was in and out in no time. No wonder he had the reputation of being the best. He even gave us back the two grand we gave him."

"Did he? Good man," Terry said. "It was well worth getting him on board. The amount of money that's gone through Baker and his tame accountant is staggering. The problem I see is trying to connect those amounts to drug transactions."

"They're in Baker's handwriting, I presume," said Jimmy. "At least that should mean he's got a lot of questions to be answered."

"I'm going to go through them bit by bit," Peter said, "and we can decide what to do about it later. Like you, Terry, I think we've got to find a connection between the money and the drugs."

"What about the other bundle?" said Jimmy, knowing that, although the money was interesting, the information in there was what might set the world on fire.

"I haven't gone through them all; what I have seen is dynamite. I recognise the name of at least two judges, a footballer and, of course, our mate Yusuf is there. Can't be sure if Baker is blackmailing them or just keeping it for ammunition, but some of the stuff I've read is enough to ruin their lives and kill their careers. "

"The stuff about Yusuf doesn't come as a surprise," said John. "Anyone permanently aggressive has got to be bottling something up."

Peter said, "I'll research all the names and make some notes. How do you think he found out all this stuff?"

"Not a clue. He has put a hell of a lot of work into it. Let's keep this under wraps. Don't make any other copies and keep yours safe."

Jimmy would keep it under wraps; of course, he would, but he couldn't wait to get home and tell Debbie what he had just found out about one of her favourite footballers.

CHAPTER THIRTY

On Monday morning, when Harry Baker opened his safe to retrieve some documents, he realised the money he kept for petty cash was missing, all eighteen thousand pounds.

"Oh shit!" he said, his heart thumping. When he left on Friday evening, he was certain the money had been in the safe. He leapt to his feet and frantically searched every drawer and cabinet in his office. Within minutes, his usually pristine desk and office were in disarray, with files and paperwork from his draws scattered everywhere.

Still nothing - where the hell could it be? He was sure he'd put the money in his safe, but he couldn't have done. It was the best safe money could buy, and he was positive he had locked it. "Shit, shit, shit," he muttered, and he searched places it couldn't possibly be - in his pockets, under the picture on the wall.

He stopped himself from tearing up the carpet; he took a deep breath and returned to the safe. He took out the folders and, making himself go slowly, he went through every document and found they were all intact.

He placed them back in the safe and locked it. Then he fell into his leather chair, the chaos of his desk at his elbows, and tried to remember the last time he saw the money. It had been last week that was it when he'd arranged a payment of five thousand pounds to a potential prosecution witness. He picked up his phone and rang his driver, fixer and general dogsbody: Frank Smith. He could trust Frank, although he had been a criminal for most of his life, serving many terms of imprisonment, that was until Harry Baker gave him a chance ten years ago. Frank now drove and dealt with any discrete and not-so-discrete jobs for his employer. He answered on the first ring. "Yes boss, do you want me to bring the car out the front?"

"No, Frank. What day last week did you drop the money off to that woman in Lewisham?"

"That was Wednesday, boss. She isn't looking for more, is she? I warned her against trying that."

"No, nothing like that. Did you count what I gave you?"

"Yeah, I counted it out in front of her. It was five thousand pounds in £50 notes. Is there a problem, boss?"

Harry swallowed and wished for a cigarette - he'd not smoked in years. "No, just checking." Then he came clean. If he couldn't trust Frank, he couldn't trust anybody. "There's money missing from the safe. It's gone over the weekend."

"Are you kidding me? That safe? Why that safe-"

"I know, I know. Listen, I need you to scout around our neighbours, speak to their security or receptionists and see if any of their CCTV covers our front door."

"Will do, Boss."

Harry didn't need to say what he said next. He did it anyway. "Be discreet. I don't want anybody to find out about this."

"No problem, boss; I'll say we think we've got issues with a vagrant sleeping in the doorway over the weekend and just want to confirm it. Leave it to me."

Harry took a breath for what seemed like the first time in twenty minutes. Perhaps they could sort all this out. "And, speak to our receptionist," he said, "that ex-soldier, find out if anything unusual happened on Friday or last week, but remember, be discrete."

"I understand, boss. I'll report back to you if I get anything."

After he rang off, Harry drummed on the desk. What next? Oh, yes, there were two keys to the safe. He rang home and sent his wife to check if the second key was still in the top drawer of his antique desk.

"Yes, it's there," said his wife. "What is this all about? You sound a little anxious, darling."

"Oh fine," he said. "Everything's fine." And knowing he couldn't fool her for long, rang off. He went back to the safe and ran his hands over the metal, both inside and out. Were there any marks? It seemed not. So if someone had got into the safe, how the hell did they do it? Money was one thing; the folders still being there was reassuring.

The documents he kept in both folders were essential, and he couldn't imagine the fallout if they fell into the wrong hands. Although handwritten records and accounts might appear outdated, he had defended too many people in recent years whose computer hard drives had provided the evidence bringing about their downfall. If someone had stolen the cash from the safe, surely, they would have taken the whole contents, unless they didn't look or realise the value of the documents.

Harry tried to tell himself that everything was okay - that the money would turn up. He knew that should the Columbians ever accuse him of misappropriating their money; death was the only punishment. It was for this reason he kept meticulous records of all transactions in the blue folder. He had never considered cheating them - his generous commission made that unnecessary, plus the fear of death!

Perhaps I should have got out earlier; he thought to himself as he tidied the office. The problem was that he needed the money - once one was used to a lavish lifestyle, there seemed no way to go back. Although his second wife came from the aristocracy, her family had no real money.

That's why he had the green folder. It was his insurance policy and had taken many years to compile. His relationship with the tabloid newspapers and celebrity clients had made it easy to get the bare bones; it was Frank Smith's dogged enthusiasm for documenting the lives of these people that had provided the detail.

Information is power; he told himself as he put a pile of upended paperclips back in their box. And power is money. The blue folder might be what could save him now if it did all go tits up. He was sure he had enough information on people in positions of power to get him out of any trouble.

Once the office was clean, he had one last job to do. He would ring the company that had restored his safe and arrange for their top locksmith to check if someone had tampered with the lock mechanism. Apart from that, he wouldn't tell anyone of his concerns, and he would bring the two folders home and keep them in his office there.

Later that night, when he had hidden the folders in an old box of Monopoly that no one had touched for twenty years and placed the box under the bed in one of the guest rooms, he phoned Frank Smith.

"Nothing doing, I'm afraid, Boss," said Frank. There's nothing on any CCTV footage."

"Did you speak to the security guy?"

"Yes, he swears nothing unusual happened."

"Do you believe him?"

"He's an old soldier."

"Okay," said Harry. "Thank you for trying." He slipped his phone back into his pocket and went back up to the guest room. The monopoly box was still there - why wouldn't it be?

CHAPTER THIRTY ONE

Peter waited for Nicky to pick him up from outside his office. When he arrived, he had to pause while Nicky removed a racing paper and an empty bottle of coke from the passenger seat and then slipped in. "So," said Nicky as they set off towards the Woolwich warehouse, "What have you learned? No keeping it from me this time. You promised."

Peter laughed. "Okay, okay. You remember we saw a guy in the warehouse last time we came?"

"The one that owned the BMW?"

"That's the one. Well, having looked at the yard camera over the last few days, I think he works entirely on his own. His hours are nine to five, exactly. A moody company based at the warehouse is the registered owner of his BMW 3 Series."

"Toffee?" said Nicky, pulling out a pack from the pocket in the door.

Peter held up his hand. At his age, and sitting in front of a computer every day, he had to watch his weight. And, of course, that wasn't the only reason.

"Open one for me, would you?" said Nicky, one hand on the steering wheel, the other still proffering the bag. As the paper crackled, Nicky asked, "So there's never anyone else there?"

"Nope."

"What time is it now?"

"Five minutes until five. Perfect timing. Drop me here."

Nicky veered on the curb. The warehouses were a few minutes walk away: they had just enough time to catch the worker. Peter slid out of the car and walked away. Just before he turned the corner, he looked back to see Nicky's cheek bulging with a toffee.

Peter went through the gates and walked into the warehouse.

The worker, who had been staring at his phone, jumped.

"Sorry to bother you," said Peter. "I'm looking for a job. Have you got anything going?"

"No, no," replied the man in broken English, "we don't want workers."

Peter persisted. "I can do anything: warehouseman, night watchman, cleaner, anything."

"No. We have no jobs. I told you; you must go." The man looked at the clock on his phone.

"Maybe I could talk to your boss. When will he be back?" said Peter, moving around the warehouse.

"I've told you, no jobs here. Now go." The man stood with folded arms and his voicc loud.

"Ok, thank you. I apologise for the intrusion," Peter said. "Sorry, may I use your toilet, please?"

"No, you must go."

Peter made as if to leave, then turned back. "I have terrible problems with my prostate. Please."

The man assessed him and Peter made his face a mask of desperation.

"Okay, okay," said the man, "be quick." He pointed to the corner of the warehouse where there was a door to the toilet under a wooden mezzanine.

Peter ran, as though desperately needing the toilet, and went straight to the toilet window and released the handle. The window was ajar enough to be opened from the outside, as he also wedged it closed; it looked shut from the inside. Now all he needed was a bit of luck. He peed into the bowl for good measure, thinking that the longer he kept the man, the more likely he would simply rush off and not bother to check the toilet too carefully before leaving. He had observed from the cctv camera, that this man liked to leave on the dot.

Peter zipped up and trotted back to the man. "Thank you so much! You're a lifesaver."

The man waved him away.

As he walked back to Nicky, still a couple of minutes away, the grey BMW 3 series sped past him. He got into Nicky's car.

"Good?" said Nicky through a mouthful of toffee.

"Great!"

"Spill the beans then, Mr Bond."

"There's a wooden mezzanine with stairs leading up to it. We could conceal a camera there. Good news: no sign of any alarm system. Let me ring the office to tell them what equipment we need. We can drive there now and pick it up."

"Okay, boss," said Nicky.

Within half an hour, they were leaving the offices with the equipment to head back to Woolwich, together with a slim technician that Peter chose not to introduce, mainly because he could never remember if the man's name was Rob or Bob and it was too late to ask him now. He could see Nicky was itching to ask the man's name; he let Peter keep this one secret. He also didn't moan too much as they left him in the car on the same corner. "Don't worry about me; I've got my toffees and my paper," he said.

Peter and his colleague walked to the back of the warehouse. With a bit of jiggling, they got the toilet window open. Peter sized up the space and knew he'd been right to choose the smallest member of his team.

"In you go then!"

Rob or Bob climbed in and Peter passed the equipment through the window and directed his man where to go. About thirty minutes later, the screen on Peter's Apple Mac buzzed to life. He came closer to the side of the warehouse where the shadow was deeper and saw the inside of the warehouse. The angle could have been a little better, so he gave his man instructions via his mobile phone. Finally, satisfied, he made sure they cleaned everything up inside the premises.

"Every speck!" he said. "These people cannot suspect anyone was in here."

When he had finished, his guy handed back all the tools through the window and snaked his sinewy body through to the outside. They pushed the window closed, Peter raked over the shingles where he had been standing, and they made their way back to Nicky.

"Good?" asked Nicky.

Peter opened up his laptop and showed him.

"Well, I'll be buggered," said Nicky. "That's a better picture than on my telly."

Peter only smiled; he was proud. Quietly proud, as always. And wasn't it better to share his success with someone? Since his wife had died, there wasn't anyone who appreciated him. I mean, the guys at my office are alright, he thought, glancing at Bob-or-Rob in the backseat, who seemed to be playing some kind of game on his phone, but it isn't the same as old friends.

After they had dropped off Bob-or-Rob, he turned to Nicky. "Fancy a curry? There's a good place near here."

"Cor, yeah, I'm starving."

Peter decided not to tease him about the toffees. Over a balti and a jalfrezi, he and Nicky chatted. The success of the day had buoyed him, and the two lagers helped to relax him too. Nicky was good company, open and funny.

'Sorry I didn't keep you in the loop with everything at first."

Nicky waved his fork. "That's alright. I was only joking really. I know it's in your nature."

"When you rang me and Terry came to the office, the idea of joining you guys on this adventure was a lifeline for me," said Peter.

"What do you mean?"

"I needed something to look forward to. I'm enjoying every minute. Getting back with everyone has been brilliant." Peter took a slug of lager. "I wouldn't want to be in the police now. I think our time and our ways have long gone."

Nicky pointed a piece of poppadum at him, which had broken into a long triangle. "You say that," he said, "but here we are trying to sort out something their methods haven't been able to resolve."

Peter grinned and slumped back in his seat. "That's true. I'm just going to make the most of it for as long as it lasts."

"Don't worry, mate. I reckon now the team is back together again; we might get more work. I never want this to stop."

Peter tried to smile. He knew for him things would stop soon. There was nothing he could do about it. He felt a sudden urge to tell Nicky. This was too big, and he'd been keeping secrets for too long. So why not? Who else could he tell?

"Nicky," he said. "I don't want this spread about, the story about the prostrate I told you I was going to tell the man in the warehouse… Well, it's true. I have got a bit of a problem."

Nicky's fork clattered on his plate. "Cancer?"

Peter nodded.

Nicky screwed up his face. "Don't they say that more old men die with prostate cancer than die of it?"

"They do. Problem is, it's secondary. I'm riddled with it."

Nicky blinked, obviously unsure of what to say. "I'm sorry. I… Do you…?" He shook his head. "What about treatment? It's amazing what they can do nowadays,"

"Not for this. I left it too long. I guessed a while back; I suppose I didn't want it confirmed; anyway, all the treatment can do now is keep me alive longer. The quality of life I'd have with the treatment isn't worth it. Even the consultant said he would have made the same decision if it were him," said Peter.

Nicky looked as though he was close to tears. "How long have they said?"

"If I keep healthy, possibly six to nine months." He grinned. "No toffees for me." After a moment, he continued, "I don't want anyone else to find out. I couldn't stand people feeling sorry for me. For the first time in years, I'm enjoying what I am doing and I want to see it out until we're finished. I'm sure you understand."

"What about your daughters in Australia? Do they know?"

At the question about his daughters, Peter felt his own eyes welling. "No, I haven't told them yet. I want to tell them only I just can't bring myself to make the phone call. Every time I've tried, I always end up changing the subject. They're so happy in their new lives."

Nicky patted his hand. "I think you should tell them sooner than later; it's only fair to them."

Peter nodded. "I don't want anyone else to find out. Promise me you won't tell the others… except maybe Terry. Will you tell Terry for me?"

"Of course," said Nicky.

They both sat in silence for a moment. Peter didn't want the night to end on such a sad note. "Remember when we were in the force and you arrested that punter who turned out to be the superintendent's brother-in-law?"

"Do I?" said Nicky and launched into the tale which had the same old reassuring grooves as the last time Peter had heard it twenty years ago.

CHAPTER THIRTY-TWO

After Terry had received the phone call from Nicky, he'd had a terrible night's sleep. What was he supposed to do? Nicky had said Peter was desperate to stay on. What they were doing wasn't easy, and it was only going to get more dangerous. Stress like that could send Peter even earlier to his grave than the doctors had said. Bleary-eyed, he made his morning cup of coffee and sat at the kitchen table to talk to Denise about it. After all, it was only a short while since she had died of cancer. What should I do? He asked her silently.

What would you want?

I'd want to carry on.

Well, there you are then.

He chuckled. He should have come down here hours ago. He whistled to his dog. "Come on, time for a walk."

It wasn't until he'd dropped the dog back at his neighbours and gone to the Peacock that his worries revisited him. He kidded with Diane before he went upstairs, although his heart wasn't really in it. One day she'd be gone too. They'd all be gone. It would simply be Peter that would be next.

"Could we have a pot of really strong coffee, please?" he asked Diane. "And some biscuits?" It was too early really. Who cared?

"Oh, I've got some jammy dodgers that I know Nicky loves."

"Right you are, darling," he said and headed up the stairs.

He opened the windows and waited for the others to arrive. Peter was the first to walk through the door. As Jimmy, John, and Nicky followed him, he had no chance to say anything. Nicky caught his eye and said, "Terry, you should see the quality of Peter's work at the warehouse. You won't believe it."

Peter grinned and set up his laptop in front of Terry. When he showed the two views of the site on a split screen, John and Jimmy, who were peering over Terry's shoulder, both shouted out.

"Wowee!" said Jimmy.

"That's amazing," said John. "Shame there's no sound."

"With a bit more time," said Peter, "we could have done that. The trouble is that the more kit, the more likely it will be found."

"Listen," said John, "I'm only joking. I can't even work the new pop-up toaster I just bought."

Terry had said nothing until Nicky tapped him. "Isn't it amazing, Terry?"

"Yes," said Terry, looking up at Peter. "It's brilliant. Fantastic." He was aware his words didn't sound as cheerful as they might. Peter seemed to understand why.

"I love this work," said Peter. "I want to continue doing it."

"Well, why wouldn't you?" said Jimmy.

The arrival of Dave saved Peter from having to answer. As the others teased him about his latest choice of tracksuit, Terry said quietly to Peter. "You're an important part of the team and you're not going anywhere."

Peter's shoulders inched down. "Thanks, Boss."

"No, thank you. By the way, did your man drop that present off for us?"

"Yes, no problem."

The others looked on for an explanation. None was forthcoming.

When Dave was finally sitting down, Terry turned to Nicky. "Kenny Pierce is back from visiting his sons. Nicky, will you update us?"

"Because he's just got back from Morocco, he's even keener to help. He's desperate to get the boys out of the prison they're in. We're going to meet in the next couple of days."

"It's all going brilliantly," said John.

Terry nodded. "Sure. We've got further in a few weeks than the Met did in two years; unfortunately, it all means nothing if we don't get Mehmed off the streets. Because there is only a week until the cocaine arrives, we haven't got a lot of time."

Diane came in with the coffee. "Found your favourite biccies," she said to Nicky and swept out before he could even thank her. The men dived in, chewed on sticky biscuits, and drank the strong black coffee as Terry ploughed through the plans. "Dave," he said. "Make sure Jones doesn't get to know any of these details. As the cocaine drops on Wednesday, we won't be telling him a thing until Monday. And then the version we choose."

Dave doffed an imaginary cap to him.

"Oh, and ask him not to involve the press."

Dave laughed. "Some hope. We ought to call him 'News at Ten' from now on."

"Can you imagine that footage from Peter's camera on the telly?" said Jimmy.

Terry stared at him. "No, mate, no, that camera is for us alone. The defence barristers would have a field day if they found out. We'll have to get it out again after the arrests." He turned to Dave. "You're the only one with a warrant card, so you can retrieve it."

Dave looked a little unsure.

"Peter will give you instructions."

Dave grinned. "And it means I won't be with Jones, right?"

The men laughed. "Every cloud," said John.

The conversation then switched to Balfour House on The Browning Estate and taking out the drug dealers there.

Terry started, "I don't want to put any pressure on you if we're not ready to go. However, I'd like to get this done before we concentrate on Mehmed. What do you think, Jimmy? It's your job, so it's your call."

Jimmy took a handkerchief out and blew his nose before saying, "We're ready to go. Nothing's going to change by waiting. John and I had a long talk with Ali and Elgin and they're up for it. John and I are seeing the informant this evening. Unless he has anything that will alter things, I'm happy to go anytime you are. We'll meet him tonight and report back tomorrow morning when we can make the final preparations."

"Do you need any extra kit for this one?" asked Dave.

Jimmy replied, "We'll need a door opener, those tasers just in case, and a few radios would be handy. If this is going to work for us, timing is all-important."

"No problem, I'll sort out the radios," replied Peter.

"Right," said Terry, picking up the last biscuit before Nicky could get it. "Let's meet here tomorrow at ten."

CHAPTER THIRTY-THREE

Jimmy shuffled in his chair at the Chrisp Street Market Cafe. It was the type of plastic chair attached to the table with steel bars, which was fine if you were thin, but if you were as big as Jimmy and sitting next to someone as big as John, well, they weren't very comfortable. He looked around at the customers and knew that he and John fitted in well. While they were bigger than everyone else, they had that hardened, weathered look of a street trader. Although strangers, no one had given them a second glance. In this part of London, it was best to keep yourself to yourself. It was a lot healthier to mind your own business.

Jimmy was checking his watch when Jerome, their informant, walked in. He was no stranger here and responded to their greetings with handshakes and hugs. His dad had been like that too - someone everyone loved and wanted to share the time of day with.

"Jerome," he said, shaking his hand. "This is John."

John stood, extracting himself with some difficulty out of the chair.

"I've been following them every night," Jerome said as soon as he slid opposite them, "and I know where they go to get paid."

"Slow down. What are you talking about?" asked Jimmy.

"The kids who work for Monty Johnston meet in the Red Lion just up the road. The publican lets them use his backroom and Mitchell pays them out there."

Jimmy glanced at John - they'd thought Johnstone's flat was where all the financial transactions took place. Their plans may have to change. He knew he had to control Jerome's enthusiasm. He leaned forward and lowered his voice, hoping Jerome would follow by example. "What time do they meet?"

Jerome took the hint and crouched forward. "Every night around ten, they'll be there tonight. The publican deals cocaine out of the pub as well."

Jimmy nodded. "Right, Jerome, I need you to leave this to us now." He leaned across the table and gripped his forearm. "Thanks, you've been a great help."

"There's more," he said, "They're talking about a load of guns Monty's got. They reckon they're going to war with a team from East Ham, who are trying to muscle in on Canary Wharf. They're well excited."

Jerome's voice had got louder as he'd spoken, and Jimmy noticed one punter glance over. Jimmy lowered his voice to a whisper. "Have they seen these guns?"

Jerome matched his whisper. "Yeah, Monty brought them to his flat and showed them off. Everyone is talking about it. There are handguns and automatics with plenty of ammo."

"You've done brilliant, Jerome. You need to step back now."

Jerome looked disappointed - as though he'd expected to be asked to help with the arrests.

Jimmy squeezed his arm again before adding, "If Monty even suspects something is going on, he might change his entire operation, which would mean us starting from scratch and him getting away with this."

As Jerome left, John ordered two more teas and said, "I hope you've got him under control. He seems like a nice kid. I hate to say this but he could end up getting seriously hurt."

"Yes, that's what worries me," said Jimmy. "The sooner we get this done, the better. I'll phone Terry now and tell him about the pub and the guns and see what he wants to do."

~❖~

The next morning, back at the pub, Jimmy went through Jerome's new information. "I've already told Dave."

"That's right," said Dave. "I checked all the records and had a chat with a few of the guys at the station. The publican is a low right life. The local Old

Bill has fancied him for handling most of the stolen gear out of the estate for ages. They have heard the rumours about drugs there, but have got nothing concrete."

"So why hasn't he had a spin before now, then?" asked Nicky.

Dave shrugged and Jimmy said, "That's the way it is now. Without firm evidence, they don't even get search warrants."

"Fucking ridiculous," said Nicky. "No wonder things are out of control."

"These guns complicate matters," said Jimmy, "although I don't see them changing our plans. We've got the element of surprise and that worked when we took out the McCullens. I'll let Dave explain what he's found out about our targets, the guns, and the potential war."

Dave stood up and shuffled papers in front of him. The men laughed at his sudden enthusiasm, and he sat down again.

"Sorry, mate," said Jimmy, "Carry on."

Dave cleared his throat. "Well, it will come as no surprise that both of them have got form, Johnston's mainly for violence, four convictions in total and he got eighteen months for grievous bodily harm in 2017; other than that, he's kept himself out of the courts. Mitchell is a cokehead. At twenty-four, he already has ten convictions, all drugs-related. Extraordinarily, he's never been in prison."

"Bloody hell," said Nicky. "What the hell do you have to do to get banged up these days?"

"On the aggravation with another gang," continued Dave, "both the Drugs Squad and my firm, Trident, have heard that a team from East Ham calling themselves the Road Warriors have been tooling themselves up for a war. Their information is from separate sources, although they've got nothing firm yet. As for the guns, there's no surprise they would get themselves ready; from what Jimmy and John have seen, the amount of cocaine they're serving up to Canary Wharf must be worth a goldmine; they won't give that up without a fight."

"Great work, Dave," said Terry, then sighed. "Looks like we're in a catch-22 situation. If we don't take Johnston out, there's going to be a war; if we take him out, there will still be a war, anyway."

"Why's that boss?" said Jimmy.

"Think about it. The sort of money involved here, once there is a gap in the market, more than just the Road Warriors will try to get in on it."

"All the rats scurrying in," said Nicky, and then, "Is Diane going to bring up that coffee or what?"

"Biscuits, you mean," said Jimmy. He put his elbows on the table. "So, what do we do? None of us wants a blood bath." He grinned. "Except John, maybe."

"Not me, mate. Keeping myself beautiful for Jilly."

The men laughed.

"No," said Terry. "We still take Johnston and his mate Mitchell tomorrow. If Johnston has got the guns in his flat, we need to get in there quickly and get them off the streets. If not, we need to find out where they are." He pointed at Jimmy and John. "That's down to you two. You got the plans and pictures?"

Jimmy picked up his backpack and took out a file. He then handed out photographs of Johnston and Mitchell, together with plans of the estate "Mitchell's flat is on the ground floor about a hundred yards from the entrance to Johnston's flat on the second floor of Balfron House." he said, pointing to the two flats on the plans. "We've seen a runner go from Mitchel's flat to Johnston's five or six times a day from about eleven A.M. onwards. It's this runner we are going to target."

He took out a photograph of a young boy and passed it around.

"Ali and Elgin are going to ambush him in the lobby of Balfron House and 'encourage' him to get us into Johnston's flat. Once we have our targets wrapped up and, with any luck, the guns, we'll crash the other flat."

"Okay," said Terry. "Problems?"

"As we depend on the runner going to Balfron Tower, the timing is a little fluid. We need to be in position by noon. However, we can't afford to be hanging about the estate for too long."

"Okay. And Ali and Elgin are up for all of this?" asked Terry.

"Yes. John will pick up the boys from the Old Kent Road in the morning and take them straight to the plot."

Terry clapped his hands. "Excellent."

"Are we all going?" asked Peter.

Terry smiled at him. "Of course - all the team except Dave, who will be with Jones. If the rest of us meet here tomorrow at 10.30 am, it gives us plenty of time to get kitted up and deal with any updates. It's only five minutes from here up the Commercial Road."

Just then, Diane came in with the coffee. This time there were fondant fancies too. Jimmy took two. Why not? By tomorrow night, they would have cleared another estate and stopped a gun battle. A man needed to celebrate his oncoming success, didn't he?

CHAPTER THIRTY-FOUR

Terry had rung Alan Jones as soon as the meeting was over and was now sitting by a window overlooking the Strand. For a bit of variety and to keep Jones on his toes, he had chosen the first-floor bar of the Clermont Hotel. It was a Grade 2 listed railway hotel, built over Charing Cross mainline station and still provided the opulence of the nineteenth century when it was first opened.

Uniformed waiters hovered between tables, precariously serving drinks off silver platters carried at shoulder height on one hand. Terry was thinking about the problem of clearing the next estate of drug dealers and getting the guns when he realised Jones was standing in front of him. As he stood to shake hands, he noticed Jones had a smile on his face. Blimey, he thought, I've never seen that before. We must be doing well.

Jones ordered a glass of Merlot. "The Commissioner and Home Secretary have asked me to thank you for the work you have done to date. They're both extremely impressed and pleased at the success you have had so far."

"They may not be so pleased by the end of this conversation," remarked Terry, just to see the smile drop off his face. "We are going to hit another estate in East London tomorrow."

"Another? Tomorrow?"

"If you are going to do a job, you may as well do it pro-"

"Agreed. But tomorrow? You really must-"

Terry couldn't bear another speech about due processes and interrupted. "Detective Sergeant Evans will be with you if you could muster some men in the yard at Limehouse Police Station from noon. The same as last time, I will phone him when the estate is clear and give him the location and the details of the flats that will need boarding up."

Jones looked like he was about to interrupt, and Terry ploughed on. "As a bonus, you'll find drugs and stolen property in a pub near the estate which the gang members use. They are being looked after by the landlord of the Red Lion Pub near Chrisp Street Market. Detective Sergeant Evans will get a search warrant and give it to you when you meet tomorrow morning."

Jones bristled at his junior officer being given the go-ahead without his say so, Terry didn't care. He continued, "The pub is going to be busy, so I suggest a couple of TSG units and some local CID to deal with any evidence found. No matter what happens, the pub needs to be closed down."

"How do you suggest doing that?" Jones snapped.

"Get the local licensing officer on the raid, together with the local environmental health officers. I'm sure they'll find something," replied Terry. "That search can't be until about ten-thirty tomorrow night."

Jones searched his eyes, then seemed to decide that there was no point trying to stop the tide especially if the tide washed up more drugs for Jones to brandish at Press Conferences.

"There is another matter we need to discuss," said Terry and then explained in as much detail as possible how a drug war was about to break out over the prize, that was Canary Wharf.

"Surely, as you have so succinctly put it, plans are in place to stop the practice. Therefore-"

"It won't matter. More gangs will move in. Everything we achieve will count for nothing, as the only headlines will relate to the bloodbath that is about to occur."

Jones sat up straight in his chair and waved his hand at a waiter. "So what are you suggesting?" asked Jones after he'd ordered a large Merlot.

"We have a few days to play with, as it will take time for word to get around that nobody is catering for the one hundred thousand office staff or the seventeen thousand residents' cocaine habits."

Terry took a sip of his coffee. "How about this?" He said, "The Home Secretary puts in place the Ring of Steel terrorist policy around Canary Wharf.

The police have done it plenty of times over the years. Everything is ready. They built it with security in mind. There are only four roads to get on and off the Wharf, and the barriers are already in place. A huge police presence will deter any would-be drug dealers and give Trident and the Drugs Squad enough time to do their thing."

Jones had turned pale. "Surely, you don't think the Home Secretary is going to lie about a terrorist threat. You realise it would mean locking down the City of London as well?"

Terry grinned, "Of course, I don't expect her to lie, and she doesn't need to lock down the City of London, either. She only needs to declare it as a security exercise to ensure preparedness for the real thing. I'm sure the residents and employees of Canary Wharf won't be happy. They're the ones flaming this war."

"The city and Canary Wharf are the engine house of our country."

Terry tried not to roll his eyes and failed. "With all respect, Chief Superintendent, they're the ones responsible for the stabbings and murders - remember - no users means no dealers. This isn't only a working-class crime; it's just as much a middle-class crime."

Jones sipped at his wine, obviously not agreeing but unable to find any holes in Terry's argument. Terry knew he had to find another way. "This is a win-win for the Home Secretary," he said, "Because it shows she's not only strong on drugs and knife crime, she's also strong on terrorism. A couple of weeks should do it. Remember what the alternative is."

"Perhaps a Terrorism Threat Practise," said Jones. "It makes sense."

Terry accepted he would repackage the whole idea as his own. That was fine. All Terry wanted was to get the job done.

"I'll try to sell it to the Commissioner," Jones said. "He's very close with the Home Secretary. I'll inform you of the outcome. There are some questions I need to ask you. What is happening regarding Mehmed? Are you making any inroads into his empire?"

"Not yet," said Terry, taking a sip of his coffee to stall for time. "We've got some irons in the fire that might come good. We haven't been on this very long. These things take time to develop."

Jones held up his hand. "It's not a criticism; it's just events are moving so fast on the other issues you are dealing with, and we were just wondering." He picked up his wine glass and looked over the top of it at Terry. "There is something else. It's a little delicate.... On the Brandon Estate, the residents have reported back that the McCullen brothers, who were the dealers on the estate, have disappeared."

Terry had a good poker face; however, he found it hard to keep it in place.

"Nobody has seen or heard of them since the day of the raids," said Jones.

"Has anyone filed a missing person?" said Terry. Perhaps their mum was kicking up a stink.

"Oh, no," said Jones. "There's no complaint from the residents. We were just wondering if you knew anything."

Terry shook his head. "I know as much as you. I can only assume that they got away when they realised their business was over. Their father lives in Jamaica, doesn't he?"

As he let that thought gain momentum in Jones's brain, he looked across the room. By now, there wasn't an empty table in the hotel bar, and Terry noted a huddle of people around the entrance desk, plainly negotiating for the next free table. Alan Jones ordered another large Merlot and Terry had a small glass of house white.

Terry doubted Jones was a heavy drinker - you didn't get far in the police service these days having boozy lunches - so he guessed Jones was building up Dutch courage to confront the Commissioner with the latest request. After paying the bill, Terry said his goodbyes and left, unsure if Jones was staying or not. Outside, he noticed a chauffeur-driven black Jaguar police car parked by the entrance to the hotel with its engine running. Jones was making full use of the perks of the job.

CHAPTER THIRTY-FIVE

Terry's phone rang on his drive into The Peacock the following morning. It was Jones. He quickly pulled into a side street and answered.

"Good news," said Jones. He sounded full of himself once again. "The Home Secretary loved our idea. She will make a statement in the House of Commons on Friday outlining her crack-down on drug and knife crime in the capital. Furthermore, she will announce an initiative to ensure preparation for any future terrorist attacks, including security exercises at potential target locations in London."

"Great," said Terry, overlooking, for now, 'our idea.' "When will the security exercise start?"

"On Monday at 5 A.M."

Jesus, that was quick. Then again, the government had been plummeting in the polls. What better than a show of strength - against a potential terrorist threat, no less - to bring their approval ratings bouncing up again? Terry had worked through eight successive governments in all their guises and colours, and essentially they were the same at heart. All politicians looked after their own interests before the public interest. It just so happened that now these two things were colliding. They would get drugs out of Canary Wharf. What did it matter who reaped the benefits as long as it wasn't the dealers?

He restarted the engine and drove to The Peacock. Diane shouted "Good Luck" at him as he sprinted upstairs. My God, is there anything that the woman didn't know? - He would bet his life that none of the men had spoken a word. She just seemed to sense things. When he opened the door upstairs, all the men, except John, were already there and chatting excitedly. The buzz was the same as forty years previously when they were all young operational police officers. Nerves disguised with quips and jokes.

Dave's clothes were the subject of much of the laughter as Jimmy asked him, "I didn't get the memo. Is it fancy dress at work day? Can't you afford a new pair of jeans instead of all torn ones?"

By now, Dave could well defend himself with this group and replied, "What? Do you want me to dress like you? What is that look, by the way? Our man at Marks and Spencer?"

Jimmy nearly fell off his chair, laughing.

Although the open windows provided a cool draught, they released none of the tension from the room. Three empty pots of coffee were already sitting on the table, which showed to Terry that they had ignored his advice about drinking the previous evening.

Jimmy went through the briefing one more time, positioning them at locations on the estate. He would watch Mitchell's flat and identify the runner when he was heading for Balfron House. Peter distributed radios, tasers, door openers and cable ties.

Terry's last words were, "We now know we are looking for an extensive collection of guns, so I want these flats ripped to pieces before we leave them."

The mood turned sombre as Dave left to join Mr Jones at Limehouse Police Station while the others headed off in convoy to the Brownfield Estate.

~❖~

John was already at the rear of Balfron House, sitting in the back of a van with Ali and Elgin. In his hand was the radio supplied by Peter the previous evening. It crackled, but still nothing came through. He gave it a couple of taps on the side of the seat like he used to do with his old one, and the next message came through loud and clear.

"Suspect has left premises heading towards target location,"

John and the other two scrambled out of the van and were in the lobby by the lift as the runner walked in. The man knew something was up as soon as he looked at them and made a run for it; he was too slow. Ali grabbed him by the lapels of his jacket and dragged him through the door towards the staircase, his feet hardly touching the floor. Elgin produced a large hunting knife from his belt and held it to the runner's throat. Jesus thought John. He stifled a gasp as the knife broke the skin and a trickle of blood ran down the man's neck.

"What is your name?" growled Elgin.

"Wesley, Wesley Brown," he replied.

Well, using a knife had one advantage - it worked damn quick, thought John.

"Well, Wesley Brown, do you want to live or die here with your throat cut open?" asked Elgin.

"I want to live," croaked Wesley.

"We are going upstairs to your boss's flat if you get us in with no problems. You will live. If you don't, you will die. Do you understand?"

Wesley nodded before stuttering, "Y-yes, I understand."

The others arrived, panting and red-faced, as Ali and Elgin started dragging Wesley up the stairs to the second floor. Leaving the others on the stairwell, John crept along the landing and listened at the flat door: all he could hear was loud grime music. The neighbours are going to be pleased when we get rid of this lot, he thought as he signalled for Ali and Elgin to bring Wesley over. Before he could knock on the door, Jimmy produced a handkerchief and wiped the worst of the blood from Wesley's neck. With Elgin squatting behind, holding the blade to his back, Wesley stood in front of the spy hole and knocked on the solid front door.

After a moment, Tony Mitchell slowly opened the door. The force of Wesley and the door as Elgin and Ali propelled them threw Mitchell to the ground, and Wesley landed on top of him. John and Jimmy scrambled over the bodies and ran to the living room. Monty Johnston jumped up from the sofa as they entered, trying to retrieve something from behind him.

Jimmy punched him square on the jaw and hit him with a left hook that splattered his nose before he could fall to the floor. "That's for Winston Campbell," he said.

Johnson gasped for breath. He deserved it, that was for sure. John could see where this might lead. He tapped Jimmy on the shoulder as he stood over Monty, fists raised, and simply said, "Later."

As Jimmy secured cable ties around Johnson's wrists and ankles, John saw he was trembling with rage, although his face was calm now and the vein in his neck stopped bulging.

Johnson couldn't yet speak and they left him moaning in pain as they recovered a machete from under the sofa cushion. Terry found some other knives scattered around the room and they made quite a pile in the corner. No sign of any guns yet, though.

Terry cable-tied Wesley and laid him next to Monty, who was bleeding profusely from his nose and mouth.

It was time to search the rest of the flat.

Nicky went into the kitchen and found Tony Mitchell there, quivering in a chair. Elgin had cable-tied his arms and legs to the chair and was now standing over him with the blood-splattered knife in his hand. Ali was going through the cupboards.

"Anything?" asked Nicky and received a huge grin from Ali, who pulled out a Tesco bag filled with twenty-pound notes. It wasn't the only bag stashed with cash. Altogether, they found over £250000 in all denominations, including euros and dollars. Every bundle was helpfully, marked with the amount it contained.

Terry shook his head when they showed him everything they'd found. "And they say they built canary Wharf on crypto-currency and gold Amex. Nah, they find cash when it suits them." He gave John a wry grin. "Come on, let's talk to one of the venture capitalists."

John and Jimmy followed Terry into the kitchen, who signalled for Ali and Elgin to leave. Terry closed the door behind them and calmly said, "Where are the guns?"

Tony Mitchell's head snapped up. "What guns? I don't know anything about any guns."

"I'll give you one more chance." He gestured at John and Jimmy. "These guys will get you to tell them. It's only a matter of how much pain you'll endure first. You may suffer long enough to wish you were dead. Where are the guns?"

Tony sat in silence, his whole body tensed, straining at his restraints.

As Terry turned to walk out the door, he said to John, "Just make sure he doesn't need to see a doctor."

Tony, visibly relaxed with that comment just before John took a pair of pliers from inside his jacket pocket.

Jimmy nudged him. "He said he didn't want him needing a doctor."

"I heard him," said John, "except he didn't say anything about a dentist. Did he?"

It didn't take long. Just Jimmy holding open his jaw and the clunk of metal against ivory. He hadn't even got a proper grip on a back tooth when Tony Mitchell squealed the truth.

Less than one minute later, John was in the bedroom with Terry. "We've got a problem; the guns are in the cellar of the Red Lion pub."

"Oh shit," said Terry, "I hope Dave hasn't given Jones the search warrant yet. I need to make a phone call. Get this cleaned up here."

As John had a last search through the flat, he listened in on Terry's phone call. "Dave," Terry said, "have you given Mr Jones that search warrant yet?"

John kept still so he could hear the answer - something about a delay.

Terry smiled and turned to John. "The press went to the wrong location." He turned back to the phone. "Thank God for the press," he said. "I need to meet with you and Jones away from prying eyes before we go any further, don't part with the search warrant till I see you."

As John swept his fingers along the back of the cupboard, Terry made plans to meet Dave and Jones outside Domino's Pizza at the top of West India Dock Road.

"Hungry, Boss?" asked John.

Terry didn't bother smiling at him and was already halfway through the door when he said, "When you've finished here, search Mitchell's place. I'll be back in twenty and we can toss everything in the boot of my car."

Leaving Ali and Elgin with Mitchell, Johnson and Wesley, John grabbed Jimmy and with Nicky, they went to Mitchell's flat. The door opener worked perfectly on the standard council door. There was a lot of growling, although little resistance from the three youngers who had been weighing and packing a mound of cocaine from a kitchen bowl into small bags. They had piled more than a hundred bags of cocaine on the table and hundreds of empty ones were waiting to be filled. It looked as though they were selling them as quickly as they could fill them.

John and Nicky left Jimmy watching over the kids in the kitchen and ransacked the flat, practised now, as though they had never been away from the game. John found another two one-kilo blocks of cocaine, hidden in the toilet cistern and about three thousand pounds in bundles at the bottom of the wardrobe.

With a wad of cash in his hand, he looked around him. Why didn't they think of spending some of their money? The flat was nothing more than a squat with a single bed covered with filthy sheets and bedclothes, the kitchen had no utensils, and the fridge's contents comprised nothing other than dozens of cans of Pepsi Cola and Red Bull.

He walked back into the living room and found nothing new: just the large table adorned with drugs and paraphernalia and a couple of chairs scattered around. The only sign of wealth was a flat-screen 55-inch television connected to a PlayStation and a large sound system banging out grime music. He turned it off and his ears buzzed in the silence.

He swept all the drugs and money into a large plastic bag and walked back to the kitchen. Nicky had torn every cupboard off the walls and doors were now hanging off base units. Jimmy had dispossessed the youths of their phones and one boy was trying not to cry, while the other two were sullen. As he and Jimmy walked out, one of them piped up, his voice breaking, "Mitchell is going to kill you."

"Oh, no," said John, swinging around. "Tony Mitchell isn't going to be bothering anyone for a very long time." He gave Jimmy a wink, and together they walked out of the flat back to Ali and Elgin.

CHAPTER THIRTY-SIX

Dave and Alan Jones were already waiting for Terry on the pavement outside Domino's Pizza.

"What's happened? Is everything alright?" said Jones.

At first, Terry thought Jones might be worried about his men. He then realised that Jones - of course - was mainly concerned about letting down the press he'd assembled. "Everything's fine," Terry said. "But there's additional information that requires immediate action. One of the drug dealers was building an armoury for the drug war we discussed yesterday, and those weapons, including firearms and ammunition, are in the Red Lion pub."

Jones furrowed his brow. "How does that affect things?"

Next to Jones, Dave looked up to heaven, and Terry resisted the temptation to snap his finger in front of Jones' face to wake him up. "You need to get an armed response unit down here now and the pub searched before word gets around," Terry said. "The publican may either dispose of the guns or worse still, hand them out to the low-life from the estate."

"What about what you're doing?" asked Jones.

"That's going fine. I'll ring Dave with the two addresses for the council to board up in about half an hour. You only need to send two TSG units with them. By then, hopefully, the Armed Response Unit will be here, and Dave can brief them with the plans he's got for the pub."

Jones turned to Dave. "You already have plans for the pub? Why wasn't I informed about this?"

Dave grimaced.

"And a search warrant," said Terry. "Remember I told you about that in the hotel last night? At that stage, we only thought you would find stolen property though," Terry was getting exasperated. "We've only just found out about the guns,"

"Why was I not informed of this?" asked Jones.

Because we didn't want the press all over it, thought Terry. Raising his voice, he said, "Because I've told you, we've only just found out that the guns are there. That's why I'm here."

Jones took off his hat, wiped his brow with a hanky, and put it back on again.

"A word of advice," said Terry and watched Jones bristle. "First, get some experienced CID officers down here. You'll need people capable of dealing with exhibits properly and arresting and interviewing any suspects. You don't want to lose this at court because of a technicality."

"Obviously," said Jones, "These days-"

"Second," said Terry, "keep the press away from the scene. If anything goes wrong, it will be down to you."

Dave made a sputtering sound, which he turned into a cough. Terry only grinned once; he had walked away. He knew exactly which buttons to press with Detective Chief Superintendent Jones.

When Terry returned to the Brownfield estate, he found John, Jimmy, Ali, Elgin and their three prisoners in the kitchen at Johnston's flat. "The other place secure?" he asked.

"Yes," said Jimmy. "We left three young 'uns there with Nicky. I reckon we could let them go so they can run home to their mammies. We've got their phones."

Terry nodded and inspected the bag of cash and drugs John held open for him. He raised his eyebrows. "Nice haul, lads."

Johnston sneered. "Who are you, old men?"

Jimmy slapped him across the head without even looking at him.

"Get them in the van," said Terry. He pointed at Wesley. "Except for him. He can go." With a knife, Ali freed Wesley from the cable ties and they laughed as he scarpered out of the flat.

Outside, Peter had the engine running of the van. Nicky joined them to help Jimmy and John bundle Johnston in. Elgin and Ali threw Mitchell in behind. They were both cable-tied with black plastic bags over their heads. Standing with Nicky by his side, the bag of loot over his shoulder, Terry waved the van goodbye and checked his watch. He reckoned they had about ten minutes before the TSG units turned up to clean the estate and board up the flats.

He walked to his car, opened up the boot, and slung the bag inside.

"Imagine if we got stopped," said Nicky.

Terry grinned. "We would have loved that when we were young officers, wouldn't we? Stopping two dodgy old blokes and finding a tonne of coke, cash and weapons."

"Then drinking all night at The Peacock," said Nicky, "to celebrate."

Terry's phone rang. It was Dave confirming the armed response unit was on its way to The Red Lion. He and Nicky climbed into the car and Nicky took out a packet of toffees. "Want one?"

Terry shook his head. Everything had gone to plan up to now; what was coming next was something different. He'd never had a love affair with guns that some of his colleagues had. He hoped all those young men and women in the Armed Response Unit, knew what they were doing. God knows how their wives (or even husbands these days) slept at night. "Ready to see some action?" he asked Nicky and drove as fast as he could towards The Red Lion.

CHAPTER THIRTY-SEVEN

Peter was glad Ali, Elgin and Jimmy were in the back of the van with Monty Johnson and Tony Mitchell. It was chaos back there! Johnston wouldn't stop fighting, kicking out at every opportunity.

John turned around in the passenger seat and shouted. "Sit on him!"

So, Ali settled his eighteen-plus stones on him. They could now just hear muffled grunts.

At the smallholding, Peter leapt out, ran to the second unit, and released the padlock. Wondering how much the McCullen brothers in the first unit could hear; he decided not to check on them and instead get Johnson and Mitchell in their hut first. He opened the back of the van and, while Ali and John wrestled with Johnston, picked up the supplies and placed them at the far end of the Nissen hut. John and Ali dragged Johnston, still bound hands and feet, into his new home. Tony Mitchell walked meekly behind. John first cut Mitchell's cable ties and said to Johnston who was lying on the ground, "I'm going to cut the ties off, but give me one excuse and I'll batter you around this hut before tying you up again and leaving you, it's your choice." Johnston didn't reply and when John released him, he lay there for a few seconds before jumping to his feet and running for the door.

Johnson's mouth hung open as John stood to one side, letting him run past. As he got to the door, Jimmy confronted him. Monty threw a wild haymaker of a punch, which Jimmy effortlessly avoided, and returned with three punches in quick succession. Monty staggered backwards; he was still game and attempted to kick Jimmy, who parried it away and hit him square on the chin. As Monty fell to the floor, Jimmy straddled Johnston, punching him: "That's for Winston. For letting him die in the gutter. That's for-"

John interrupted him by tapping him on the shoulder. Jimmy stopped, got up, and walked out of the hut without looking back. Peter had never seen Jimmy shy away from violence and he always seemed untouched by the pain and injuries he was capable of inflicting - so why stop now? Maybe with age came wisdom. No point in having dead bodies to deal with. As it was, Johnston seemed more embarrassed than hurt as he lay curled up on the floor.

The men locked the door of the second hut behind them and Peter grabbed more supplies from the van to give to the McCullens. On opening the door, the stench was breathtaking. The brothers must have heard the ruckus as they were standing in the middle of the hut, legs wide and chins held high. Gerald said, "What the fuck do you want with us? Who are you? Why are you keeping us here?"

"So many questions," said John, strolling toward them.

"You need to take it easy on those crisps. You're getting fat," said Jimmy.

Gerald took a step forward but then retreated. "We just want to know what's going on," he said.

Peter almost felt sorry for him - the hard man laid low, "We will reveal all in good time," he said. "Now empty those slop buckets. It stinks in here."

Once they had supervised the McCullens emptying their buckets, they put them back in their hut.

"Remember, go easy on the crisps," said Jimmy as they locked the door behind them. They walked away and then Jimmy tapped Peter on his arm and mimed that he was going back to the hut to listen to their new prisoners.

Peter crept back with him and they placed their ears to the door. They heard Johnson say, "What did you tell them?" and the frightened voice of Mitchell replied, "Nothing, I told them nothing."

"Don't fucking lie to me," shouted Johnson. "They were ripping the fucking place to pieces till they took you into the kitchen. When they came out, they stopped searching. What did they ask you?"

"They just ask if there were any more drugs. I told them to fuck off."

"Did they ask you about your flat?"

"No, they never mentioned it."

Peter and Jimmy grinned. So they didn't have a clue they had all the drugs and money.

"When we get out of here, if I find out you've lied, you're a dead man," said Monty.

Jimmy banged on the door and shouted, "I hope you two fuckers kill each other in there!" He and Peter walked away laughing.

At the side of the van, Peter phoned Terry. Above him, the lark was singing. He rang off and turned to the others. "Terry and Nicky are waiting to see what happens when they raid the pub. He doesn't think there'll be anything else for us to do today but suggests we go for a drink and he'll ring and give us an update."

"A drink, you say?" said Jimmy.

John put his arms around Ali and Elgin. "You coming, lads?"

Peter was aware that now they had collected the money; the brothers could go when they liked, although it didn't surprise him when they agreed. They all wanted to discover the eventual outcome. Would they seize the guns? Would they arrest Mehmed?

They headed to Bexley Village. "There's a pub on the right," said John. "Used to have a right good time with the publican's missus there."

Jimmy punched him on the shoulder. "Bonking her upstairs while the poor old fella was downstairs pulling pints!"

"When was that?" Asked Peter.

"God knows," said John. "Twenty years ago? Thirty?"

"You have been a stallion for a very long time," said Ali, seriously, and they all fell about laughing.

"They'll be long gone by now," said Jimmy, wiping the tears from his eyes.

It had seen many changes of ownership over the years, and the boozer was friendly and, somehow, had escaped the anonymising decor of the big chain pubs. They settled down at a sticky table with their lagers and listened to another one of John's escapades. Peter sat back, content. Life was good. Sure, he hadn't long to live; he was in no pain; the beer was cold and his friends were all he needed right now.

CHAPTER THIRTY-EIGHT

Jones looked over the heads of the gathered press, through to the empty Limehouse Police Station. He could see Detective Sergeant Driscoll in front of the Flying Squad and Firearms Officers, gesticulating. He wondered if he should have left him to do the briefing - to be honest; it wasn't as though he, Jones, had all the details down pat. A familiar sinking feeling came, (the same sinking feeling he'd had ever since Terry and his crew had been on this job), and he wished he could be in two places at once: briefing the Firearms Unit and in front of the press. He turned on his smile - the smile that had cost a pretty penny at the private dentist - and welcomed the press. Their hubbub settled, and they turned to him.

"Ladies and Gentlemen, apologies for the delay, I am sure," he turned up the voltage of his smile, "it will be worth your while. This afternoon, we took back control of a nearby estate plagued by drugs and drug dealers. This estate has been the scene of stabbings and murders over the years. As we speak, my officers and Tower Hamlets Council are boarding up premises used by these miscreants and restoring CCTV to the estate." He waited as the hubbub got louder and the press scribbled in their notebooks."

Without raising a hand, a young woman at the front said, "Why aren't we there instead of here?"

He gave a little bow, as though this was the most pertinent question he was ever likely to hear. "The reason you are not, at this stage, being invited onto the estate is that during the operation, we discovered our targets had concealed an arsenal of weapons, including firearms, on another property."

This was gold to the assembled press. Jones pictured the headlines: GUN HORROR ON STREETS OF LONDON; POLICE SCOOP GUN HAUL: GUN TERROR FOILED. He knew for the press they would much prefer it if an actual gun battle was about to take place and although that was not what he wanted, he knew enough to offer the possibility. "It's going to be highly dangerous as our officers from The Flying Squad and Firearms Unit will shortly search that venue. IF," he held up his finger, "and only if this is successful, I will invite you all to witness the outcome."

The crime reporter from the Sun turned to the crime reporter for the Daily Express and said quietly, "He's going to look like a right dick if they don't find any guns." Unfortunately, he wasn't quiet enough, and it hurt Jones to hear The Daily Express reporter reply, "I think he qualifies for that title, with or without guns." Nor was he best pleased when he saw the other reporters nod their heads in agreement.

Through the window, he saw the Flying Squad exit. One keen young woman at the back noticed too and looked as though she was about to charge away.

"We must stay here to wait," said Jones. "That is imperative."

The press looked at him expectantly. What else was there to say? There was no way he wanted to answer any tough questions. He dragged from his memory an old speech about what he had done since being in office and tried as best he could to ignore the eye-rolls and the Sun reporter, not bothering to lower his voice, saying, "God, he's a bore, isn't he?"

~❖~

Dave was in the passenger seat of one of the Flying Squad cars and behind him were four other vehicles containing the rest of the Flying Squad and the Firearms Unit. He held on as they drove fast against the one-way system and entered East India Dock Road towards Chrisp Street. They squealed to a stop outside the Red Lion and as Dave leapt out, he noticed Terry and Nicky parked up. He resisted the temptation to wave and called the men to gather outside.

Made larger than life by flak jackets and Heckler and Koch semi-automatics across their chests, the armed officers stormed the Red Lion, followed by their Flying Squad colleagues. Dave felt a rush of excitement as he watched the customers (about fifteen of them) raise their arms. How funny it was, he thought, that it was what all humans did in those situations - when had we been taught that? Only through films and television. This was surely a once-in-a-lifetime experience for a group of sad old drinkers drawing their sorrows on a weekday afternoon.

"Get on the floor!" shouted an officer and the punters, docile as children playing Sleeping Lions, slumped to the ground. There was the thump, thump of heavy police boots running up the stairs. Dave ran after them and was there as Lenny King, the publican, was being handcuffed and read his rights.

"Where are the guns?" Dave demanded. The man was pale and stubborn and would say nothing. They searched the flat to no avail. Shit, thought Dave, maybe they aren't here.

"Take him to the cellar," he said and knew at once he had hit the jackpot by the look on King's face. In the vinegar stench of old beer, they found a sports bag stuffed with guns among a stash of obviously stolen electrical items.

Dave watched as a firearms officer ensured all the weapons were safe, being careful to preserve any fingerprints.

"Four 9mm automatic handguns, one Glock, three sawn-off shotguns and a variety of ammunition," said the officer, adding, "We'll need forensic to confirm, although I reckon these are ready to go."

"Good job," said Dave. And it had been. It had been a great job and the first time he'd been in action since joining Terry's team. As he walked back to the van, he kept his fist close to his leg and raised his thumb when he passed Terry's car. There was no need to talk to him just yet. They'd be meeting soon.

Once in the van, he telephoned Jones. "All done, sir." He could hear the babble of the crowd of the press as he gave all the details.

"Wait," he heard Jones say. "Wait!" It wasn't Dave he was talking to, it was the press. From the noise, Dave guessed they were ahead of Jones with the news and were already heading towards the Red Lion in the hope of bodies, guns and a picture of King doing the walk of shame with his hands handcuffed behind his back. The only thing they'd find was a group of disgruntled punters hanging around outside a pub with blue Metropolitan Police - Do not Enter tape festooned across the entrance.

"Drop me off here," said Dave to the driver.

The woman gave him a look.

"Just at the corner there."

The vehicle slowed down, and Dave leapt out, shouting to the officers in the back. "Good job, people." He watched them drive away with his hand held high, then doubled back on himself to wait under the DLR railway arches at Willis Street. Within seconds, Dave and Nicky pulled up. He got in the back seat.

"Good to see some action?" said Terry.

"Yes," said Dave and told them in detail the exploits in the pub. They knew nearly everything already, but they were good enough to humour him. They let him out a few hundred yards from Scotland Yard and unlocked the boot. The bag of cocaine and weapons from the flats was heavy, and he felt like he was taking his life in his hands as he walked along Victoria Embankment with it bouncing on his back. I hope to God, I don't get mugged, he thought; nobody would believe me. He looked over his shoulder and it reassured him to see Terry and Nicky still sitting in the car, obviously waiting for him to enter the building.

Inside Scotland Yard, Jones was busy directing how to arrange the chairs for yet another press conference he had called. There was panic in the air, as was expecting the reporters to arrive en masse in less than five minutes. On a table by the microphones, the cache of guns found at The Red Lion was on display - shining like museum exhibits. Dave opened his bag and showed Jones the Johnston takings. "Excellent!" said Jones, rubbing his hands, and called for another table.

It seemed there were no further questions for Dave: questions that - if Dave were in Jones' position, he would have asked - for example, wasn't any money found on the premises? Were the flats empty? What has happened to the suspects?

All Jones cared about was how things looked.

Which, now he came to think about it, suited Dave fine. Terry and Nicky had told him to come to The Peacock as soon as he could for a little celebration. Not that the job was over by any means... but, yes, they all deserved to let loose a little. It had been a good day: guns and drugs off the streets.

"May I go now, Sir?" he asked Jones, who wasn't listening - he was tapping the microphone and gesturing for the journalists to be let in.

When Dave got back to the Peacock, the party was in full swing. The locals didn't know if it was a stag party, birthday party or impromptu piss-up; they didn't seem to care and just joined in the fun. When Peter started playing the piano, knocking out songs from years gone by, everyone, including Diane, realised it was going to be a long night.

Dave laughed as Elgin and Ali turned bright red in the face, being unused to alcohol, and sang a melancholy song from their boyhood.

Peter sidled up to Dave, "They're sad because it's their last night. Ali said if he'd known police work was like this, he would have gone on the straight and narrow years ago."

Dave grinned. "I wish it was all like this,"

Peter raised his eyebrows. "Sick of paperwork?"

Dave nodded.

"Enjoy this while you can then," said Peter, clinking his glass with Dave's. "Life is short and for living."

CHAPTER THIRTY-NINE

The next morning, Wesley Brown found himself cable-tied for the second time in twenty-four hours. On this occasion, he had been in a café in Chrisp Street market enjoying his burger and milkshake when, from out of nowhere, two thugs came and put a hessian bag over his head and threw him in the back of the car. There had been no chance to call for help, but surely, he couldn't help thinking someone would call the police. Not that he wanted to see them, either.

The car started, and the bag whisked off his head. Next to him was the vast bulk of Arian Mehmed and he tried not to flinch.

"So, tell me. Exactly what happened yesterday?" said Arian Mehmed.

"I don't know what you're talking about," replied Wesley.

Wesley saw Arian smile, although it didn't reach his eyes, and then nod towards one of the "huge Turks" sitting in the front passenger seat, who reached over and hit him across the face with the back of his hand. Wesley saw stars and tasted blood inside his mouth. He tried not to cry. Life wasn't fair. It was only yesterday when he was stabbed in the neck and today he was being slapped across the face.

"I was taking money over to Monty," he said quickly before he could get another slap, "and when I got into his building, these two big Turks dragged me into the stairwell and held a knife to my throat," he lifted his head to show the cut on his neck, "and told me they were going to kill me if I didn't get them into Monty's flat. When we got upstairs, I think four or five more were there; they were from London and old. Two of them were as big as the Turks were. Once they got into Monty's flat, they tied me up, threw me on the floor, and I saw no more. After about an hour, they let me go."

He searched Mehmed's eyes. He had to believe him. There was nothing left to say. What if he didn't? They had left the city now and were travelling towards Essex and the industrial units - towards the kind of places, he'd heard, where they liked to torture a man - hang him up by his feet, flay his skin, that kind of thing.

"Who else was in the flat?" asked Mehmed.

"Just Monty and Tony,"

"Were the Londoners Old Bill?"

Wesley blinked. This had never occurred to him. "Can't see it," he said. "They were old, maybe sixty or seventy. One of them could have a row and gave Monty a good hiding,"

"And what happened to Johnston and Mitchell?"

"They put bin bags over their heads and took them away," replied Wesley.

"Where did they go?"

He would have thrown them up if Wesley hadn't had his hands tied. "I don't know, honest," he said. "Nobody has seen them since. Those dudes bust Tony's flat up and took all the coke from there as well. In the afternoon, the council came and boarded them both up."

"What about the pub? What's that about?" asked Mehmed.

"It's the pub we use. Monty must have stored his guns in there because the Old Bill turned up yesterday afternoon, all tooled up and nicked Lenny, the owner. Last night on the news, it said they had found a load of guns. They must have been Monty's,"

Mehmed stared out of the window for a moment, thinking. "What guns did Johnston have?" he said.

"I haven't a clue about guns, I promise. There were all sorts, like handguns and shotguns. He showed them to us in his flat and said we were going to war with a firm out of East Ham. I promise I don't know anymore. I didn't even realise, he had put the guns in the pub."

"Are you sure they were Turks who grabbed you?" asked Mehmed

"Yeah, they were just like you guys."

"We're not fucking Turks; we're Albanian," spat Mehmed.

"No offence," said Wesley, "you all look alike to me." He regretted it as soon as he said it and braced himself for another slap.

"Get him the fuck out of here," was all Mehmed said.

They stopped the car and, thankfully, cut his ties. As they roared off, Wesley looked around him. He hadn't a clue where he was, but he had never been happier.

~❖~

Back in the car, Mehmed leaned forward and spoke to Ismet, his most trusted man. "Who the fuck is trying to take me on? Have we spoken to all the police we know?"

"Yes boss," said Ismet. "They know nothing. They haven't heard of any unknown faces in town, and they're sure those old blokes aren't Old Bill."

"Fuck!" said Mehmed, slamming his hands on the back of the driver's seat so that the driver swerved a little in shock. "You're sure neither the McCullens nor these last two haven't turned up dead anywhere?"

"No, Boss," said Ismet.

"It's got to be the Hassans," Mehmed hissed. "It has them stamped all over this. Who else could it be? Drop me at the cafe, go get him and bring him back to me."

Normally Ismet was without expression, but now he widened his eyes. "Do it!" screamed Mehmed and slumped back in his seat as they raced back to the cafe.

He paced up and down at the cafe, refusing all offers of drink and food. "Come on," he muttered to himself. "Come on." He looked up at his heavies behind the counter and asked again. "You prepared?"

They nodded and one of them showed him their gun again.

Half an hour later, Yusuf Hassan walked into the cafe, followed by Ismet. Unlike his brothers, he was a spindly specimen, but Mehmed could see from the look on his face that he'd like to kill them all - probably would make plans to kill them later. It had been a risk bringing him here under force, but enough was enough. He couldn't have his best men kidnapped (killed, possibly) by this man and say nothing.

He waited until Yusuf sat down and then sat opposite him. "Thanks for coming to see me, Yusuf."

A braver man might have said I hardly had a choice, did I? But Yusuf only grunted.

"I've got a problem," continued Mehmed, "and I'm hoping you can help me with it." Without waiting for a reply, he continued, "Two Turks and four or five old blokes have been running riot with my dealers. What do you know about this?"

"Absolutely nothing," said Yusuf.

"You must do. I just told you two of them are Turks."

Yusuf spread out his hands. "Arian, you probably know more Turks in London than I do. My firm is serving up cannabis and you've got the cocaine trade. Everyone is happy. If someone is challenging you, it isn't anyone involved with me."

"Are there any new people who have arrived from Turkey or Northern Cyprus? Who would think they could take me on?"

"I don't know anybody new in town; anyway, it makes no sense. Knocking over a few of your dealers won't get to you, will it? I think it's probably a little gang just trying

their luck robbing some dealers. The chances are they don't even realise the dealers work for you."

"It's more than that. Every time they hit a dealer, the dealers disappear. That's hardly a little gang robbing them. Is it?" barked Mehmed.

"Mehmed, I don't know anything about it, other than what I've seen in the papers and on the news."

Mehmed stared at him. Had all this been for nothing? Yusuf was a pipsqueak. He was also a man who held grudges. "Thank you again for coming to see me. I will get you dropped back."

Yusuf lifted his chin. "Next time," he said, "You could ask me to come. Didn't your mother tell you about manners?" He narrowed his eyes. "There are consequences for those without manners."

This time Mehmed's men didn't bundle Yusuf into the back of the car; they opened the door for him and closed it gently behind him.

Mehmed watched them go through the window and sighed. He knew Yusuf had been lying; however, he didn't want to start a war right now. With a large shipment arriving next week, the last thing he needed was additional police attention at the moment.

He looked up at Ismet. "I should have eradicated the Hassans a long time ago."

"Ossie and Omer are now both in Belmarsh prison," said Ismet, meaningfully.

Mehmed nodded and said, "It might be difficult to get Mustafa out in Northern Cyprus, but the two in prison are easy. Ignoring the sister, that only leaves Yusuf." I will enjoy killing him myself, he thought.

CHAPTER FORTY

Upstairs in the Peacock, there were soreheads all around. Terry opened the window to allow a much-needed cool draught to run through the room. When Diane brought up the third jug, they had already gone through two jugs of coffee and packets of paracetamol. "Great night, boys," she said. "I've been thinking about putting on entertainment once a week. Now I think I'll just get you a lot back instead."

"Sorry Diane," said John. "At our age, I don't think we could do a night like that every week."

"Wimp," she said as she breezed out.

The men laughed.

Terry clapped his hands to bring order. This was fine celebrating their successes, but their final mission was the most important one of all. Unless they could intercept the huge delivery of drugs and take Mehmed out, the same old cycle of violence would start all over again. "Great work yesterday, everyone," said Terry. "Today's Friday and we've got till next Wednesday when the shipment arrives. After this meeting, John, will you come with me to see Yusuf and give him the cash from yesterday?"

"No problem," said John.

"Nicky, could you get hold of Kenny Pierce and arrange a meeting with him this evening or tomorrow morning? I just want to keep him on his toes."

"I'll ring him as soon as we're finished," said Nicky.

He turned to Peter, checking as he always did since he heard about Peter's diagnosis if he looked pale. Peter seemed as hearty as ever. "What's happening down at Woolwich?" he asked.

"It's the same routine every day, just the same man on-site between nine and five, Monday to Friday. He moves the same pallets and boxes back and forth with the forklift all day, just to make it look like it's being used."

"Nice work if you can get it," said Jimmy.

"He didn't open the yard last weekend," continued Peter. "I'll monitor it again over this weekend."

Terry turned to Dave, looking as youthful as ever in his bright white Adidas hoodie. "Dave, I know we said we'd leave it till Monday. While he is in good humour, I need you to give Jones a full briefing today."

Dave grimaced. "Oh, good,"

"We've got a location for them to plot away from the warehouse," Terry said. "Kenny Pierce told us it never arrives before midday, he only gets a phone call when it's on its way, so my guess is the driver rings when he's off the ferry. However, we can't take a chance, so Jones needs to brief at the local nick at seven and be in position by nine A.M. at the latest."

Dave took out his notebook and wrote this down.

"It may end up being a long wait," said Terry. "Better safe than sorry, though. Tell him under no circumstances is he to invite the press to this one."

Dave laughed. "I can try. But he's obsessed with them."

"Here," said Peter, sliding a folder across. "That'll keep Jones busy. It's a briefing pack with plans and photos."

"Tell Jones I'll ring him when the lorry arrives," said Terry, "and Mehmed is in the warehouse. Please emphasise he mustn't show out. I don't want him doing a drive-through to look at the plot. I'm sure he'll pester you to discover how we will find out they've arrived at the warehouse, so do the usual. Play dumb and blame me."

Dave nodded. "Got you."

"We will all be together watching the cameras, about three miles away," said Terry, "except for you, Dave. I hope to have a much more proactive role for you on this occasion."

A huge smile filled Dave's face as John slapped him on the back and said, "The boy's going to become a man."

He paused and looked around at each of the men. "All of you have a quiet weekend," he said. "It's a big week next week. Unless Kenny Pierce comes up with something that needs dealing with, I won't need to bother you till Monday. Let's have a lie-in and meet here at eleven."

It seemed the men were glad of an excuse to rest, and they sloped off with barely another word. Only John remained and he was checking his phone. He whistled as though shocked.

"Anything good?"

John smiled. "Jilly and I like to sext."

Terry waved his hands. "Too much information, mate, way too much." They laughed. "Come on," said Terry, "Let's go and see our old friend Yusuf."

When Terry and John arrived at the bookmaker in Old Kent Road, Yusef was like a raging bull, pacing around his office, screaming expletives making no sense at all. Even the contents of the bag John was carrying didn't improve his mood. Eventually, Terry got him to sit down and explain the problem, but every time he got to where the men had grabbed him, threw him in the back of a car and paraded him in front of Mehmed, he lost it again.

Terry and John could hardly keep from laughing until Yusuf said, "I'm going to get Ali and Elgin to kill Arian Mehmed before they fly home. He needs to understand the consequences of disrespecting me. They need to kill him slowly, and he must know it came from me. I might even get them to bring him to a lock-up I've got, so I can hear the screams and watch him die."

Terry felt his eyebrows shoot up. Although getting these men off the streets would be no bad thing, he wasn't sure if this would spark the biggest bloodbath London had ever seen. Have you spoken to Mustafa about this?" he asked.

Yusuf's chin snapped up. "I don't need to ask my brother's permission to do what's right,"

Terry spoke as calmly as he could. "I think Mustafa might see things differently. For a start, Ali and Elgin are his men, and Mehmed has plenty of protection. It will need a lot of planning to get to him. Should they fail, you will start a war."

"War!" Yusuf screamed. "Me start a war? Mehmed started the fucking war when he sent his thugs to kidnap me. This has all come about because of your involvement in all this. I told Mustafa we should never have got mixed up with you lot."

Terry glanced at John, who shrugged. They could say nothing to calm down Yusuf's lust for revenge.

At the car, Terry said to John, "We've got to put a stop to this or Yusuf is going to screw everything up for next week. Phone Ali and get him and his brother to meet us at the Lord Nelson pub now." Once John made the arrangements, Terry said, "I'll drop you at the pub to keep the boys company and I'll phone Mustafa in Northern Cyprus from the car. I have a feeling this could be a long and uncomfortable conversation."

About twenty minutes later, Terry walked into the pub to a waiting pint of lager. He took a large gulp and said, "I've just been talking to Mustafa; he's booked you, boys, on the four-fifty-five flight from Gatwick this afternoon. Your tickets will be at the Turkish Airlines desk. I need you to collect your stuff from the flat and leave without talking to Yusuf or any of the others."

Ali put down his drink and was about to protest when Terry continued, "John will drop you at the airport. I'm sorry it's such a rush, there is a bit of a problem and Mustafa wants you home straight away." To John, he said, "You take my car and I'll get a cab back."

"It is sad," said Ali.

"You must visit us," said Elgin.

None of them was in the mood to finish their drinks and so, after some formal handshakes, John shepherded the brothers to his car. Terry watched the three big men disappear and doubted he'd ever see the brothers again. But that is what this job was like. You became like brothers over a few short days and then puff; they disappeared out of your life.

CHAPTER FORTY ONE

That evening, Terry was listening to Cool for Cats by Squeeze on his only CD and singing along, at the top of his voice, as he drove to meet Nicky and Kenny. Beside him, his phone buzzed and seeing Dave's name flash up, he turned down the music and pulled over.

"How did it go?"

"Jones was so impressed by the notes he asked if you had recommendations for what they should pack for lunch, too."

Terry laughed. "His nose is out of joint, as usual, I see."

Dave imitated Jones. "Explain to me how he'll know when either the drugs or Arian Mehmed will turn up and at what time. And how does he know he's going to be receiving one hundred kilos of cocaine and have with him over one million pounds in cash?"

"What did you tell him?"

"I said you were confident in your sources, etc."

"Any signs he's going to attempt a reccy or inform the press?"

"I mean, I'm not a hundred per cent but he promised he wouldn't."

Terry sighed. "Well, we tried. Thank you, Dave."

He rang off and put his music back on. As he drove, glass and steel gave way to redbrick houses and then there were fields and trees. He was glad they decided on a quiet country pub near Westerham to meet up.

When he arrived, Nicky and Kenny were already there, sitting in the garden under the shade of a willow tree. Even Kenny seemed relaxed and recounted the events of his few days in Morocco.

He looked across at Terry. "You will fulfil your side of the deal?"

"Of course," said Terry.

Kenny barked out a laugh. "God loves those boys. They have always been trouble, but I've got to get them home with me."

"After Wednesday, as long as it goes to plan," said Terry. "They'll be released. Don't doubt it."

"I haven't told them what's happening," said Kenny. "Trouble is, although they're good boys, they can't help shooting their mouths off. I haven't told the missus either, although that's different. She has never asked me what's going on in my business, but she's always been there for me."

"It was the same with my wife," said Terry, and then wished he hadn't spoken because he had to turn away. He had unexpectedly teared up. He cleared his throat and got to business. They went over the plans for Wednesday - the minute Kenny got the arrival time; he would ring Nicky first, then Mehmed.

Kenny kept laughing and Terry supposed that this was like a retirement party for him. After this one last job, he would be out of the business of crime and informing forever. Kenny was lucky, Terry reflected. People like him normally end up dead or doing a long stretch in prison in his game. Kenny would be one of the few he'd met who'd paid no consequences.

In the pub car park, after they'd said goodbye to Kenny, Nicky turned to Terry and said, "He comes across a nice bloke, doesn't he?"

Terry nodded. "Maybe he's mellowed in his old age."

"Do you think?"

"Don't you?"

Nicky thought for a moment. "Maybe. I wonder if he ever looks back at what he did to his mate's sons or if he just carries on enjoying his great big house and all his money?" He shook his head. "Anyway, can I have a lift?"

"Why? What happened to your car?"

"Wouldn't start. Had to get the train and a taxi out here."

Terry cuffed him. "You should have said." He tossed him his car keys. "You drive mine and drop me at a station. I've got a meeting in town at 9 p.m."

"Who are you going to see? Do you want me to come with you?" asked Nicky.

Terry ignored this and said, "No, you get home. It's been a long week. I'll go through everything on Monday morning."

~❖~

Nicky dropped him outside Orpington Station and arranged to get his car back to him on Saturday morning.

As Terry walked into The Sports Bar above Victoria Station, a giant of a man rose from his stool to his full six-foot-eight-inch height; he seemed to get up in sections, He warmly shook Terry's hand and in a booming, coarse and distinctive East London accent, said, "Hello, Terry, good to see you again. I'm Toby Russell and this is Detective Sergeant Paul Wright."

"Have we met before?" asked Terry.

"You won't remember me. When I left training school, which was nearly twenty-five years ago, they posted me to Bethnal Green and I went to the police sports club in Chigwell to play rugby. I think it was one of your last couple of games before you retired from playing. You were a fullback, weren't you?"

"Bloody hell, you've got some memory. I don't know about twenty-five years; it was at least four stone ago for me." They laughed. "By the look of your cauliflower ears and the size of you, I assume you played in the second row. I've got to say, no disrespect, but you neither look like nor sound like a Toby."

"I know," said Toby. "I come from the Ocean Estate on the Commercial Road in Stepney. My mum had delusions of grandeur. There were five of us boys and we all got posh names. It could have been worse. She called one of us Sebastian and another Giles."

All three of them laughed before Paul Wright went to the bar to buy three pints of lager.

While he was away, Toby updated Terry on the difficulties he was encountering running a proactive unit like the Regional Crime Squad. Even as a Detective Chief Inspector, paperwork and accountants tied him down.

"How about promotion?" asked Terry. There'd be time to get to the crux of the matter later. In this job, it was all about making connections and showing support.

"That won't happen. I've been on one superintendent's promotion board. As soon as I opened my mouth and they heard my accent, I could see it was all over. One of them even asked me what I'd studied at university. Bearing in mind, they had all my records in front of them; he had the gall to feign surprise when I told them my formal education ended at a secondary modern school in Stepney Green."

Terry took a mouthful of his lager and got down to business. Although he'd been able to play Jones like a puppet, he didn't trust him in the long term and he needed these guys to help him bring down Arian Mehmed. The problem was - it wasn't exactly kosher for a Detective Chief Inspector of the Regional Crime Squad to keep things from Detective Chief Superintendent Jones. After Terry had outlined his idea (hinting at the possible repercussions from Jones once he knew of their plans), he said, "I know when I went through all this on the phone, you fancied the job, but I understand if you don't want to get involved."

"You must be kidding, Terry," said Toby. "It sounds like a brilliant plan and we're definitely in. As for Mr Jones, let me tell you, I've already had dealings with him. When he was a Superintendent and working for the Anti-Corruption Unit, he accused one of my men of stealing money meant for an informant. He threatened to arrest him and send him to prison. I confronted him and explained that as the job hadn't come off, there was no money due to be paid to the informant, so he needed to get his facts straight before accusing my officer. He didn't like it, especially when I told him that in my experience, time spent in research is seldom wasted."

Terry laughed and said, "I thought it was only me he didn't like."

Terry handed over the map of the area Peter had compiled, together with plans of the warehouse and photographs of Arian Mehmed.

Once Toby placed all the documents in his briefcase and Terry had bought another round of drinks, Terry said, "What's going on with the Met today? Everything I read in the newspaper and see on the news about incompetence and corruption. I don't recognise it as being an organisation I was a part of."

Toby and Paul looked at each other and both smiled before Toby said, "It's weird, you bringing that up. We got here a bit earlier and were talking about the same subject when you walked in."

"I read a report yesterday," said Terry. "The Met has recruited one hundred police officers with criminal records in the last two years. An Assistant Commissioner they rolled out to face the press commented, 'some were for very minor offences'. The interviewer didn't pick him up, but in my book, that means some weren't minor offences. It's unbelievable."

"Terry, they're accepting people with previous convictions for theft, assault, and even sex offences," said Toby. "Nowadays, you need a university degree or the equivalent to get in the Met."

Paul nodded. "The likes of us three wouldn't get a look in."

"They don't want working-class recruits; those brought up on the very estates that need policing," said Toby. "When these new kids join straight out of university or from out in the sticks, they don't know what's hit them."

"That's right," said Paul, putting his elbows on the table. "They're not street-wise, and, as you know, there's no course where you can learn that. When they face a difficult situation, they can't differentiate between good guys and bad guys."

Toby laid his hand on his chest. "They don't have the gut instinct people like us have."

"So, who's guiding them?" asked Terry.

"Don't get me started on the quality of the senior officers leading them. They've no interest in serving the public, just keeping their noses clean to get their next promotion," said Toby.

Just like Jones, Terry thought.

"The new recruits have no chance," said Toby. "I've been in the job for nearly twenty-five years, and sometimes I'm embarrassed to tell people what I do. Imagine being a police officer and feeling ashamed of the job you do."

Terry remembered his graduation day. How proud his mum and dad were of his smart uniform and his gleaming brass buttons. The first time he met Denise, he'd been wearing his helmet. She'd no idea he was six feet tall. He'd felt like it, for sure.

"Someone told me you can join the CID straight from recruitment. Is that right? Asked Terry,

It is," said Toby. "You can opt to join the department at eighteen, straight after your initial course and never having the experience of being in uniform on the streets. Imagine them dealing with some of the people we have. They'd get eaten alive,"

Terry shook his head. "This is all very depressing. It sounds like it will only get worse."

"They need to have the guts to accept they've made a mistake and change the qualifications to join. Then they need to target kids from the estates," he said.

Terry thought about the McCullens, Johnston and Mitchell, locked up in the sticks and wondered if they'd have turned out differently if there had been more options. Not them, maybe they'd have always chosen the wrong path, maybe the others who worked for them - the ones like Wesley, who'd seemed harmless enough. "There are plenty of good youngsters out there," he said.

Toby agreed. "And also target those leaving the armed forces. We then might get a combination of shrewdness and discipline."

After numerous pints of lager, they parted company. On his way home, Terry smiled to himself and reflected that another piece of the puzzle was now in place.

CHAPTER FORTY-TWO

Terry had just gotten out of the shower on Saturday morning when he received a call from Peter Rhodes. His heart leapt in his chest, afraid it might be bad news about his health; Peter said, "I don't know if you're busy today, but I've been through that second folder found in Harry Baker's safe. There are some worrying aspects I'd like to show you. Are you free for lunch at my place?"

Terry hadn't been sure how he was going to fill in time over the weekend and was grateful for the distraction. "Definitely," he said. "I'm meeting Nicky to get my car and I'll see you at two."

A few hours later, he arrived at the beautiful detached Victorian house in Dulwich Village, with a blue Bentley Continental on the drive. With a broad Irish accent, a woman in her mid-forties answered the door and led Terry into the living room. Terry looked around and smiled at the large imposing room, decorated with William Morris' wallpaper and some sturdy mahogany furniture. He thought of the rest of the team in their more modest homes and was glad at least one of them had raked in the money after leaving the force. Peter came in and sat in a grand leather armchair. Before sitting down in an identical chair, Terry saw an oxygen tank and mask just behind Peter's seat.

Peter must have noticed Terry's face as he flapped his hand and said, "I don't use it, it's just in case I may need it in the future."

"You've got a beautiful home, Peter, and staff?"

Peter puzzled for a moment then said, "No, that's Mrs Doyle. She cleans the house once a week. I'm hopeless at cooking. If I can't get it delivered or put it in a microwave, I'm lost. I asked her to come in and rustle something up for us. Anyway, while we're waiting, shall we go through these documents Jimmy found in Baker's safe?

They moved into the dining room. It was as equally impressive as the living room, although the walls and drapes were dark green. It should have been a dark room, but the floor-to-ceiling window flooded light in. Peter had arranged the documents and photographs on a large oak table into different sections. Peter's organisation skills always impressed Terry.

"We have twelve different people involved," said Peter. "I won't go into all the details, although I need to highlight a common thread running through several of the dossiers." He moved to the top of the table and pointing to one section, said. "There are two judges; each has a different sexual preference, one for young girls and the other for young boys." He hesitated before saying, "We're talking about twelve or thirteen years of age."

Terry glanced at the photographs and looked away. "Holy shit," was his only response.

"I know. Sickening, isn't it? There are two barristers and three solicitors. They are all married and there are photographs of them in bed with various women. The common thread, if you look at the photographs, is they all appear to be taken in the same hotel room. By the quality of the furniture and fittings, it has to be one of the high-end establishments: the Dorchester, Savoy, Ritz, or somewhere like that."

Terry studied each photograph again and said, "So, someone has set them up?"

"Definitely. Moving on to the other dossiers; this man," Peter said, pointing at a photo of a man walking down the street, "is the CEO of the largest energy company in the UK. According to these notes, he has been taking bribes from a French rival for information. Then," he said, picking up a picture of someone Terry vaguely recognised, "there's a premier league footballer. He got a gagging order through Baker's solicitors. It stopped a girl selling her story to a newspaper about a weekend of debauchery with him and two of his mates."

"Same old, same old," said Terry, glad to be away from the judges and their predilections.

"The funny thing is," said Peter, "in the documents; someone took a statement from the girl the day after her financial settlement."

"Could that have been the newspaper?" asked Terry.

"I wouldn't think so. They take statements on their headed paper, anyway at that stage, she had already got £100000 from the footballer, so there was no story." He moved down the line and picked up another picture. "This is an actor."

Terry had never seen the guy before.

"He's a soap star and is married and gay. Big deal, right?" he said sarcastically. "And this is a backbench MP who has moved vast sums of money from his family business off-shore to avoid tax."

"Well, that won't shock anyone,"

Peter shrugged. "It might, as he's a Labour MP and is the main aggressor from that party, relating to Tory sleaze."

"An MP who is a hypocrite is hardly big news nowadays," said Terry, though he could see what Peter was getting at. Someone was collecting information on these guys - big and small - but for what?

"Last but not least," said Peter, grinning and holding up a picture of someone Terry recognised, "is Yusuf Hassan."

Terry took the photo of him. "God, he's an ugly bastard, isn't he?"

"We know the type of work Harry Baker has done for Yusuf. He set up an off-shore company for him and helped him buy a penthouse apartment in Nell Gwynn House just off Kings Road in Chelsea and a townhouse in Brighton with money from that account. We don't know why Harry also photographed his every move and wrote everything about him in log form."

Terry sat down at the table to think.

"His file is indicative of the rest," said Peter. "A hell of a lot of time and energy has gone into each of these subjects. Whoever put this together has spent ages following him. There are photographs of Yusuf entering and leaving his private members' club in Soho. In Brighton, where he spends every weekend, there are pictures of him in various nightclubs all over different men. When you read the reports, he's openly gay in Brighton and calls himself David."

Terry hadn't expected that at all. "Really?"

"The point is, these dossiers must have taken forever to put together and are both detailed and current. According to the documents, Yusuf was in Subline Nightclub in Brighton a couple of Saturday nights ago and they followed him back to his house with a new conquest."

Looking through the mountain of documents in front of him, Terry said. "To be honest, Peter, I'm not sure what we should do with this, bearing in mind, we have no originals, only copies of photographs and the defence would always say someone has doctored them." He paused, looking at the far end of the table where the judges in their Saville Row suits were. "Then again, we can't just ignore what those judges have been up to." He rubbed his hands over his eyes. "We've got plenty to worry about first. Let's revisit this after we've dealt with Mehmed."

Peter nodded and set about clearing the table methodically. Terry watched him as he did so: worried he might be breathless and pale after such a long presentation; however, Peter simply seemed like Peter: affable and organised.

They settled down to the tastiest shepherd's pie Terry had ever had; he realised this was the first proper meal he'd had in a few weeks. Mrs Doyle soaked up the praise like a sponge.

~❖~

The rest of the weekend had dragged by for Terry. He'd had little sleep and was feeling weary as he sat in the room above The Peacock on Monday morning. It seemed like the others felt the same. They were all waiting for Wednesday and the stress of it was making them tetchy.

He talked through Yusuf's death threats.

"All hot wind," said Jimmy decisively.

"Maybe it was still best that Ali and Elgin returned to Northern Cyprus."

Jimmy pouted and said nothing.

Nicky piped up as though trying to change the atmosphere. "We had a good meeting with Kenny."

"And we can trust him to tell us exactly when the drop-off will be?" asked Peter.

"Yes," said Nicky.

"Are you sure?" asked John.

Now it was Nicky's time to pout. "I said so, didn't I?"

Luckily, Diane came in just then with some millionaire's shortbread and a pot of coffee. "I put a dash of whisky in," she said. "Thought you all needed a bit of cheer."

Terry wasn't sure if that was a great idea.

"Cheer up, fellas," she said as she left. "Only a couple more days to go."

Terry shook his head when she left. "How does that woman know everything?"

Jimmy laughed. "Beats me, boss."

John joked, "Do you think she's got the room bugged?"

Peter replied seriously, "Definitely not; I sweep it regularly,"

They all stared at Peter.

"What?" he said, "It's better to be safe than sorry."

"Oh, Jimmy," said Terry, as the coffee-whisky mixture hit his stomach. "Have you spoken to Jerome Campbell for an update on what's happening on his estate?"

"I have," said Jimmy and blew his nose before speaking. "There's total confusion. Nobody can work out where Monty and Tony have got to. As for the pub, they're just gutted; they've got nowhere to flog their nicked gear, as the brewery has now boarded it up. It doesn't look like any outsiders have yet tried to move in." He snatched a piece of shortbread before Nicky could take it and said, "And that kid who got us into Johnston's flat, Wesley, got grabbed by Mehmed's men and taken on a long drive to talk to him. Mehmed wanted to know what happened. He thinks we could be the police."

"Is the boy all right?" asked Terry, thinking of the kid who'd been so open-faced and scared. He hoped to hell Mehmed hadn't hurt him.

"They roughed him up a bit," said Jimmy, "and put the frighteners on him. Other than that, he's fine."

"That's good."

The men sat back and Terry watched Nicky lick his finger and pick up crumbs from the edge of the table. It was warm in the room and drowsy; the hum of traffic outside sounded like waves on the shore. Terry felt himself blink slowly and was afraid he would drop off to sleep. What else to say? "The Home Secretary," he said, startling the others.

"What about her?" said John.

"Mmm? Oh, yes. On Friday, she announced to the House of Commons that she was clamping down on terrorism." He took the coffee pot and moved it out of everyone's reach. The whisky had been a bad idea. He continued, "And on Saturday morning, the police started the security checks on Canary Wharf with a full lockdown starting this morning." He turned to Dave. "That's right, isn't it?"

Dave nodded and took out his notebook. "The Drug Squad and Trident are working together," he said. "They have some solid information and are looking at doing a series of raids for drugs and firearms by the end of the week."

"Great," said Nicky.

"I spoke to one guy on Trident this morning. They've had a productive weekend and are now sure they've got the address where the guns are housed and are just waiting to confirm a drugs' stash location. They've got twenty-four-hour surveillance on both properties."

"That's good news, Dave," said Terry. At last, it wasn't only them doing all the grunt work. If they kept this up, a good part of London could be free of drugs and guns for a long time. "Keep us up to date with any progress."

"Boss," said Nicky, looking at him out of the corner of his eyes. "Anything you'd like to tell us about that meeting in town the other night? You know, when I dropped you off at the station."

Terry grinned. "Met an old Rugby pal," he said, and then, "Okay, you got me - I met with Toby Russell who's head of the Regional Crime Squad."

John sat up straight in his seat. "Is he going to help us?"

Terry nodded and then grinned.

"Is he not worried about Jones?" asked Dave.

"He's about as much of a fan as you are," said Terry.

Terry then glanced at Peter. There was only one thing the rest of the group didn't know, which was to do with the dossiers of information on those judges, football star and D-list celebrities. Should he let them in on it? No, he decided, it would be too distracting. What they had to do now was concentrate on the job at hand - and for that, he'd have to raise morale. They couldn't be sitting around here like a wet weekend. "I've got plenty of money left over from Mr Jones," he said, "let's have a bit of lunch. Does anyone fancy an Indian?"

"Cor, yeah," said Nicky.

"I'm in," said Peter.

John stared at the table. "I'm sorry," he said. "I just don't get this Indian or Chinese food thing. When we were kids, we only ever had rice for pudding, not for dinner. It's just weird."

"Right," said Nicky, "I suppose it's Italian then."

CHAPTER FORTY-THREE

Terry knew Tuesday had been a tough day for the entire team, with nothing to occupy their time other than the thought of the imminent events of the following day. For no useful reason, they met up once again and went over every eventuality. There was common agreement that handing the information over and taking no part in the proceedings was the most difficult. They had become so invested in Arian Mehmed's downfall that having no control over the outcome was challenging for them all.

Terry thought he was probably the worst of all of them as he paced his kitchen once more on Wednesday morning. The dog looked at him expectantly; Terry felt guilty. He worried that if he left the house to take him for a walk, he'd miss the important phone call: which was stupid - Nicky would ring him on the mobile.

At eleven seventeen precisely, his phone rattled on the kitchen counter. He snatched it up.

"Hi, Nicky, have you heard?" he said.

"Kenny just rang. The lorry will be at the warehouse at about two. He's just going to ring Mehmed and tell him,"

Terry stared at his phone for a split second before running out of the house. He had his phone clamped to his ear and was ringing Dave.

~❖~

Waiting in a railway siding, about half a mile from the warehouse, Jones held court in front of the assembled press and television crews. In the back of his mind, Terry's warning kept sounding - no press! But what did Terry know about running the police force these days, or at all?

"Who are the suspects?" the man from The Sun shouted over the heads of his colleagues.

Who indeed? Thought Jones. "We are not at liberty to divulge that just yet," he said.

The Mail reporter threw her hands in the air. "At least tell us how many."

"I'm afraid that is also classified."

The crowd got even more restless and quite a few peeled off. It's no good talking to the uniform officers, Jones thought. It's not as though they knew what is happening either. Although the day was a little cooler than it had been the last few weeks, Jones felt beads of sweat on his brow and his mood didn't improve when he remembered the briefing at the police station and the look of disdain on the faces of the armed officers of SO19 and the uniform police officers of the Tactical Support Group. The Senior SO19 Officer had sidled up to him afterwards and clarified that she was considering pulling the whole operation. Why should she put her men at risk with so little information? He'd managed - through a mixture of pulling rank and extreme deference - to change her mind, but it'd been touch and go.

A woman from ITV asked if they had a specific time. "We'd like to go live." And there were unstifled groans when he trotted out the same line about "Classified information."

Jones wondered if he should have involved CID after all. The problem with the CID was that they took the limelight - and some had press training and one of them could have stood in his place. He took out his hanky and mopped his brow.

~❖~

Terry was in his car three miles from the warehouse. Propped on the dashboard was a laptop. Nicky sat on the backseat and peered between Terry and Peter to see the screen. It showed a split screen with a black and white view of the yard and a colour vision of inside the warehouse. Nicky pointed out the BMW 3 series sat in its normal parking space and, in silence, they watched the warehouseman sweeping the yard with a stiff brush.

Terry looked through his side window at the car next to him. John and Jimmy sat bolt upright; faces turned towards him. He signalled it wasn't time just yet and as a man, they gave the nod. They could hear Peter's running commentary and all five of them were listening to Peter's description of the empty parking lot and a man sweeping as though it was the FA Cup Final.

At 1.45 p.m., they finally saw something different on the screen. Terry felt his stomach tighten as two vans led by a black S-Class Mercedes Benz with dark tinted windows pulled through the gates and swung into the empty warehouse.

"Look," said Nicky, as Arian Mehmed got out from the back seat of the Mercedes and leaned on the bonnet with a large black holdall in his hands. None of them had seen him before. There was no doubt it was him and matched the photo Terry had in his hand. When Peter relayed Mehmed's arrival to the others, Terry saw them tense, too. If only they could all be there, not sitting watching this on a screen.

"Four men are now climbing out of the cabs of the vans," said Peter. "They are opening the rear doors of the vehicles." His voice was professional, monotone almost. Terry felt his heart beat a drum solo in his chest.

"2 p.m.," said Peter. "Suspect Mehmed is looking at his watch."

There were some breathless minutes as they watched Mehmed pace. Terry checked his watch, too.

"2.05 p.m.," said Peter, his voice rising a little with excitement. "A motorcyclist is pulling into the warehouse. He dismounts. He is taking off his helmet. 2.06 pm. The motorcyclist is talking to Mehmed."

God, thought Terry, why hadn't they wired the place for sound?

"Time?" he said to the others, though it wasn't a question. All five men got out and Peter placed the laptop on the roof of his car. They huddled around, and Terry took two phones out of his pockets and held one in each hand.

"2.12 pm," said Peter; Jimmy nudged him. "We can see it now," he said, and they all watched in breathless silence as a Heavy Goods Vehicle trundled down the road, drove through the yard gates, and then into the warehouse.

"That's got to be it, right?" said John and the others shushed him.

They watched as two men pulled the warehouse sliding doors behind the lorry, and the driver jumped down from his cab and opened the rear trailer doors without speaking to the others. The men from the vans went to the back of the lorry; two climbed in and started moving boxes onto the tailgate.

Terry pressed the preloaded numbers on both phones he held in front of him and, when answered screamed, "ATTACK, ATTACK, ATTACK".

Although it was less than a minute, none of the men spoke until a convoy of vehicles roared into the yard,

"There they are," shouted Jimmy, "there they bloody are."

Pulling back the sliding doors, armed police officers flooded the warehouse with raised guns. Mehmed was still holding the large black holdall and although there was no sound, Terry knew the armed officers were screaming for the occupants of the warehouse to get to the ground. Some quicker than others, they all started descending to their knees and eventually lay flat on the ground. Mehmed was defiantly the last to comply, still gripping the holdall.

When he finally slid to the ground, the men erupted in cheers. After a few seconds of hugging, they turned back to the screen to watch the men being handcuffed and photographed where they lay. One officer yanked the holdall from Mehmed's grip.

"You get it, boy!" said John, and they all wished they could leap through the screen and look inside the bag. It must have been something good in there as the officer held it open for the others to see and they took a tonne of photographs. There appeared to be equal excitement relating to the contents of the lorry.

"We did it!" said Jimmy, giving John a high five and Terry found himself lifted off his feet by Nicky, who was shorter and much fatter than Terry.

~❖~

When Terry had shouted ATTACK, ATTACK, ATTACK, Jones had leapt into action and led the raid on the designated warehouse.

At his heels was a convoy of press and television reporters in close pursuit.

He ordered the doors smashed open and stood slightly to the side so the press could watch the excitement of the Armed Police followed by the Tactical Support officers running into the warehouse. He imagined a huge haul for the bad guys - sorry, the suspects - with them lying on the floor begging for their lives, large bags of cocaine piled up next to them. The lead officer signalled him.

He puffed out his chest and walked into the warehouse. The press, cameras on shoulders, phones out, notebooks in hand, walked in after him. He looked around, unable to register what he was seeing. The warehouse in Dagenham, Essex, was empty; completely empty.

All the way back to Scotland Yard, Jones cursed under his breath. He knew Terry Reid had conned him; humiliated him in front of the press. There was no way out of this. His job, for sure, would be on the line as soon as the Commissioner and Home Secretary heard about this - which he reckoned, checking his watch, was probably right about now, knowing how embedded the journalists were in Westminster. Why did he ever let himself get caught up in this? Why didn't he trust his gut and refuse to work with those bent old coppers? Now, their mess would taint him forever.

When he got out of the lift at New Scotland Yard, Jones braced himself for ridicule. He was so caught in his own fears that it wasn't until he was in the corridor jogging to his office that he registered the sound of a party. Could it be that they had already heard and were celebrating his demise? No, surely not, he wasn't that hated, was he? He steeled himself against running away and went into his office.

There stood the Commissioner and an array of senior police officers with drinks in their hands. What the hell was going on?

The Commissioner came over and slapped him on the shoulder. "Fantastic result, Alan. The Home Secretary has contacted me to offer her congratulations and informed me the Prime Minister sends his congratulations."

Jones smiled weakly, buying time.

"I didn't think it was possible," said the Commissioner, "especially in such a brief space of time."

Jones bowed his head to hide his confusion and said, "We try our best." Making his excuses, he walked to the drink trolley and, with a flute of fizz in his hand, pulled Police Constable Ball aside. Ball was the Commissioner's driver, and he didn't have to impress him. "What's going on?" asked Jones.

PC Ball raised his eyebrows. "They've arrested Arian Mehmed with a hundred kilos of cocaine and recovered over one and a half million pounds in cash."

But the warehouse had been empty. God damn it, there was about fifty press who had witnessed his humiliation. "Who arrested him?" he hissed

"Regional Crime Squad," Ball answered, "however, I believe it was down to the crew you and the Commissioner recruited." Ball raised his glass and said, "Congratulations, Sir," and Jones wasn't at all sure if this junior officer was mocking him.

He plastered on a smile and said, "Of course, I was simply wondering if you knew the name of the arresting officer," and then breezed away before Ball could answer. It was time to shake hands; it was time to take credit.

~❖~

Dave wasn't at the party - thank God - he was in the warehouse in Woolwich, waiting for those few minutes between Mehmed and his men being taken away and before forensics arrived. He grinned as the vans, with the prisoners, kicked up the dust as they drove out of the Industrial Estate. Toby Russell and a few other Regional Crime Squad officers were the only ones left. He'd been lucky enough to stand with them when the raid took place and have a front-row seat, unlike Terry and the rest of the gang. As he walked into the warehouse, he stored up details for the others - the way Mehmed's bright white shirt had got muddied, which seemed to cause him more distress than being arrested; the way one detective had shoved a packet of cocaine up his t-shirt and claimed he had a beer belly. "Pregnant, more like," one of the other officers had quipped.

Toby and the other officers looked the other way as Dave took the stairs two at a time to the mezzanine area. He located the camera and battery pack and removed them, as instructed by Peter. He placed them in an Ikea carrier bag he'd kept folded down the back of his jeans and walked out of the warehouse, giving a quick nod to Toby, who returned the gesture with a wink. In the car, Dave laughed and laughed. "Oh, Dad," he said. "I wish you'd been there - the boy done good." Now, the only thing left to do was go to the station and see if Mehmed had rolled over yet. Then, of course, a wild celebration.

CHAPTER FORTY-FOUR

It was tight in the one car with Terry, Nicky, Jimmy, John and Peter. There had been no point taking two cars to release the prisoners in Dartford, as they were going to The Peacock afterwards for a drink. "Guys," said Terry to the three in the back seat, "You are going to have to rearrange yourselves. Nicky needs to go in the middle."

"How come? He's the fattest," said Jimmy.

"Oy," said Nicky.

"He's the shortest too," said Terry, "and I need to see out the back. You two are like the Berlin wall."

"Defunct," said Nicky and got jabbed in the ribs by the other two as they rearranged themselves. "Ow."

None of them suggested Peter should sit in the middle, as there was an unspoken agreement that he should at all times get the best of everything.

The men were looking out of the window as they passed Woolwich Station when Nicky's phone rang. Terry watched him through the rear-view mirror. Nicky answered laughing, but immediately his face fell. "No. When?" The other men fell silent, knowing something was seriously wrong.

Nicky rang off and sat in silence.

"What?" said John.

"That was Kenny," said Nicky. "The boys are dead."

"Which boys?" said Jimmy.

"His boys."

"How?" asked John

"They had their throats slit,"

The men were silent, and John put his head in his hands. Terry didn't know whether to pull over. He carried on, focusing on the car in front of him. They waited, knowing an explanation was coming.

"Kenny doesn't know all the details yet. Apparently, they were in their cells. Kenny had told them yesterday, they were about to be released and he doesn't know if they blabbed it out. He reckons it has Arian Mehmed's fingerprints all over it."

"Shit," said Jimmy.

"Does he blame us?" asked John.

Nicky shook his head. "I don't know. He said that he shouldn't have told them so soon and said something about God's revenge for Joe Brown's boys."

"Who's that?" asked Peter.

Nicky said. "Some years ago, Kenny was involved with Brown in a huge Fraud. Brown got nicked and implicated Kenny. Next thing, the police found Brown's eighteen-year-old twin sons in a burnt-out car. Both had bullet holes in their heads. The rumours were that Kenny had ordered it." He paused, looking straight ahead. "Maybe they were more than rumours."

Terry felt a little sick. He hadn't seen the point of living when Denise had died. How would you cope with losing both of your sons?

"I wish I didn't know," said Nicky.

You and me both thought Terry. Their feeling of jubilation had flown away, left by unease. Had it been their fault the boys had died? No, of course not. They had lived in a dangerous world of their own making. Then again, Terry and his men stirring the pot hadn't helped. So far it'd felt like a game - but now, he saw, it was a game with far-reaching consequences.

Peter put a hand on his shoulder. "Remember why we did this," he said. "Isaac Okoro, that's why. And with all the guns and drugs off the streets, there will be far fewer deaths. It's like the trolley problem."

"What are you on about?" said Jimmy.

So Peter told them about the trolley problem and how you had to decide if you would switch the tracks on a runaway tram, so it killed just one person, other than the five it was aiming for.

"I'd roll Nicky into its path," said Jimmy. "It'd stop and he'd only get dented."

The laughter and the mock fight in the back cleared the air. When they had settled down, Terry asked Peter to call Dave and put him on speakerphone.

"My man," said Terry. "How's it going? What's happening with Mehmed?"

Dave's voice came through loud and clear. "Mehmed lawyered up straight away and said nothing. Toby isn't worried, though; they've got more than enough to convict him. The warehouseman has rolled over and is telling them everything. He's got no living relatives here or in Albania and doesn't want to spend the rest of his life in prison. Also, when they searched the warehouse office in Woolwich, they found copies of a handwritten log with enormous amounts of financial transactions on it. Mehmed's name was all over it, and with it, they found personalised headed paper belonging to Harry Baker. They sound very similar to the documents we saw."

"That's careless of them," said Jimmy, laughing.

Under his breath, Terry said to Peter, "Nice to see they found our present."

"Toby's looking to get a search warrant for Baker's office now,"

"Hope you reminded him he's got a safe," said Jimmy.

"Yes, I did, although I think he thought it strange; I knew about that," replied Dave. "He's very grateful for the information and wants us to meet up with his team for a drink. I've invited him over tonight. Hope that's okay?"

"Absolutely," said Terry. "He's one of the good guys."

When Dave had rung off and the others were chatting in the back, Peter leaned over to Terry and said, "What do you want to do about the other documents we've got from Baker?"

"What's that?" said Jimmy.

They hadn't been as deep in conversation as Terry thought. He shrugged and said, "Go ahead, Peter, you may as well tell them what we've got."

Jimmy, John and Nicky were unfazed by the D-list celebrities' shenanigans but when it came to the judges…

"Fuck me," said Jimmy, "That's awful."

"Do we know where they live?" said John, curling his fist.

Terry considered this vigilante action for a moment. "It's difficult to see what we would gain by handing the documents over to the police at this stage," he said. "I'm still worried we haven't got the original photographs, just copies."

"So we take it into our own hands," said John.

Terry waved his hand - there had to be a better way. "They may well find them when they search Baker's safe. I'll speak with Toby Russell and get his views if they don't. Let's see what happens to Harry Baker first."

That settled and they sat in silence until Peter said, "I bet Jones was livid with what happened. I would have loved to have seen his face. Shame I didn't have time to put a camera in the warehouse in Dagenham."

The men in the back laughed. "I bet he ran into the warehouse all puffed up and there was bugger all there," said Nicky.

"We certainly brought him down a peg or two," said John.

"Yes," said Terry. "And he'll think I did it to humiliate him, but the press could've jeopardised the entire operation; we all know nicking them is the easy bit, convicting them is a different ball game. Mehmed can afford the best barristers money

can buy."

They reached the smallholding and let the McCullens out first. Terry could hardly recognise them. Each of them looked years older and all the fight had gone out of them. As they adjusted their eyes, they blinked. Monty Johnston and Tony Mitchell looked no better, despite having spent less time in their hut. Terry couldn't help but notice the dried blood all over Johnston's face and a deep cut over his left eye that certainly should have had stitches but was healing, anyway.

Standing out in the yard, it seemed to dawn on the four of them, without anything being said, that, although in different huts, they had endured the same confinement without knowing the others were there.

"What are you going to do to us?" Monty Johnston was the first to speak, although the others probably thought the same thing.

John said, "That depends on you. Life is all about choices and you've got to make some."

"That's deep," remarked Peter.

"Right now," said Terry. "We're going to let you go. Should you go anywhere near your old estates, we'll be back and this time, we won't be so nice."

"We don't know where we are," said Johnson.

Terry pointed. "London's that way." The men looked at each other and started walking. They had no mobile phones and no money. It was going to be a long trek.

The men watched them disappear into the shrub. "They should be home by Christmas," said Jimmy, and the men laughed. Terry went to the boot of his car and took out a bottle of champagne. There were no glasses, only plastic cups and after he'd sprayed them with it, they rested against the car as the sun went down over the Nissan Huts. "Here's to us," said John.

"And here's to Kenny," said Nicky.

None of them had wanted to think about Kenny's sons, but now, in the peace of the countryside, it seemed right to lift their cups and take a solemn moment.

Terry checked his watch. "Diane is going to kill us," he said. "There's only an hour before the party starts."

CHAPTER FORTY-FIVE

There had been barely any time; however, the men had managed to get home, change, and dash back to The Peacock. They'd scrubbed up well, thought Terry as he surveyed them in suits, Flying Squad ties and polished shoes. On the door was a "Private Party" sign and young Jake was the doorman, only letting in those that had helped. Diane had done them proud with a big buffet and a free bar (Well, not free - Terry was going to foot the bill). She'd also decorated the place but must have only had Christmas decorations as there were red and green balloons, gold streamers and random bits of tinsel over the chairs.

She came over and hugged Terry. "I knew you could do it," she said.

"Do what?" he said innocently, and she laughed.

"Terry! Terry!" John blundered over with a small, dark-haired woman in his arms. "This is Jilly."

Terry took her small hand and kissed it and Jilly twinkled. Gosh, she was a good-looking woman. Not a patch on Denise, of course, but… Wow!

"Thank you so much," said Jilly. "The estate's a different place these days."

"I told you," said John. "We did nothing."

She squeezed him and planted a kiss on his cheek. "Oh, my big bear."

Jilly excused herself and went to speak to Diane.

"Well, what do you think of my Jilly? Asked John.

"She's stunning," said Terry. "You're punching way above your weight."

John smiled and said, "I know."

Terry went to Toby and shook his hand. "Thank you," he said simply.

"No, thank you, and thank you for inviting me and my team here tonight. We should be the ones putting on a party."

"How has Jones taken it?"

"A bit discombobulated at first. You know him; within the first hour he'd put a spin on it and was taking all the credit." He caught Dave's arm and brought him in. "We couldn't have done it without this one," he said, and Dave beamed from ear to ear. "Now, listen both of you - I hate to bring work to the party, but we raided Baker's offices an hour ago and the safe only had some cash and other innocuous documents."

Terry knew there wouldn't be anything in there - it had been a long shot that Baker would have put anything of importance back in the safe after Monkey Gregory had cracked the lock - although he arranged his face into a mask of disappointment.

"They've arrested him. I'd say it's unlikely they'll have enough evidence to charge him. When they executed a warrant for Tanner Accountants, there was no sign of Geoffrey Tanner and the offices were empty. There was no office equipment or computers, not even any paperwork. It was bare. However, they were moving the money; those offices were just a front."

"Let's wait and see what happens with Baker," said Terry, knowing they had plenty of leads for the future.

"No more job talk, I promise," said Toby. "Let's enjoy the evening."

Terry was about to agree when Jimmy grabbed him and shoved a phone in his face. "It's Ali and Elgin," he said. "Say hello." Terry did as he was told, and then Jimmy moved away, bellowing down the phone. "I wish you guys could be here. Can I come to you? I fancy a holiday." Jimmy's wife rolled her eyes a couple of yards away and turned to chat with Jerome, Winston's son. How had he got the news about the party? Jimmy must have told him, Terry supposed. Was it a good idea he was here? How safe could they keep him? But then he watched him laugh at something Jimmy's wife said and knew it was fine. They were all safe now as Mehmed was off the streets.

Terry spotted Peter and Nicky sitting in the corner. He walked over to them and clapped them both on the shoulders. "You okay?" he said to Peter.

"Of course," said Peter, "Never better." And then, as if knowing Terry needed more, "You have to stop worrying about me. I have. This job gave me a new lease of life."

"Men," said John solemnly, coming up to the table. Jilly was no longer on his arm. "I have something I need to show you."

He slid into a seat and beckoned Jimmy over.

"What?" said Jimmy,

"Shut up and sit down."

Jimmy did as he was told. Then John opened up his jacket and stealthily handed each of them a thick brown envelope under the table. Terry looked around before opening his. Jerome, Jilly, and Diane were chatting at the bar; Toby, with his team and Dave, were piling their plates with sausage rolls; and Jimmy's wife was now with Jake at the entrance, blowing her cigarette smoke out of the door. He could see the profile of another woman chatting to them and recognised Mrs Doyle from Peter's house.

Sure that none of the guests was taking a blind bit of notice, Terry opened his envelope and found it stuffed with £50 notes.

"Sorry, Terry," said John, "I couldn't give it all to that dickhead Yusuf, especially after the way he spoke to you."

"How much is in here?" hissed Terry.

"Twenty grand each. I've left a bit more upstairs to pay for tonight."

"Jesus. What about Ali and Elgin? Did they know what you were doing?" said Terry.

John grinned. "Oh, definitely. I gave them an envelope each before they got on their flight."

The men sat in silence, and Terry knew they were waiting for him to take the lead. This was wrong; plainly, this was wrong. They hadn't come into this job to get money; they'd come to get drugs off the street. Whatever the management thought, they all had been police officers, and good ones at that. Would they be any better than the dealers if they took this money?

And yet… What harm would it do? The money would only have gone to Yusuf and the Hassan family - probably used to buy more drugs.

He felt like he was diving off a cliff.

He looked up at the men, patiently waiting, winked at John and said, "You're fucking murder, John. You make the Devil seem like a Saint."

EPILOGUE

After a plea of not guilty and a five-week trial, the jury convicted Arian Mehmed, and the judge sentenced him to twenty-three years' imprisonment. As Mehmed was denying any knowledge or involvement in drug dealing, his legal team chose not to mention the group of 'old blokes' and two Turks, who had been kidnapping his dealers and stealing his cocaine. The documents found in the warehouse showing the movement of vast sums of money provided the police with the opportunity to apply for an order under the Proceeds of Crime Act. The court directed Mehmed to return eight million pounds or serve an additional five years in prison. Regional Crime Squad officers hoped he would refuse to comply with the order.

Yusuf Hassan contended, to anyone who would listen, that it was only the arrest and imprisonment of Arian Mehmed that had saved his life, as Yusuf would have most definitely murdered him.

At the next available Parole Board hearing, Ozzie and Omer Hassan applied for parole and succeeded. They started making plans for their permanent move to Northern Cyprus once their license permitted it.

In Northern Cyprus, Mustafa Hassan's legitimate businesses went from strength to strength, with Ali and Elgin 'encouraging' new customers to use his services and equipment. Mustafa had purchased land near his own on behalf of his brothers to prepare for their arrival.

Once Kenny Pierce had eventually repatriated his sons' bodies to England and buried them. He sold his house in Westerham, Kent and moved with his wife to his home in Marbella, Spain. The outward-going Kenny became almost a recluse and other than a regular round of golf, he and his wife kept a very low profile.

When they arrested Harry Baker in his office, his safe provided nothing to substantiate the suspicion of Baker's involvement in the laundering of drug money. Although questioned at length, there was not enough evidence to charge him with any crime and the police released him. However, various appointed officers of the Law Society mysteriously received copies of the documents found by the police in the warehouse. This forced Harry Baker to resign from his position with Baker, Radcliffe and Wright Solicitors. The company changed its name to Radcliffe and Wright Solicitors and Harry Baker's invitations to Law Society functions ceased.

A few months after the trial, they awarded Detective Chief Superintendent Jones a Commissioners Commendation for the role he played in the downfall of Arian Mehmed and his empire. His proud wife and parents attended the ceremony. A short while after, they promoted him to Commander and transferred him to the Public Order Operational Command Unit (OCU). He handled the development of policy concerning public order events. OCU was a unit staffed solely by uniform officers.

With his health failing, Peter Rhodes took Nicky's advice and flew to Australia to inform his daughters of his condition and prognosis. They had placed him on a strict, no-alcohol diet, feeding him the healthiest ingredients available. After six weeks, although he missed his daughters, he returned home to his weekly curry.

Before leaving for Australia, Peter had offered Jimmy Smith the opportunity to set up a security guarding division for him. This included doormen for pubs and clubs, night watchmen for building sites, and security guards for shops and supermarkets. Jimmy dealt with all aspects of the new section, including sales, recruitment and invoicing. On his return to England, Peter couldn't believe Jimmy's progress and provided two additional office staff to deal with the administration. This gave Jimmy time to find more clients and expand the division even further.

John Olde had gone back to collecting money, only now it was daily and from laundrettes in South London. His relationship with Jilly Jones was going well, but who could predict the future for him?

Having returned to retirement, tending his garden and playing golf twice a week, Nicky Wybrow, made a point of keeping in touch with the others. He arranged occasional lunches that always spilt into the late evening.

Once the trials were over, Dave Driscoll received invitations to join both the Flying Squad and the Regional Crime Squad. He chose the Flying Squad, like his dad before him. His outlook on life had changed, and he was enjoying work again whilst studying for the Inspector's examination.

Terry Reid was on his fifth cigarette and fifth coffee of the day, after having taken his dog for a walk. The same routine since his wife had passed away from cancer. When his mobile phone rang and he recognised the number. One thought ran through his mind. 'Surely, not again?'

Book Two in the series: A Deal with the Devil coming soon.

www.tomfinn.net

tomfinn999@yahoo.com

ACKNOWLEDGEMENTS

Mike Sullivan, crime editor of The Sun, whose advice and encouragement at the early stages of this project, gave me the confidence to keep going.

Petra McQueen, is an extraordinary editor. Thank you for your patience and knowledge.

My incredible wife who always has been and always will be the better part of me.

Printed in Great Britain
by Amazon

38219131R00136